A JULIET FRENCH MYSTERY - 1

SHED GIRL

MILANA MARSENICH

Black Rose Writing | Texas

ISBN: 978-1-68513-355-9
Library of Congress Control Number: 2023942567
PUBLISHED BY BLACK ROSE WRITING
www.blackrosewriting.com

Printed in the United States of America
Suggested Retail Price (SRP) $21.95

Shed Girl is printed in Book Antiqua

Cover art adapted from a photo by Koolshooters on Pexels.com

*As a planet-friendly publisher, Black Rose Writing does its best to eliminate unnecessary waste to reduce paper usage and energy costs, while never compromising the reading experience. As a result, the final word count vs. page count may not meet common expectations.

To all who struggle to find love and safety.
May you find your true homes.

Acknowledgements for *Shed Girl*

I would first like to thank Reagan Rothe and Black Rose Writing for taking a chance with me and *Shed Girl*. A huge thank you to Carol Carreau, for taking the time during a tumultuous news cycle to read *Shed Girl* and give me detailed feedback on the manuscript. It is a much better book because of her. Thank you to Maggie Plummer for her editing at the beginning of this endeavor. Her support and feedback for the story helped me find my way with it. Thank you to Susan Sage for being a beta reader and giving me valuable feedback. Her enthusiasm for this story helped me to find the courage to send it out for publication. Thank you to Judith Bromley for my author photo, and for being an early beta reader.

Thank you to my brother, Ed Marsenich, for his enthusiasm for my writing. Thank you to my brother, Bob Marsenich, and my sister-in-law, Karen McMullen, for giving me a place to write and for their ongoing faith in my writing efforts. Thank you to Jan Myers for giving me a place to write. Thank you to Women Writing the West and Western Writers of America for supporting my writing efforts. I've made many friends along the way and am happy to be a part of both organizations. All my stories begin with my family and early friends. They shaped my life, my language, and my stories. They taught me to love. Without them, this book would not be possible.

SHED GIRL

CHAPTER ONE

Juliet French knew magic. The soft wind in the cedars, the haunting howl of the coyote, the smell of the weather when the clouds grayed, and waves crashed against the rocky cliffs of the Northern Washington coast all filled her with wonder. She lived in Annie's Court for that ocean smell and the trance it threw over her. She had come from a long line of magic lovers, her mother, her grandmother, her great-grandmother, and all the mothers before. They had found their paths in life with beauty, prayer, tarot cards, and dreams. But when the blood-curdling scream pierced the ocean fog, primal instinct and fear grabbed hold of Juliet. Not magic.

She turned and saw a man in a brown hooded sweatshirt hovering over a blond-haired boy of about ten. The man held him tightly around the waist, squeezing him like a teddy bear. Annie's Court, a tourist town, and a town of quiet reverence, started slowly on Sundays, with few people wandering the streets. Overhead, seagulls circled and squealed. Out in the bay, the ferry coming from the San Juan Islands sounded its horn. A long mournful hum slid over the town.

"Let go of me," the boy yelled and flung his arms at the man.

"Shush now," the man cooed, like a father trying to calm a hysterical child.

The boy kicked his legs hard, hitting only the thick dense air the fog had brought in.

The man grabbed him by one leg, picked him up like a calf he'd roped, and dumped him upside down. The boy's face turned red and stiff. The man turned his head toward Juliet. Just under a rubber mask that covered the top half of his face, she saw him smirk.

The masked man couldn't have known the fierce terror this abduction would set off in Juliet. She'd been pinned and held against her will. She knew the horror of fighting someone else's weight until every muscle burned and went still. A raging anger bullied her fear aside and sent adrenaline surging through her. She launched herself across the street and leaped at the man's back. A dank smell nauseated her. His head reared up; the smile gone. He smashed the back of his skull against her forehead.

The trees, sky, and ground shattered into confetti, and she nearly went down. But not quite. Touching the road with her fingertips, the fall heat lifting off the pavement, she came up roaring and jumped at the man's back again, throwing her whole hundred pounds against him. She was only five-feet-two-inches, but she was strong. In her dark leggings and t-shirt, she moved with the nimble speed of a ninja. She pulled off the man's hood, grabbed his hair, and yanked his head backwards, tilting his face to the clouds.

Like the Douglas fir in the park, he resisted and stood solid. He turned his head toward Juliet. She clawed at his cheeks and forehead, but her fingernails bounced off the rubber mask. Lightening cracked in her brain. She dug her nails into his skull, digging into the hair roots and pulling hard as the man tightened his grip on the boy. The boy's blond hair stuck out in every direction. His shirt, jagged at the hem, inched up toward his neck, showing the pure white flesh of his belly. He shot Juliet a look of terror.

She strengthened her grip on the man, but he threw her off, an unseasonable fly. A desperate hope fogged her brain, and she couldn't think. But then, thinking wasn't necessary. She needed to act. She stood, ready to pounce again, as the boy vanished behind the man's great hulk. The two disappeared into a white van with a cleaning company emblem on the side.

A man sat in the driver's seat. Another man's flannelled shoulder propped the side door open. His bushy beard covered too much of his face, shaking Juliet's senses. The door slid shut and the van sped down the road, leaving her with nothing but a tuft of brown hair in her hand. Two blocks into the escape, the van's back door opened suddenly, and the boy tumbled out, all arms and legs, spinning like a carnival ride, landing right side up and running.

Juliet ran after him, but the boy was fast. She couldn't catch him. Her lungs burned only minutes into it. The boy was gone, down a side street, toward the water. The seagulls mocked her; they cheered him on. Run, boy, run.

When she stopped, a short bald man lumbered behind her. He wore navy pants and a gray sweater that was too tight around his midsection. He stopped, leaned on his knees, and breathed hard. Except for her bafflement at his sudden presence, Juliet would have done the same.

"Sorry, I didn't get here sooner," the bald man said. "I was having coffee at the Hungry Bear when I saw what was happening. I called for back up and ran out."

Before she could open her mouth to reply, a siren screamed and a patrol car skid to a stop at the curb. The bald man stuck his head in the open window and talked with the officers. She panicked and held her breath. The van was gone. The boy was gone. They were there for her.

"How well do you know that kid?" the bald man asked.

Juliet lifted her eyebrows. "Doesn't matter. He's gone now." Shame filled her belly. She had wanted to help the boy. She'd wanted to stop that man from stealing him, bring the boy home, and feed him soup, give him a blanket and a pallet to sleep on until social services came and returned him to his parents.

"Detective Benson Picard." He handed her a business card.

She gazed at it and handed it back. "So, you say." She looked from him to the cop car parked at the curb. They had been useless. Both the boy and his temporary captors were gone. She turned to walk away.

"Wait," the man said. "Do you know where he'll go?"

She turned back. Listening to the squeal of the seagulls, she shrugged. "Since you're the police, can't you do more to help him?"

"I saw you grab him," Picard said.

Juliet's chest swelled with fear. A cop misunderstanding her was a bad sign. She hadn't seen it in the tarot cards. Innocent people ended up imprisoned or thrown out of town all the time. At least he couldn't send her back to her aunt in Arizona. She'd already celebrated her eighteenth birthday, if you could call eating a stale donut alone in an abandoned shed celebrating.

"Is he your brother?"

"No." Curiosity, that persistent cat, got the better of her. "Why?"

"The hair. You've got the same haircut."

Juliet patted her head. After eighteen years of long hair, she'd cut it off. Now her hair stuck up in a thousand black cowlicks. Something she hadn't counted on.

"Where would he go?" Picard repeated.

Most likely to the tent town, she thought, shrugging again, a refined teen gesture. "Hopefully home. Where he belongs."

"You could help me." Picard rubbed his shiny head. "Unofficially."

She could hear the lap, lap, lap of the waves rocking the shoreline. The seagulls squawked out a warning. Deft at recognizing danger, Juliet tilted her cowlicks and looked at Picard sideways.

"For money. For food. You look like you could use some nourishment."

"I won't narc on the kids, if that's what you want."

"Walk with me and I'll tell you."

She hesitated, didn't know if she could trust him, didn't like entanglements.

"I'll buy you a sandwich," Picard said, and gave her a crooked tooth smile.

The fog had lifted and the breeze off the water came in soft and fine. A silken mist rose to the sun and washed her face. Light on her feet, ready to flee, she went with Picard, the seagulls' warning a dainty handkerchief dropped at the curbside.

•   •   •

Old Victorian mansions sat on the hill. Long grasses reached toward the water like outstretched hands. Ranch houses and condos, tucked in between the industrial docks, stretched down the shoreline of Annie's Court. Main street went from the highway to the waterfront. Small artsy shops with beads, bohemian clothes, and paintings lined the street. The Hungry Bear Café sat in the middle of the shops.

Juliet had fled her aunt's home in Arizona and headed to Alaska, landing in Annie's Court, never getting further north than Washington. She loved this town, with its quaint flower parks and large leaf maples lining the streets. The abandoned shed she called home suited her just fine. Perfectly, in fact. The shed had just enough room for her and Wilma, the calico kitten.

She followed Picard back to the Hungry Bear where his cold coffee waited for him. He ordered a ham sandwich and told her to get whatever she wanted. She wanted a ham sandwich.

"Two," he said to the waitress. "And a chocolate milkshake?"

Juliet nodded. Why not? She was hungry. He was buying.

"Annie's Court has a problem with runaways," he said. "I don't like that they show up here so often. They aren't safe. And then, something seems to happen to them. They disappear, maybe go home. But I don't think so."

She knew this. She shook her head and blinked. "And?"

"I need help understanding what kinds of dangers they face. Where are they going if they are not going home? Most of them are too young to be on their own, to understand the hellish nature of predators."

"Most of your runaways are runaways because of predators," Juliet said, turning the saltshaker on its side and spinning it like a top.

Picard nodded, seemed to think about that. "You might be right. More reason to help them to safety."

"If you are talking foster homes, some of those aren't safe."

"I just need a pair of eyes on the street," he said. "To alert me to nefarious doings."

"And you want me to be those eyes?"

"Yes."

"How dangerous is it?"

"That's the tricky part," he said and rubbed his bare chin. "I only want you to report to me. We'll handle the trouble."

"I said it before. I won't narc on the kids."

He smiled. "Don't report on the kids. Report on the adults that may be taking advantage of the kids."

Juliet let her gaze soften. She scanned The Hungry Bear. The wooden wall panels had just been stained and polished to shine. A ramp with a railing led up to the cook's window where he pushed hot plates onto a silver metallic counter and called out numbers. The rich scent of pancakes and bacon frying wafted out and smelled heavenly. The waitress walked by with three platters of French toast balanced precariously on one arm.

"And how will I find these adults?" Juliet asked.

His smile broadened. "Something tells me they'll find you." He pushed a twenty-dollar bill across the table to her. "Think about it. In the meantime, buy some food to eat at home."

Picard acted like he knew she had a home. But that charade was an act. No one knew she lived in the small, abandoned shed in the same block where the old ship had landed a hundred years ago. Juliet had made sure of that.

"I've seen you at the Farmer's Market," Picard was saying. "A lot goes on there."

She raised her eyebrows at him, felt a wicked edgy sensation in her chest. Had he been watching her? The thought made her want to stand straight up and leave.

The waitress arrived with two ham and cheese sandwiches, chips on the side, and one chocolate milkshake. Juliet picked up a chip and popped it in her mouth. The ham sandwich was delicious.

It soothed her soul and her stomach. It quieted her fear. She was being ridiculous. He'd have no reason to spy on her. When she finished her sandwich and the milkshake, she took the twenty and stuffed it in the pocket on her leggings, next to the pocketknife she usually carried. "Okay," she said. "I'll see what I can learn."

.   .   .

She had gobbled her ham sandwich down so fast that Picard bought her second one, one to take home. She shared that one with Wilma. Nearly a week had passed since that meeting with the detective. She'd taken the twenty and bought some cat food and couple of bagels and put a five-dollar bill in her savings can.

Skimping on food made her weak and irritable, but she didn't know when she'd have more money. She didn't know if she'd learn anything useful to Picard, didn't know if he'd be good to his word and pay her. Better to plan for failure, she thought.

Juliet rolled up the camp table that sat at the end of her bed and slipped it into a jean bag she'd made for it. She tucked her tarot cards into the pocket on the side of it. A few feet away, at the other end of the shed, Wilma poked her head out of the box that served as Juliet's dresser. Wilma usually liked to climb under the army blanket, making herself at home in the comfort of Juliet's bed.

That day she climbed up a nearly clean t-shirt that hung over the side of the box, where Juliet had thrown it. She jumped from there to a pile of folded clothes on one of Juliet's camp chairs, knocking the pile to the plywood floor. On a mission of some sort, Wilma jumped to the jean jacket hanging from a nail Juliet had pounded into the wall as a clothes rack, pulled herself up the denim, until she slid back down into the pile of jeans, shirts, and leggings on the floor.

"You crazy cat," she said. "Stay here and hold down the fort." Even though she knew Wilma wouldn't stay put. Wilma had a small hole someone had kicked in the shed where she came and went as she pleased. Juliet and Wilma were alike that way. They liked their escape routes.

She grabbed two camp chairs and the bag with her table and cards and leaned them against the outside of the shed wall. Little bits of green paint fell off onto the denim material of the bag. From behind a nearby boulder, she pulled a silver latch with the padlock already in it, and a screwdriver. Setting two screws into the holes in the wooden door, Juliet attached one side of the latch. She repeated the process on the wall, firmly attaching the lock to the door. Not a conventional lock, but it kept the shed secure, while looking like a shed rather than a home for a wayward girl.

She thought back on the flowered wallpaper lining her bedroom wall at Aunt Gloria's house. There, she'd had her own bathroom with thick white towels and makeup, brushes, and toothpaste scattered across the sink counter. Here, in Annie's Court, she used the public bathroom in the park across the street from the shed. Inside, she pulled a paper towel off the rack, turned on the water, and washed her face and armpits.

Once she was semi-clean, and with the shed locked up tight, she picked up the table and chairs and headed toward the Farmer's Market. On Saturdays, she provided tarot readings to tourists for petty change. At least she'd earn a few bucks there.

She crossed the wet street and followed the red brick road to the open mall. Seagulls picked at bugs on the street and a few stray cars moseyed by. Juliet attempted to count her blessings: sixteen good years with her mother, an aunt who cared enough to take her in when her mother died, an aunt who cared enough to feed and shelter her, to fight with the school principal about lost credits during and after her mother's funeral.

Sure. Aunt Gloria cared about her.

She just didn't care enough to believe her when Juliet told her about Layne. Layne, her aunt's boyfriend, had snuck into Juliet's room at night and forced sex on her. Aunt Gloria was a gentle, trusting woman in her fifties. She couldn't believe her boyfriend of three years had that kind of mean streak. He got drunk and sometimes got rough with Aunt Gloria. On those nights, her aunt retreated to her room or took the Buick out for a ride.

Still, her aunt couldn't believe Layne would go after Juliet, pressing her against the wooden dresser and forcing her to do things with him. Aunt Gloria figured her niece was lying and needed attention because she was missing her mother or wanted to keep her aunt all to herself. Or Juliet just feared being alone.

Aunt Gloria didn't see the truth: Juliet was suffering from her boyfriend's sexual violence and wanted to protect them both from Layne's cruelty.

"Stop it," Juliet scolded herself. That episode of her life ended two years ago. It was water long past washed up on the shoreline and gone back out to sea.

Let it be. Go back to counting your blessings.

She had a dry shed to sleep in, and no siblings to worry about. But then, if she'd had a sibling, they could take care of each other.

Since she had run away from Aunt Gloria's, she'd made her way alone from Arizona to the Northwest coast, hiding in make-shift shelters. She'd eaten food from dumpsters behind grocery stores–food too old to sell but not too old to eat.

Either that or she went hungry.

On her eighteenth birthday, she learned no one looks for you anymore once you turn eighteen. If they had looked for her before. She wouldn't put it past Layne to forbid her aunt from searching for her only niece.

Okay. Enough. Counting her blessings was impossible. Juliet hated it when her mind raced into nonsense like this.

She set up her table and chairs at the Farmer's Market and shuffled the tarot deck, waiting for the waves to wash her sailor up on the shore. She'd tell him about the blond boy, and how she searched for him in the old boat, out by the tent town, and in the caves at low tide. It was odd she hadn't seen the boy again.

She'd ask her sailor to find him and make sure he was okay. If her sailor asked why she didn't go to the police, she'd explain she had talked to them. They, too, had lost track of him. They asked for her help. If her sailor wanted to know why she didn't consult the cards about the boy's whereabouts, she'd tell him how the cards never betrayed a pure heart. And Juliet was sure the boy had a pure heart.

Of course, she realized her sailor wouldn't literally wash up on the shoreline, especially with all the ferries and docking boats, tugs, and timber floats in the water. She wasn't even sure she could call it a shoreline, with its rocky beaches, marinas, and smokestacks spewing stinky stuff into the air.

Nevertheless, the tarot cards said she'd find him here. She must've gotten to Annie's Court before he did, that's all. Juliet had spent a lifetime, all eighteen years of it, being patient. It wouldn't hurt to wait a little longer.

In the meantime, she had Wilma–a calico kitten Juliet named after a hurricane, one of her customers had told her about. The man had been caught in Wilma's dark winds, his boat ropes breaking from the storm's fierce anger. But that storm was on the east coast, and Wilma, the kitten, lived with Juliet on the west coast.

Wilma had her own dark winds. She chased the shadows of sea eagle wings, but when the real wings showed up, she scooted under the shed, barely escaping the birds' powerful talons. Juliet thought those wing shadows would make a perfect tarot card: a ghostly image representing a real threat.

Juliet's table stood across the market's courtyard from a stand with yellow squash and overgrown pumpkins. To her right, a pastel woman with a toddler sold handmade soaps. She wore a soft paisley skirt, and the child wore a matching dress. Juliet would check out her selection later when she had some money.

She'd love a new bar of fresh lavender soap to take back to the shed. Last week she'd traded a tarot reading for a black plastic bladder she filled with fresh water, warmed in the sun, and used as a sixty-second shower. That warm water was sixty seconds more shower than she'd had all month. It was so much better than the sponge baths she'd been taking. Juliet loved it. The only thing missing was good soap. Maybe the woman would even trade one of her bars for a reading.

Two barefoot twin girls and a man that might be their father flanked the other side of the vegetable stand. She had a clear view of the wild assortment of wooden toys they sold. Most of the toys were animals, including a warthog and a wolverine, fish jumping off ledges and girls holding tiny kittens. Some carvings had thin copper wire twirled around to create little cities, caves, and sailboats. A white wolf stood on a coiled-copper rock. Three miniature teens drove a copper convertible.

The twins wore teal rayon jumpers. Juliet wondered if the man made the jumpers too. The girls stared at her with tired, blank eyes, like maybe they'd been in the sun too long, or were sick of being at the market. Maybe they just wanted to go home to their mother and have a good nap.

Across the street, behind the mall, almost directly behind Juliet's table, a woman with a long-haired spaniel held a sign that said, "We need help." She had long, stringy hair that matched the dog's hair. Juliet worried about the dog and the woman, in that order. She'd give the woman some money once she had some. Begging was a tough profession-about the toughest one around.

Juliet hated asking for help. Beg, borrow, or steal was not for her. Well, she might steal if she had to, for the dog's sake.

"You tell fortunes?" the man from the toy booth asked. He had a soul patch under his lower lip, thick brown and gray hair cut short, and bright green eyes, eyes a woman could fall into-eyes that made Juliet lose her balance for a minute. But then, she saw the wrinkles at the corner of his mouth when his lips turned into a smirk. He was at least twice her age. Too old for Juliet.

Aunt Gloria had swooned over older green-eyed men, and Juliet had seen where that attraction had gotten her. Of course, Juliet knew it wasn't a man's age or his green eyes that posed the problem. It was some little rock of darkness in a man's heart that collected dust and grime year after year.

The toymaker held a cinnamon roll in one hand. Its scent drifted up and seduced Juliet in a different way. Her mouth watered as she looked across lettuce bins and new snow peas at the bakery booth. She only needed one customer. Then, she could buy her own cinnamon roll.

He stared at her and took a bite of the roll, bumping it into his soul patch. It was as if he didn't quite know how to locate his own mouth. The white frosting glittered on his lower lip, reflecting the late morning sun. He smiled, revealing white teeth with little bits of dough in them.

Clearly, he was not her sailor.

But there was something about those eyes.

They looked into her, looked through her, investigating her, down to the very bottom of her thick, heavy heart. She thought he saw the good and bad lurking there, hiding, waiting, wanting to be drawn out.

"Well, do you?" he asked with his mouth full.

"What?"

"Tell fortunes?"

"I read the tarot and the cards talk. Would you like your cards read?"

"The cards talk. Cute. How much?"

"Twenty dollars." She'd jacked the price up five dollars. Juliet didn't like being called cute.

"I can turn twenty into eighty in a poker game," he said, rubbing the soul patch and smearing the frosting. "Oh, okay. Deal me some cards."

Comparing the tarot to poker was like comparing night to the day, the coast to the desert, witless idiots to geniuses of the western world. But she needed the money. She fixed her eyes on him, shifting the cards. She calmed her mind with a prayer that the cards would inspire helpful decisions in the man.

"A person does not deal tarot cards," she told him. "It's called a spread. And I'd be happy to." She smiled a not-so-sincere smile and handed him the deck. "Shuffle the cards and think about your questions."

He raised his eyebrows at her. A non-believer. She wasn't sure what he wanted. He wanted anything but his tarot read. The first card proved it. The reversed, or upside down, moon. The upside-down moon meant he was asking for help but ignoring it when it arrived. He'd already traded his own life for power and money. She'd known other men who'd made that mistake. Her mother's cowboy, Harrison, had a moon shadow over him before he disappeared.

"This card means there is deception in your future." She almost said "heart," but it was never good form to insult customers, even if they didn't believe in the tarot. His money would still buy a cinnamon roll and a bar of lavender soap. She turned over another card, the reversed Empress. The second upside down card compounded the first, indicating more secrecy. "This one speaks to something in your past that has been troubling you. It's about to end."

A look of surprise crossed his face. He glanced back at the twins and across the market. Juliet followed his gaze. Another girl, barely a teen, had long red trusses down her back. She sat in a chair at the hair salon booth. A peach polka dot scarf draped around her neck. The hairdresser pulled the girl's beautiful hair into a tight ponytail at the back of her head and cinched it there with a rubber band, creating a full, curly ponytail that glistened in the morning mist.

"No," Juliet gasped as the hairdresser reached for the scissors.

"Keep going," the man with the soul patch said. He looked irritated.

Yes, how dare she pay attention to something other than him? She looked back at the cards. "This card, the Wheel of Fortune, in this place is a good omen. The project you are working on will come to fruition. But this one, Justice, again reversed, sheds darkness on the whole subject. It's good to be thoughtful, good to think of others, good to take off the masks you wear. It also looks like the law will be involved somehow. Perhaps there is a thief nearby, or a snoop. Keep your windows closed and your doors locked. This many reversed cards show a need for extreme caution."

The man took a twenty out of his pocket and handed it to her. "Do you do parties? I'm having a get together next Saturday and I'd love to have you entertain the guests."

Entertain. She really did not like this man. She ran a hand through her hair, flattening the cowlicks and popping them back up. The short hair did nothing to hide her sharp cheekbones. Instead, it stressed the soft curves in her face, her full lips, and her long lashes, the very things that drew men to her.

But she didn't want this man drawn to her. He had strange powers. He turned his gaze on her and she felt dizzy, like he could toss her around with just a shift of his eyes. She stiffened her neck and stood tall, trying to regain her composure. Like him or not, she set up a booth that morning for two reasons. To earn money with tarot readings and as an informant for Detective Benson Picard.

"I do," she said. "A party is expensive."

"How much?"

A hundred dollars to anyone else. "A hundred and fifty dollars."

"Sheesh. What were you in your past life? A bandit?"

"Payable now."

"How do I know you'll show up if I pay you now?"

"I'm here every Saturday. You can find me. Call the market patrol on me, report me as a swindler. I'm not booking my time without the cash up front."

"You take a check."

Juliet smiled sweetly, shook her head, and fluttered her long lashes. She had gray eyes, eyes that were dark and rich, eyes that men seemed to go crazy over, although she had yet to figure out why.

This man, though, seemed impervious. He had his own magic and Juliet was not keen on it. He pulled seven twenties and a ten from his wallet and wrote the address on a piece of paper. "Seven o'clock next Saturday night," he said. "Show up early, before the others. You'll be ready when the guests arrive. You're not there. Believe me, I'll find you."

The tone of his voice reverberated in her chest, like the tower card sitting in dark green waters, trapped in seaweed, a shard of lightning hitting the sky, the earth's warning, just before a quake brings everything down.

She nodded, tucked the money into her back pocket, and picked up the tarot deck, watching him walk to the hair salon booth. He spoke with the hairdresser. After what looked like a tense exchange, she gave him the long, red ponytail. He took it and went over to the girl with the now-short red hair, grabbed her by the arm and tugged her along.

The twins watched, huddled together.

As Juliet did after every reading, she turned the final card in his layout. The hangman, upside down, stared at her, making her feel like she floated in that dark green water. She took a breath, and the feeling passed, leaving the bitter taste of seaweed in her mouth.

CHAPTER TWO

Gazing across the crowd, Kyle preferred the Sunday Farmer's Market to Saturday's. It amazed him how different they were. Only the locals and boat people came out on Sundays. The tourists headed for home or their next destinations. The locals had faces that were lively, honest, and chapped, with ruddy coastal cheeks. They were early risers who dressed, not in spandex and fleece, but in canvas coats, jeans, and fishing boots, ready for the fresh fall that crossed its long shadow over the last days of the market.

The afternoon sun cut through the clouds and splintered the mall, feeling too strong for the time of year. Kyle loved the fall, but today's heat felt pressured, oppressive. Something dangerous boiled up and was about to spill over, flooding out every gain he and the tent camp had made.

It scared him.

Passing booths that overflowed with beets, onions, and new red potatoes, he looked for her, the girl from the old ship. Long before he reached the bakery table, the smells seduced him. With all his might, he resisted the temptation to buy a certain chocolate cookie. The three dollars he'd spend on a cookie could buy food for the camp–proper food like fish or burgers. Kyle passed a waif of a girl with her parents, all three eating such chocolate cookies.

The girl from the old ship would be like this one. She'd be a tender sight, skirt blowing against her knees, slender arms, hoodie hanging heavy over her shoulders. She would be like this girl, only without the parents. He ran a hand through his dark brown hair and hiked up his jeans.

It would take all of Kyle's seventeen years' worth of wisdom, if he counted infancy, which he did, to find her. She'd be here, though. As sure as the sunflowers swayed in the wind, as sure as the cut dahlias graced Annie's Court kitchens, she'd be at the market. She had hit it every weekend in August.

He knew it and the police knew it. They'd be looking for her too. Crossing his fingers, a superstitious gesture that he didn't really believe in, he figured he didn't stand a chance of finding her, much less convincing her to throw in with the rest of the runaways, especially since they were asking a lot and weren't offering that much.

Stephan, the Captain of the tent camp, had sent others out to find her, to no avail. She was a ghostly runner, and good at hiding.

The crowd parted and proved Kyle wrong. Lightly moving her fingers over the leeks, she stood in plain sight, right next to a clean rack of cut broccoli. She was neither waif-like nor slender, but athletic and quick as she slipped a white onion into her Puget Sound sweatshirt pouch.

The girl was a thief. To prevent her arrest, Stephan had sent Kyle to offer a promise of security. Even though she was too young to live at the tent camp, they could find a place for her to live and keep her safe. Still, she'd have to follow their rules. Staying within the law topped the list of those rules.

This girl's slippery fingers would bring the police down on all the runaways. If she caught police attention, the cops would thunder through the tent camp like a tidal wave, sending the kids back to the streets of one city or another. The girl would land in juvenile hall and never make it free and clear to her next birthday. She was all of thirteen, maybe fourteen. She'd go to jail and then home, back in the clutches of whatever had sent her running.

She moved like an innocent among the zucchinis and exotic teas. She had none of the amateur's telltale eye-shifting. No anxiety wafted off her, and her hands weren't shaking. What scared Kyle, and he suspected scared others, was the wild, hard look in her blue-gray eyes. It was the look of someone who'd already been caught and locked down. He'd seen that look before–on fishermen who'd survived a bad storm, and on starving horses in Montana. He'd seen it after the fire on his father.

He watched the sun play off the red tones in her short hair. Word on the street was that her hair was long just yesterday. Kyle reminded himself not to fool himself into thinking he could save her. Only this girl could keep herself out of trouble. If she declined his offer, no one at the tent camp could do anything about it. They offered an alternative, and that's all. Nothing more, nothing less. Stephan said.

As fast as a pat on the back, the girl slipped behind a squash truck. She sidled up to the table and, while the farmer sacked up a half dozen summer squash for a vibrant young biker, she nabbed a twenty from the open till. But then, she bumped the table, and the farmer turned to her.

"I'll take two spaghetti squash." Kyle stepped up. He held out a handful of money.

The farmer turned toward Kyle and the girl backed away.

The squash would cost him at least three of his hard-earned dishwashing dollars, the same price as a chocolate cookie. He hoped the girl was worth it. By the time he paid for the squash, the girl had gone around the corner to the crafts section, where her pouch could really swell. Kyle hooked a finger in his belt loop and twisted the waist of his baggy pants tight as he took off after her. A rain cloud drifted across the sun, passing a shadow on the market. A police officer patrolled a few feet away from a jewelry stand where the girl stood spinning a dull pair of crystal earrings.

Kyle moved to introduce himself. He'd invite her for a cold drink and a burger after his shift at the café. If she agreed to stop stealing, they'd make sure she had food and shelter. They'd even deliver food right to the old ship if she refused to move into a safer setting. That's why Kyle and the others worked–to buy food for the runners.

He'd be kind about his offer. But firm.

Before he could reach her, she laced a lapis necklace between her fingers. Staring right at the officer, as if to perform a magic trick, she twisted her fingers into a fist and the necklace disappeared into her palm. The officer blinked twice and started for her. She flipped the jewelry table and ran toward the chocolate cookie table.

Kyle ran after her, dodging the table and dropping his squash at the officer's feet. He wove his way between colorful potholders and purses made of old jeans. He sprinted past a card table, several cards flipped up between two people, a magic trick in the making. His legs burned as he grabbed the girl by the wrist and dragged her through the crowd.

"Get your hands off me! You stupid moron. Get your friggin' hands off me!" She yanked her arms hard, and the motion pulled Kyle toward her. Too close, she pierced him with her blue-gray eyes.

He stopped in stunned silence, every instinct in him going wrong. A cloud covered the sun, and a chilly wind crossed Kyle's cheeks. Loosening his grip, he let go of the girl as she dumped the contents of her Puget Sound sweatshirt onto the street near the bakery table, the white onion rolling toward the cookies like a foreign ambassador.

Those blue-gray eyes shifted. She gave him an especially rank look of disgust before disappearing into the crowd. He wiped his arms, as if wiping that look off. Kyle felt gross, the same way he felt after a busy night of washing dishes: smeared with sweat and leftover ketchup, other people's potato crumbs clinging to his face.

CHAPTER THREE

A full week had passed since Juliet had accepted the toymaker's offer to read tarot cards for the guests at his Saturday night party. She spent the week regretting the agreement. But she was a woman of her word, another thing she regretted as she got ready for the party.

She wore her black knee-high leather boots, one of two possessions she held onto when she left home. The other was an ivory colored, oversized cable-knit sweater of her mother's. She put on black silky shorts with a loose skirt sewn over the top of them. She'd found the "skort" at The Red Door Thrift Store for three dollars.

Three hard-earned dollars.

She had worked an entire week scrubbing fishing boats for that money, plus a little extra to stow away for a rainy day, her mother's repetitive warning. Her top was a much better deal. Juliet had hand-sewn two red ten-cent scarves together to create a flowing sleeveless halter that tied at her waist. A black sweater the same length as the skort finished the outfit. She was pretty sure she looked good enough.

She pulled a red cap over her black hair. Several strands escaped the red knit and twirled around her face, outlining her sharp cheekbones. Widening her gray eyes to make them sparkle, she practiced one of her looks. People in love had large, soft pupils that made others crazy about them, even if they wore a big sign saying, "I'm already taken." Juliet had seen it with her mother and her mother's cowboy, Harrison.

Her mother had gray eyes like Juliet's, sharp elegant cheekbones, and a soft pale complexion. She had a beautiful face, one that belonged in the movies. As a girl, she had watched her mother grow soft and sleepy around Harrison. Her mother had loved Harrison, and he had been good to Juliet. Until one day he just didn't come home.

She didn't want to think about Harrison as she walked down to The Red Door Thrift Store, to meet Detective Benson Picard. It was two blocks from her shed, just far enough away so no one, especially not the police, would know where she lived. She liked her privacy. Plus, her living situation was illegal. Illegal privacy. She liked the sound of that, like she was an inland pirate.

Picard picked her up on the corner. He wore his same too tight sweater and a tweed flat cap. He turned the car engine off as she got into the front seat.

"I'll be in a meeting for an hour," he said. "Use the cell phone if you need help. I can be there in minutes. I'll bring reinforcements if need be."

"There is nothing to worry about. The guy is annoying, but not a criminal. Yet, someone there might know why the runaways come to Annie's Court."

"And where they go when they leave."

"That too."

Picard bit his bottom lip. "Nevertheless, if there is trouble, you call."

"Okay." Juliet was used to placating others. It was a type of emotional Aikido she'd learned at her aunt's house. She'd say 'okay' and do what she wanted. It kept her mostly safe. Mostly. What a terrible word.

"I mean it." He looked at her for a long minute before starting the car. "You left the tape recorder at home, right? I don't want him thinking you're spying on him. If he finds it, no one will trust you."

"Right. You told me. I left it at home." Feeling the lie in her mouth and the plastic bulk of the recorder in her pocket, Juliet didn't look at him. The recorder was a good way to catch anything questionable and have a record of the information for later. Getting information was the only reason she was on this escapade to start with—to catch the troublemakers. To keep the runaways out of danger. She should be back at the shed with Wilma, tucked into bed reading old magazines.

The detective dropped her off in front of the toymaker's condo. The building's shiny metallic front glimmered in the evening light. She heard the waves lapping at the broken edge of the shore, their constant, hypnotic rhythm drawing fishing boats home.

"Any trouble at all? You call me," Picard said again.

Juliet nodded, swung her legs sideways, and pushed herself up out of the sedan and its low seat. She closed the front door and opened the back door, grabbed her tarot bag off the black cloth seat, and shut that door too. She was going to a party.

• • •

"You made it." The man with the soul patch stood in the open door wearing a silky white shirt tucked into black pleated trousers. Diamond bracelets and a gold neck chain advertised his wealth.

The room had a high ceiling, large bay windows, and walls of slate blue, like the sea in the evening light. A cabinet full of dolls with bright satin hats and long dresses stood next to one filled with Kachinas. Her mother had collected the small carved figures dressed in soft beaded leather like ancient shamanic dancers. A third cabinet housed toys like the ones he sold at the market. But these toys were even more exquisitely crafted.

Wooden twin girls with emerald, green eyes, eyes that appeared to be real emeralds, held twin kittens. The kittens' eyes glittered with red rubies, and tufts of real fur lined the inside of their ears. Their mouths opened. Juliet could almost hear their soft meows, asking to be let out of the glass cabinet.

"Of course, I made it. I keep my word." She wrapped her arms around herself, pulling the sweater tight. It was a nervous habit she'd had as a kid.

"And you got here early. Just as I instructed."

"Yes," she said. "As you instructed." Juliet did not like to be instructed.

"We'll use a table from the kitchen for the cards and put it over there."

"I brought my own table."

"You won't need it," he said. His voice softened from an insinuated demand to something clear and easy, like the jazz playing in the background.

He pointed to a large living area where a polished wooden floor stretched out to the long windows looking out on the Inland Passage, the huge expanse of water between the mainland and the islands. She could see the shipping channel where the boats ran their goods up the Inland Passage and into British Columbia.

A brown leather sectional and a matching overstuffed chair turned their backs on the windows, a thick Oriental rug between them. A dining room table of dark wood, maybe walnut, stood near one wall. The furniture smelled fresh, like it belonged at the center of a showroom.

More exotic smells wafted up to meet Juliet. Coffee laced with rich spices, a deep musk that made her think of the forest. The smell of old quilts. That scent nearly brought her to her knees as her mind filled with images of her mother's quilts: elephants on a red background with the jungle behind them, the plaid diamond quilt, the purple star quilt. She'd left them behind at Aunt Gloria's. Grief flooded her heart and left just as quickly.

From the condo, Juliet could see the tide had come in and a light fog dusted the bay. Two small boats made their way back to the safe harbor, their lights flickering in the mist. Clouds crowded the sky, and the sun had all but dropped out of sight, turning the heavens pink and red. Something caught in the power lines looked like a blue heron, its wings splayed out, the feathers ragged. Then, Juliet saw it was just a colorful kite. The red, yellow, and blue materials swirled and resisted the wind like a dancer's skirts. Across the water, industrial smoke rose from the lumber mill's chimney, spreading soot and darkening the sunset. It dampened Juliet's mood, watching the beauty sullied by that industrial air.

But work waited, and so did the toymaker.

"What's that perfume you're wearing?" He bore those green eyes into hers, giving her that sense of familiarity again, making her stop and hold her breath.

Something wicked and not quite real poured over her like molasses. Count to ten, she told herself. Think of something else, something other than her sailor, something other than her mother's lost cowboy. Something other than the father she never knew. Something other than this man's green eyes and the way they made her lose her balance.

Every girl loses her first love, her mother had told her. The cowboy wasn't her mother's first, though. Her mother's first love had been Juliet's father, who disappeared one day and never returned. Just like, years later, Harrison disappeared, cowboy hat and all. A very unusual circumstance, her mother had said, her voice milky and faraway.

The dizziness Juliet felt around the toymaker was one good reason not to trust him. She shook her head, trying to dislodge the spell that overcame her when he looked at her like that.

"Smells like lavender," he was saying.

"Help me with this table." She leaned her own table against the wall and ignored his comment. He was right, of course. It was the lavender soap from the market, and it was heavenly. "It should be easy to get to at the edge of the room. A side attraction, but not the party."

"I can see why the guests would think it's the party." He tugged at her sleeve, rubbing his thumb up and down the soft material of her sweater. "Mohair?"

"Something cheap," she said, uncomfortable being so close to him. She pulled away to lift the table. "Grab the other end of it. When will the guests arrive?"

"Just me and you tonight, babe."

Her heart flipped, and she stopped with the table in mid-air. She should have known better. His hundred and fifty dollars and Picard's promise of additional money had made her foolish. "Tell me you're kidding?"

"What? You're paid already, aren't you?" That melodic, hypnotic voice. He narrowed his eyes at her, unblinking, holding her still, something she didn't understand. He looked away and freed her.

"I don't do private parties." Her voice had that smooth, far away sound.

The doorbell rang, and she burned a look into him.

He smiled, a smile that only half charmed her.

"OK, I was kidding. By the way, I am Tony LeCrosse."

I know who you are, she fumed inside, the spell broken. To work, she had to concentrate. She did not need the rug pulled out from under her and then shoved back in, all twisted. She could not stand on that. A fighter jet from the naval base flew overhead, screaming across the sky. Screaming like she wanted to scream. Be careful, the jet screamed, mimicking the danger in the room.

Juliet took the warning.

Mr. Green Eyes had finally given her his name. Foolishly, she hadn't even asked. She'd only asked for an address and then given the address to Detective Picard. The detective had given her LeCrosse's name.

Picard knew this business.

Juliet didn't.

"Georgy, my boy, hunter extraordinaire," Tony said to an older man at the door. The man had rosy cheeks, deep wrinkles, and brown plastic glasses. The man bobbed his way into the room. "This is Juliet. She'll tell you your future."

Juliet went cold. She did not remember telling him her name.

"If I have a future," Georgy My Boy said. Over brown pants, he wore a brown jacket that needed a tailor to let it out at the waist.

"George, George, George. You've been repeating that same soppiness since we were thirteen. I'll tell it then. This is your future." Tony gestured at the toys, a wooden clock ticking away, a dog barking in silent glee. "You're still denying it, you crazy old fool."

"I suppose you're right, Tony. Got anything to drink?"

Tony poured him four fingers of whiskey and splashed a little coke on top.

I *can* tell his future, she thought. She stepped to the table and rolled the sleeves of her sweater between her fingers, releasing the musty smell of being too long at the thrift store.

George turned to Juliet. "So, you're a fortune teller. You any good?"

"I don't tell fortunes, George. I spread cards and the cards talk."

"The cards talk. That's cute."

Cute. Just like the toymaker. She already hated this party. She wanted to go home but didn't want to interrupt Picard, even though he'd made it clear she was to call him at the first sign of trouble. This wasn't trouble, though. This was annoyance, the kind that makes your skin crawl. She could walk home, but the fresh bite of the fall air meant she'd freeze in her little black skort.

"Nice boots." Georgy My Boy stared at her boots and dragged his eyes up her thighs. "Nice skirt." He didn't stop there. He moved his eyes to her breasts, in their red scarves. "Sweet. I want my fortune told." He touched her arm, not once looking at her face.

"That'll cost you more." Juliet grabbed his wrist.

"How much?"

"A trip to the county jail."

Now, Georgy My Boy looked up at her.

"You choose," she said. She didn't know if she could keep her mind clear enough to read this man's cards. But then, she didn't have to. She'd spread the cards and his pea-brain could read them for itself.

"Whatsa matter? You can't take a joke. Okay. Tell me my future."

Juliet sat behind the table and took her cards out of her bag. She ruffled them twice and handed the deck to him. He shuffled the deck, the bad psoriasis on his hands flaking onto the table. Her mother had had psoriasis. Juliet was convinced that it was a disorder of the stomach. Her mother had vacillated between eating mainly vegetables and eating mainly junk food. When she ate vegetables, her psoriasis got better; when she ate junk food, it got worse.

George put the cards on the table. "My life is in your hands."

"What kind of reading do you want?"

He stared at her, blank-eyed.

She noticed his left eye watered, creating a face that looked half sad. The other half was bitter or resigned. She couldn't tell which. "There are different types of readings. A two-card spread is used to answer a question. 'Should I do this? Or should I do that?' A three-card spread represents past, present, and future. It helps a person look at the road they've been down, the road they're on, and where they're going if they stay on that road. A four-card spread is the one I most often do for people. It offers advice for overcoming obstacles and sometimes sheds light on the purpose of those obstacles.

"Then, there's the traditional Celtic cross, a ten-card spread that gives you a lot of information about whatever your question is." Juliet picked up the cards and widened her gray eyes at him, trying to center herself and control the situation. She couldn't hold a grudge, and she hated that about herself. "Have you ever done this before?"

"Hung out with gypsies and fortune tellers? No. Put my life in the hands of a child? How old are you? Don't answer that. No, I've never done this before."

"Welcome, welcome," Tony said to each new arrival. The crowd moved like a wave from the doorway into the large living room, some people splashing into the kitchen and bedrooms. George seemed impatient to get another drink and join the crowd.

Juliet drew in a breath and let it go, studying the room. At least forty people had arrived while she'd been talking with George. Drinks materialized in their hands. A woman stared at her. She looked to be in her late thirties, her auburn hair cut sharply at her chin. Tight jeans hugged her narrow hips. The rolled-up jean bottoms showed off her ankles and open-toed turquoise shoes.

Three older gentlemen pulled out cigars and headed for the balcony. A young man in black pants and a black t-shirt sat alone in the corner, looking oddly familiar. Sulking, he ignored the others as they came in. He might have been Juliet's age or a little younger. He had the same green eyes as Tony, and she guessed he might be related to him. Maybe an errant son. Or maybe not. Tony had gathered a menagerie of people together. Juliet should just have fun with the readings and drum up future business for the Farmer's Market, but she felt sullen, discombobulated, and out of her element.

She turned back to Georgy My Boy. "Then, I'd recommend the four-card spread."

"Fine. Toss 'em down."

The first card bore a picture of three swords stabbed through the heart, upside down. "This card represents the situation," she said. "A breakup of some kind. You refuse to look at your part in it, blaming someone else for your alienation. You keep refusing to do what needs to be done, and it leaves you depressed and bitter, gnawing on a past that can't be changed."

Of course, Juliet already knew this pattern about him. She could see the ghost of it in his clothes and the way he held himself. His past haunted him. These things she couldn't tell him.

Georgy My Boy grit his teeth and narrowed his eyes at her. "You studied up on who'd be here so you could pull off this circus trick."

"I assure you; I did not study up on anyone."

"It doesn't take a genius to see I've had a hard time." He investigated his glass as if it had the answers.

"There's more," Juliet said. "You've barely gotten started on this reading. I see you hesitating, having second thoughts about it. If you give up now, you'll never know what action to take and the likely outcome."

"I know what action to take."

"I've only laid down one card. You have three to go."

"So, you can say I've had not only a hard time, but a really hard time? No, thank you. I don't need some girl telling me what to do about my life. Tony can a man get a drink or what?" he yelled across the room and left the table.

It was a shame, too, because he had an ace of swords in the position of recommended action. The ace of swords was a good sign he could change his life and repair the relationship–she guessed with his wife–if he wanted. But an upside-down king of swords held the outcome position, signifying a person using words to gossip, slander, and pit people against each other. True to form, Juliet guessed.

"Would you like a drink?" The girl from the Farmer's Market, the one with the now short red hair, stood in front of her. She had pale blue-gray eyes, a child's eyes, with sleepy eyelids, and a slight nose that went off to one side, as if it had been broken and never set right. She wore black footless tights with a soft green tunic. Simple sandals with leather straps crossed the arches of her feet where the bones raised. The boy in black was watching her.

"No, thank you. I don't drink," Juliet said. And neither should you. "How old are you?"

"Oh, I don't drink either," she said. "I just help my father. Please don't tell anyone. He'll go to jail and then I'll have nowhere to live."

"Your father?"

"Tony. The one who hired you." She indicated Mr. Green Eyes.

They did look alike. They both had eyes a person could fall into. But Mr. Green Eyes could be her grandfather. The boy in the corner got up suddenly and left the party. No hellos or goodbyes, just an abrupt exit.

"How about a coke then?" the girl asked.

Juliet turned back to her. "Sure, why not? What's your name?"

"Twyla."

"Pretty name. It suits you. Is your mother here?"

Twyla shook her head.

"Maybe you should stay with your mother during these parties," Juliet said. "There are a lot of men, who knows what they might get up to. You should be going to the movies with girls your own age."

Tony came up and put his arm around the girl's waist, pulling her into him in a way that made him look like no one's father. "People never stop telling you what to do, right?" He gave Twyla a brilliant smile.

Light reflected off her tunic, which had jewels sewn into the silk.

The girl tilted her head to Tony, turned to Juliet and started to say something, and stopped.

The woman with the auburn hair came up behind Twyla and put her arms around her. She had brilliant green eyes like Tony's. The three of them stood looking for all the world like a good American family. Twyla slipped out from under the woman's arms and followed Tony into the kitchen.

"Enjoy the party," the woman said, leaving Juliet without really greeting her. Her auburn hair bobbed at her chin as she turned toward the door, where a new group was chatting.

Twyla brought the coke. "Let me know if you need anything. I'm the official hostess."

"Okay. Thank you."

Twyla looked over at some new arrivals. "Kyle! What is he doing here?"

Juliet shrugged. What did she know?

"He's crashing the party," Twyla said. "I'm going to tell him to leave." She stomped over to him, and Juliet could see her hands clutched into fists and held tight at her sides. She couldn't hear what she said, but she could see the fire in her eyes, eyes Juliet would not want aimed at her.

Kyle, a tall brown-haired boy who looked to be about Juliet's age, talked with his hands, palms open, like he was trying to push a genie back into its bottle.

Tony LeCrosse joined the conversation with a curious look on his face. He looked at Kyle when he talked, and then at Twyla when she talked. Juliet sipped her coke as she watched the exchange. She vaguely wondered if the two had been dating. Twyla looked too young for Kyle.

Somehow Tony settled it, Twyla calmed down, and Kyle stayed.

Juliet had nearly finished her coke when Twyla's voice took on a soft tone and they walked toward her. "Want your cards read?" Twyla asked Kyle. "Tony says Juliet is good."

"I'm glad you changed your mind about talking to me," Kyle said.

"Your cards? This is Juliet."

"Sure," he said. "Let's see what the stars have in store for me." He stood a full head above Twyla, had an athletic build, brown hair, and dark brown eyes. When he smiled at Juliet, she felt her spine turn to stardust and fairies rushed in to hold her up.

Or maybe it wasn't to hold her up from meeting Kyle. Maybe the fairies rushed in to hold her up from the coke she had just sipped down.

CHAPTER FOUR

The next morning, an atom-splitting headache wracked Juliet's brain, making it difficult for her to open her eyes. She shook off the dream of the boy dressed all in black. The boy at the party had disappeared almost as soon as she saw him in Tony LeCrosse's condo. He was nothing but a phantom figure. She wondered if he was even real. In her dream he was real enough, staring her down with LeCrosse's green eyes–staring her into some kind of submission, which she avoided by waking up.

She sat up on the bed, rubbery and faint-hearted, rubbing her head. Through her blurred vision, she saw unfamiliar surroundings. A moose on a wall quilt looked down at her as if she'd done something wrong. Small ceramic bears of all colors lined the windowsills. Copper-coiled dogs danced and jumped in a grassy field.

Photos of the auburn-haired woman covered the dresser. Rows of them looked out at Juliet. It was the same woman who had sauntered into the party last night with her hair cut sharply at the chin, looking like she could be Twyla's mother, and the boy in black's mother. One photo was a marriage portrait. She stood next to a dapper Tony, both smiling into each other's green eyes. She wore a knee-length silk wedding dress with a long chiffon veil. The dress showed off her sculpted calves and the elegant flow of her ankles. A soft perfume and the scent of young love wafted from the pictures–something forever, strong, and good.

A knock came on the bedroom door, the sound slamming a ghostly sledgehammer into her head. The pain spread down her neck and into her shoulders, the pain a living, growing thing.

"Who is it?" she asked, looking at herself in the mirror. She was dressed exactly as she'd been last night, except her boots and sweater were gone. Her skort wrinkled against her thin thighs. Her red halter-top revealed her shoulders and arms. Black cowlicks stuck up in all directions. She glanced around the room for her sweater and didn't find it.

"It's me, Kyle."

Kyle. Who was Kyle?

"Just go away," she said. Feeling awful, she didn't care to see anyone. She must have gotten hit with the flu.

The door opened and a boy in a gray fleece coat poked his head in. His brown eyes and dark hair looked vaguely familiar. Though he was thin, he filled the doorway. Even from the bed where she sat, he smelled like last night's party. The smell sent goose bumps down her arms. She remembered him. He'd arrived at the party awhile after Twyla. After what looked like a fight, Twyla had introduced him as a friend. He'd laughed at that, and said, "at my insistence."

"Kyle. From last night? Maybe you don't remember. You were pretty drunk." He stepped in and eased the door shut behind him. Her radar went off, suddenly alert. She tried not to look like a deer in headlights. A startle response was dangerous among strangers. She'd learned that lesson right after she'd run when safety became a huge concern. Predators could smell fear.

"I remember you," she said, her voice raspy. And then, "I don't drink."

"Well, you have a funny way of not drinking. Rum and cokes, anyone?" He smiled and sat on the bed.

Her world spun.

Light blazed through the sheer curtains, sharp as a razor. She put her hand up to shield her eyes. It didn't help. She put both hands firmly at her sides to keep from being swallowed by the monster that was the bed floating under her in that bright light.

"Listen," he said, putting a firm hand on his knee. His faded blue jeans hung loosely on his narrow legs. "You might be in trouble. Last night, you got very drunk, and some people didn't like the readings you gave them. Tony's not happy about it. He's not saying much and, according to Twyla, that's a bad sign."

Juliet just wanted the pain in her head to go away. Instead, it laid her flat again. "I really don't drink. I ordered a coke. That's all. Someone must've drugged it."

Kyle nodded. It was a kindly nod.

She might have resented his pity if she hadn't been so ill.

"That's what I suspected," he said. "Why would Tony drug you? To set you up for something?"

Juliet thought about Benson Picard. LeCrosse had come to town at the same time a lot of runaways had come and then left. Picard thought LeCrosse had something to do with it. He wanted Juliet to snoop around, see if she noticed anything. Snoop was something she rarely did. She let the cards talk, but as a rule, she did not get involved in other people's business.

"The usual reason people drug others is so they can take advantage of the drugged person," she said. Sexually, she didn't bother to add. She hoped nothing had happened when she was out cold. It was one of the most horrible things. Layne had taught her that. A dirt-filled shame overcame her. "I don't know why he'd drug me. I was hired to *entertain* the guests with tarot readings."

"Which didn't prove entertaining at all. Especially for some people. If they don't think you're a witch, they think you work for the police. Someone even accused you of hacking into his computer to gather information before the party."

"Who thinks I'm that good with a computer?" She wasn't. Her mother had refused to buy a home computer. All she'd learned was in public schools, the basics like word processing, research, games, power points and art brochures, a little bit of coding. Hacking? No way.

"George, Tony's gofer? I found him in here with you."

"Eww." She choked on the shame, holding it tight in her chest.

"About to disrobe."

"Double Eww. Did he?"

"I came to the rescue." Kyle smiled a big, beautiful smile, the morning light shining off his brown hair.

She must be suddenly feeling better because she didn't mind looking at that light in his hair. The hangover made her vulnerable. His smile reached into her dark, murky heart and took away some of the pain. That same smile also unraveled the shame in her chest, making it feel less dense, less ready to implode and ruin everything.

"You mean you're my knight in shining armor?"

He nodded.

"My hero," she said, more to the bed covers than to Kyle. "Thank you."

He shrugged. "I'm glad I walked in when I did."

"Where's Twyla?" Juliet stood up, but the room whirled, forcing her to sit back on the bed. She waited to find her bearings. "I need to talk to her. She served me a spiked coke."

"I haven't seen her since late last night." A door opened and a shadow slid over Kyle.

"You're awake. How do you feel?" Tony stood in the doorway in a black bathrobe loosely cinched at the waist. His gray and brown hair stuck straight up on one half of his head. The stench of aftershave wafted in. "You were quite the party girl. I think you drank too much."

"I didn't drink too much," Juliet said, holding her head. She had to admit she smelled like the day after a good drunk. But it was impossible. "I don't drink. Someone drugged me."

"Nonsense," LeCrosse said. "No one here would do such a thing." He reached out and touched her bare collarbone.

The room spun, and the dresser was bathed in brilliant white light. Dust danced in the sunny beams. A copper coiled dog jumped for joy and ran free. The vanity mirror glittered. Juliet saw herself there, wrapped in white roses. The petals floated around her like snow.

Kyle took her hand, and she instantly was back in LeCrosse's condominium again, her weight pressed firmly against the mattress.

LeCrosse sat down beside her. He smelled like an ashtray, and like whiskey. The odors pinched her stomach into a tightly revolving ball.

"Mr. LeCrosse. I don't drink. I take my jobs seriously."

He held out the tape recorder. "I'm confused then. What is this?" He pushed a button and the sounds of last night's party shouted at her. The sound of Juliet drunk.

She didn't remember turning it on. And she surely didn't remember losing possession of it, or herself, for that matter. She looked around the room for something to make sense of the night.

The vanity table held a small circle of toys, fish jumping off the ship's stern into the water, reversing time, tiny sailboats gliding in luminous colors across the sea, brilliant soldiers equipped with tiny guns, all of them pointing at her. She felt their invisible bullets fly.

She held her hand out, palm facing him, half a surrender. "Please, turn it off. It's my good luck charm. I never turn it on. I didn't even know there was a tape in it still."

"Oh, there's a tape in it."

"An accident, I assure you."

"This device is not okay at a party where we go around revealing secrets. You assured me you'd have the utmost discretion. But this? A recorder is not discreet." LeCrosse chastised her as if she were a child. He took the tape out and put it in his pocket, handed the tape recorder to her. "I better not find this or anything like it around my home again. Do you understand?"

"I'm sorry," she said, putting the recorder in her skort pocket. "It was foolish of me. I appreciate you hiring me. I did my best to help your guests, but I hear they're not happy." Something strange glimmered in his eyes and disappeared, taking the headache with it. In its place was heart-stopping despair. Juliet wondered what on earth was going on. "I'd like to talk to Twyla."

"She's gone. Ran off to her mother again. That girl can't decide where she wants to live. It drives us crazy." Those soft, green, sultry eyes caressed her face, erasing time. LeCrosse looked almost normal, like a decent, concerned father.

Through the open door, the tall living room windows beckoned to Juliet. She stood and steadied herself. Kyle let go of her hand, offering his arm. She took it. With his help, she walked into the other room and stood at the windows. Two crane barges were cleaning up the mill. The lumber mill's stacks shone in the morning sky, belching their gray smoke into the air. Two oil tankers from Canada were docking. The woman from the photos arrived and stood next to LeCrosse, leaning into him affectionately, running a finger over the soft black robe as she looked around the living room. Her gaze landed on Juliet, an outsider.

"Alice LeCrosse," Tony said. "Alice, Juliet and Kyle."

"Pleased to meet you." Alice grasped Juliet's free hand, smiling brightly at her.

Apparently, Juliet was no longer an outsider, but Alice LeCrosse's instant best friend.

The woman's eyes shone green, matching Tony's, matching last night's boy in black. They were clear and beautiful, like

Twyla's. Except for the way she hung on Tony, she could have been his sister. Her face was ivory white. Her lithe body moved with the grace of a swan. She wore a simple cotton dress, cut low. Something rough lay just below the surface, maybe long years of drugs on the streets. Or perhaps a deep, unsatisfied hunger, a thievery that drove her choices until she somehow landed in the lap of luxury with Tony LeCrosse. Underneath it all lay lost youth and innocence.

How Juliet knew any of this information, she had no idea. It was sudden knowledge that came in spurts since her mother had died. These thoughts filled a mile-deep chasm that appeared the day her family went from small to nothing.

Juliet felt Alice's cool, sharp gaze. A shiver hit her spine.

A horrible hunger was still at the center of this woman. Juliet's moment of clarity abruptly disappeared, and she was tossed into deep waters, unable to breathe. Murky seaweed clogged her brain, her nose, mouth, eyes, and ears in a thick veil she had to fight off.

Kyle slipped his arm around her waist and held her snugly.

Just like that, the watery seaweed was gone. The fog lifted and disappeared. Through an open window she heard a ferry's horn announce its departure. A siren raced through the streets. Juliet saw the boats in the harbor. The mill smoke floated across the sky. And LeCrosse's charming face waited for her to say something, beckoning her to give in and tell the truth about why she was there.

But Alice was still talking, coming to her rescue. "I told Tony the tape recorder was an innocent mistake. But you know men." She winked at Juliet, ran her hand down her red print dress. "They have to discover everything for themselves." She ignored Kyle, as if he existed only to prop Juliet up.

Even in her rag doll state, it struck Juliet as odd. The last thing she could do, even if she wanted to, was ignore Kyle. She felt his warm hand on her arm. Her legs trembled, and it wasn't residue from the spiked drink. She didn't understand it. Juliet had no room in her heart for feelings. She'd made sure of that. But Kyle's hand on her arm opened something small and fragile in her heart and let a glimmer of light in. Kyle had come to her rescue when she couldn't rescue herself, something that never happened to Juliet.

Out on the water, the morning fog sifted out of the bay and sailboat masts bobbed in the sun. Sailors navigated the Inside Passage, coaxing the wind and waves to carry them north, through the Strait of Georgia, toward Desolation Sound, the Broughton Islands, and eventually Alaska. On the water the coastal world might be sweet and elegant.

But in Tony and Alice LeCrosse's condominium, something sour twisted in Juliet's stomach. She turned in Kyle's arms, gazing over his shoulder. Her boots sat next to the chair at the tarot table, her black sweater flung over the chair. She had evidently made herself quite at home. Her cards were still on the table, the deck in disarray.

The lone figure of Death, upside down, looked up at her from his wrong-sided head.

CHAPTER FIVE

Two days later, Juliet sat on the curb across the street from the red brick mall of the Farmer's Market, the mall emptied of vendors on weekdays. A dog and its owner played in the dog park behind her. Across the street, someone in the old railroad building opened its garage doors, revealing a smooth wooden floor. A small, athletic woman in a martial arts uniform ran a broom across the floors. Juliet recognized her as the teacher.

Low blood sugar made Juliet dizzy and weak, giving her that underwater feeling, and making it hard to think. It gnawed at her, and her belly rumbled. She should've eaten before leaving home that morning. Just like she couldn't shake the hunger, Juliet couldn't shake Tony LeCrosse's face. It showed up on the sides of buildings, in trees, in the sand lining the shore. She'd wash it away only to have it appear later, on the back of her hand or in the dew wet grasses. She couldn't understand why the man haunted her. He bore down on her with his iridescent green eyes, holding her captive in her own thoughts.

She'd met men without hearts. Normal bouts of conscience didn't affect them. They looked right through people, wanting to own the agency of others, bending others to their will, staring them into submission. It worked. Others did their bidding.

She also knew the danger of assuming a darkness around others that didn't exist. It could leave her alone and isolated, in a prison of her own making. After living at Aunt Gloria's house with Layne, Juliet had closed her heart, locked it up tight, to protect herself. It wasn't a bad strategy. Just not the best.

In her palm, she cupped the magician's card. It showed up that morning, reversed, warning her, just like before her mother died, the card announcing the all-wrong timing of her mother's death. Now it sent Juliet a message about LeCrosse, if only she could decipher it.

Mindlessly, Juliet scratched pictures into the concrete with a rock. A horse, a truck, a man, a woman, one giant teardrop surrounding them all. Her mother's cowboy, whose disappearance was so much like her father's that her mother died of a broken heart. Police records said a car accident killed her, but Juliet knew better. Her mother had loved Harrison. She went crazy after he left, started drinking. Really drinking. One night, Juliet begged her to stay home but her mother, drunk and raving, got into Harrison's truck and went looking for him. All she found was a power pole that broke from the impact of the truck, taking out the power across the valley.

This morning, clouds rolled across the sky, painting frost on car windows and promising a downpour. Juliet felt it inside. Her dark hair sprang out from under a blue knit stocking cap, disheveled and wild, like her stormy gray eyes. She still felt fragile from whatever someone had slipped into her drink at LeCrosse's party. Her mind was confused, and half stolen by thoughts of the man. She'd barely managed to get dressed that morning. But here she was in black stretch pants, a blue Refuge Cove t-shirt, and the same black sweater she'd worn to the party.

The taekwondo club rented a studio space in the old train depot and Juliet watched as it filled up with kids in white uniforms and colorful belts. They lined up and bowed to the instructor. After they ran around the room several times, the teacher called out commands and the students executed kicks, punches, and steps. The young martial artists yelled as they moved down the wooden floor, eyes focused on the dark-haired woman.

In another life, Juliet had dreamed of learning martial arts. That desire was before and after Harrison disappeared. Or, more accurately, because of Harrison. Her mother had insisted someone was after him, that they needed to protect themselves. When he disappeared, Juliet watched and listened, moving through the world like a wildcat. She'd read books on taekwondo from the library, but never took a class.

She still had time. Once Juliet shook off the black cloud of loss and grief, once she got on her feet and settled in an apartment, she could take any class she wanted. Once she figured out what LeCrosse was up to, and Benson Picard paid her real money.

Detective Picard sat down on the curb next to Juliet. He wore a black turtleneck and gray slacks, looking a well-rested fifty, making fifty look good. He offered her a ham sandwich and a cup of coffee. She took both. He gave her another twenty. She tucked it into her sweater pocket.

"LeCrosse is dangerous," Picard said. "I've asked around the station. They've got nothing real on him, but they say he's a charlatan, trained in the art of black magic."

"There's no such thing," she said, only half believing it. "It's the mind playing tricks on itself, helped by someone who knows how to manipulate others."

"Your tarot?"

"That's the mind working with images, bringing forth what it already knows. A bit of love and magic. Definitely not black."

"How did you learn?" Picard asked. Juliet looked sideways at him. He seemed genuine, like he honestly wanted to know. She didn't trust easily but couldn't see the harm in telling him.

"My mother taught me." A dog barked in the park behind them. Crows cawed and gathered in a tree. The wind picked up leaves and tossed them around. Clear my mind, she prayed to the wind, feeling a bit of grace in it.

"Your mother must be very open-minded."

"Yes," Juliet replied. "She was."

Picard drew in a breath. His eyes drifted away from Juliet. "Was. I'm sorry. How long ago did she die?"

"About two years ago, after my sixteenth birthday."

"I'm sorry," he said again.

"Me too."

"Are you okay?" Picard asked. "You don't seem yourself."

Juliet raised an eyebrow at him. How would he know? He'd barely just met her.

"Just sleepy. That's all."

"Well, be careful. Don't take unreasonable risks."

Juliet raised both eyebrows at that.

•   •   •

After Picard left, Juliet stayed sitting on the sidewalk and finished the sandwich. Wind rattled the fence surrounding the dog run behind her. Leaves from the large maple fell into her hair and lap, cast about by a whim of nature. "You and me," she said to the leaves, "we're kindred souls."

"Remember me?" Kyle stood above her in his gray fleece, his brown hair combed back off his forehead. His square shoulders relaxed into a bear-like shape, making him look old and young at the same time.

"I was drugged for a night, not forever," she said. "You're Kyle, my knight in shining armor, my knight of swords, the one who rescued me."

"I'm glad I walked in when I did. It's not a joke. We should call the police."

"No. I have a friend on the force. I'll tell him." She bit her lip at the lie. Picard had just been with her, and she hadn't told him.

Kyle nodded and let it go. Behind them, two more dogs entered the run. They chased balls and sticks and each other. Their owners laughed and sounded delighted.

"Have you seen Twyla?" Kyle asked.

"No."

"I haven't been able to find her since the party."

"Tony said she went back to her mother's."

Kyle didn't seem satisfied. "She didn't seem too keen on her mother. It makes me worry." He sat down beside Juliet.

She felt so comfortable and relaxed with his closeness. Sudden energy pulsed through her veins. She hated that effect, hated herself for being soft and vulnerable, for falling in slow motion, for wanting to lean into him, for feeling out of control. "Maybe she did go home to her mother. Maybe it's that simple."

Kyle looked away and sighed. "She said you were watching her at the Farmer's Market when she got her hair cut."

"The hair Tony took from the stylist?"

"She said her dad wanted to donate it for a cancer wig." Kyle rubbed the sleeve of his sweatshirt, rolling the cuff and unrolling it.

"He's not her dad." Juliet pulled the long sweater tight around her.

Kyle nodded. "Was she there for drugs?"

"Maybe. I don't know. What's your part in all this?"

He looked at her and shifted his shoulders.

"Oh, I see. It's a secret." Her own bitterness surprised Juliet. She had secrets, too. Still, she hated being iced out, especially by someone who had just made her swoon.

A gaggle of geese flew over, honking one long noise.

Kyle nodded.

"It's the tent town, isn't it?"

He stared flatly at the brick mall and the taekwondo class, giving her nothing.

"I lived near the tent town before. When I turned eighteen, they ran me off, out of the area, threatened me, saying I'd bring disaster to all of them. Just for being eighteen. I wasn't even in their camp. You're a heartless bunch."

"Stephan ran you off. He's nearly eighteen. So am I."

"My advice is, find a place to go because he won't cut you any slack. Once you turn, it's a regular 'Lord of the Flies' out there."

In the dog park, Juliet heard one owner tell his dogs to be nice and mind their manners. She figured her mother was talking to her from the other side. Be nice and mind your manners. Would anyone kick Stephan out? Maybe. She didn't care anymore. She was much happier in town, in the shed. A hundred square feet of bliss. Shelter from the wind and rain. The only rules she had to follow were her own. And, of course, the town laws.

"I knew he had his quirks," Kyle was saying. "I didn't know he was so callous." He tugged at the back of her stocking cap, tucking a strand of hair inside. "You have an escapee," he said. He let his hand rest on her back. "You should let it grow. It shines a very pretty red when the sun comes out."

"Who needs the sun?" she asked, softening her tone, surprising herself, her heart running wild, "when my knight in armor shines so brightly?"

• • •

That evening Juliet heard sounds in the old ship and caught its musty odor as she walked up to it. Rotted wood left holes in the hull, the molded planks falling to the ground. Vines climbed the bow, sprawling onto the deck as if to capture the ship's huge wooden hull and hold it hostage. The ship had sailed into the rocky Annie's Court beach long before anyone had settled there.

It started the seed of the town, landing close to where Juliet lived. There it stayed, dry-docked for more than a century.

The sounds bothered her. Sometimes animals got trapped inside the old ship and panicked, calling out in terrible ways. Their terrified cries reached her shed and haunted her, insisting that she help. Searching for them was dangerous, but she hated the idea of the animals being caught with no escape. Juliet hated animals suffering, period. The mold alone could sicken and kill them. She wouldn't want to be trapped in that musty air. She had to find the animal and scare it off the ship.

This cry sounded a lot like childhood pain. Probably a young cat. Juliet held an old can of bear spray in front of her like a beacon lighting the way. The last thing she needed was some cougar jumping on her when she tried to free it. The ship was dark. She should have brought a flashlight along. "Hey kitty-kitty," she said, alerting the animal to her presence. "Hey kitty." The sounds stopped. Some animal knew she was there.

The moist wood had grown a carpet of green moss and she pressed her feet into its mat. The ship had plenty of years to collect the morning dew and let it settle in the wooden seams of the vessel. She tried to stay in the lit areas. A scratching, wheezing sound came from below. Against her better judgment, she climbed down the old staircase, certain that if the animal didn't get her, the rotten wood would break, and she'd crash to her death.

Before she died, she should say her prayers and ask forgiveness for her sins: running away and abandoning her aunt to a ruthless boyfriend. Maybe if she'd stayed, her aunt would have tossed the guy out. Maybe Juliet could have kept her mother's cowboy from disappearing, too. Then, her mother wouldn't have vanished in that blazoned moment of too much love and too much wine, a moment Juliet would give anything to erase from their lives. Her gut hurt, knowing she'd never have another chance to save her mother, to stand by her and be a good daughter.

At the bottom of the stairs, a soft light flickered across the inside of the boat's hull. A candle burned next to a huddle of rags on the aft wall. Tufts of red hair stuck out from a green hood. Twyla looked up, slant-eyed from droopy lids. Her nose ran. She pulled an old army blanket around her shoulders and coughed, looking like a real Four of Cups, abandoned and alone, the cups knocked over and completely empty, one last chance for something good.

"What are you doing here?" Juliet asked, noting the wrappers, the small fire pit, and the cabinet covered with a soiled print cloth. Stupid question. She was living there. "You can't stay here. The boat is probably making you ill. It's full of mold. Spores get into your lungs and make you sick."

Twyla nodded a slow, sleepy nod. "I don't have anywhere else to go."

"What about your so-called father, Tony?" Juliet didn't like the man, but living with him was better than living on an ancient, moldy boat. "What are those marks on your arms?"

"You're right, he's not my father. Besides, he kicked me out. He won't let me come around when I have bruises. He's afraid he'll be blamed." She held her arm up.

Juliet took a closer look. "He did that?"

Twyla stared at her, blank-faced.

"We'll call social services and get you home. How old are you?"

Twyla turned her head into the blanket and curled up against the wall. "Like they'd care," she said. "Please just go away."

"Sure," Juliet said. "I'll go, but you're coming with me."

"No. I'm fine here."

Juliet knew fine. Fine: terrible but tolerable. Fine: it sucks, but I can handle it. Fine: leave me alone right now; I don't want your help. Fine: just give me some time. Fine: I'll do it myself. Juliet had been fine many times over the years. Her muscles tightened at the thought of it. A brief ray of streetlight shone through a crack in the wood, landing on Twyla's pale face. Her eyes drooped, watery and dull. Her lips quivered and her skin hung on her cheekbones, like the skin had been wrung out and dried.

Twyla was not fine.

"You're coughing and sick," Juliet said.

"Go away."

"If I go alone, I call the cops and they come and get you. You come with me and tell me what happened at Tony's condo, who spiked my drink, who gave you those bruises, and why you left Tony's place. Where's your mother?"

"Seattle."

"You can go to her."

"No. I can't. Her boyfriend is... No."

. . .

After much coaxing and, well, bullying, Juliet got Twyla out of the old ship and into her shed. She fed her some Ramen Noodles and tucked her under a blanket on a foam pad. Twyla had made Juliet promise she would not go to Social Services.

Juliet relaxed on her own bed, thinking.

"They had their chance," Twyla had said, petting Wilma. The calico kitten purred against the girl, slinking in close, bits of hair coming off in Twyla's hand. Wilma turned her belly up, four legs reaching to the sky, trusting the affection, like the world had just gotten a little sweeter.

"Whatever that means," Juliet had said. "Tell me something real. I'm trying to be a friend. I might be able to help you."

Twyla said that social services would send her back home to the same circumstances. They'd done it before. They didn't believe her when she told them her mother's boyfriend was after her. She was in danger with him in the house. The boyfriend had convinced everyone that Twyla lied so she didn't have to follow their rules. He had his own set of rules for Twyla–rules her mother knew nothing about or ignored if there was meth in the house.

Twyla's mother didn't want to believe that he'd cornered Twyla and threatened to hurt her mother if Twyla didn't do what he wanted. She'd already chosen the boyfriend over her daughter. Her mother was too drug-addled to notice the gleam in his eye every time Twyla walked into the room. She didn't notice the too-close touch, or the boyfriend grabbing Twyla by the waist and pulling her on top of him until she fought like a banshee. Once, her mother called the police on Twyla, filing assault charges on her and threatening to send her to juvenile hall.

Juvenile hall would have been preferable to living with her mother's boyfriend. But the justice system gave her one more unwanted chance and sent her back to her mother's house. It had been her demise. One night, when the adults were passed out, Twyla stole away, dressed in warm clothes and carrying a little food and a handful of money. She took a bus north to Annie's Court, thinking she'd reason with her mother when she came to find her. Her mother never arrived.

Juliet wanted to give Twyla a chance to get over her sickness and recover on her own, now that she knew what she feared. She understood being held down and groped and not wanting to go home. She understood it too well. They would figure out something, a foster home, maybe. The girl was too young to live on her own.

But when Juliet awoke in the morning, Twyla was gone.

CHAPTER SIX

The morning after Twyla disappeared, Kyle caught a ride to the city with a truck driver named Arnold.

"My friends call me Arnie," he told Kyle. "You can call me Arnie."

The drive took about two hours in the thick of traffic. Arnie pulled into a warehouse parking lot to drop his goods at a lumber yard. Kyle turned backwards in the cab, thanked Arnie for the ride, and let himself down out of the truck. He started off down the cracked sidewalk toward the center of an old industrial neighborhood.

"Wait!" Arnie yelled.

Kyle turned back to him.

"I've got some errands to run," Arnie said. "If you come back before dark, I'll haul you back up to the Court."

"The Court," Kyle said and smiled at the truck driver's nick name for Annie's Court. He wasn't sure what he'd find in the city, but he'd like to be home by nightfall. "I'll do my best to be here."

After walking several blocks, he stood in front of an old department building. About a decade before, the building had been refashioned into a youth shelter. The windows to the Phoenix Center, a not entirely wholesome place where lost and forgotten teens rose from the ashes, were dim and smoky. He pulled his hands out of his sweatshirt pocket and pushed open the dirty glass door.

The place smelled of cigarettes, sweat, and mold, all mixed into one odorous cocktail, creating a pungent, not exactly inviting, aroma. The walls had been smoked up, painted over, and smoked up again. Kyle wondered how many teens had wandered into these rooms.

Running a hand through his brown hair, he made eye contact with a teen playing pool in the corner. The boy wore tight jeans and an oversized t-shirt. His dark, curly hair bubbled up, adding an extra two inches to his height. He was maybe thirteen, close enough to Twyla's age to know her. The boy went back to the game and made a bank shot off the one ball. He called the eight ball in a corner pocket and banked it. It went right in. Not bad for maybe thirteen.

"Can I help you?" The boy waved the pool stick at Kyle.

"Is the manager around?"

"Looking at him."

"The adult supervisor?"

"Adults," the kid said and shook his head. "Jamison," he yelled at the ceiling. He racked up the pool balls, shifting and shaking them in the plastic triangle, until he seemed satisfied, removed it, and hung it on the side of the pool table.

Kyle glanced up. A fiftyish man with brown, flyaway hair stood behind a sliding glass window gazing down on him. When Kyle waved, the man did not wave back. Behind Kyle, the cracking sound of pool balls breaking apart, and falling into the pockets filled the silence.

Kyle reminded himself of his mission. He was there to find out where Twyla came from, or, more specifically, where her mother lived. Perhaps the girl had returned home. If not, once he found Twyla's mother, he would talk her into leaving the boyfriend and coming to get the girl.

At the Farmer's Market, Twyla had been angry with him for — of all things — rescuing her from the police. She'd yelled at him that Tony LeCrosse was her father, that he could find her there. He showed up at one of LeCrosse's parties and Twyla was mad as hell at him for coming there, evidently forgetting that she'd told him to find her. After he'd tracked her down, he found Tony posing as a father. Nothing real in it. She told Juliet that her mother lived in Seattle and had a boyfriend who liked little girls.

Now Twyla was sick and needed her mother. And she had disappeared again. Kyle crossed his fingers that if she had come home, she was safe, and Kyle's trip was for naught. But he doubted it.

"Jamison here." The man from the window appeared in person and loomed over him with an outreached hand. He wore glasses and had a tan that peeled where his jaw jutted out from his neck. A flannel shirt hung halfway out of his jeans.

"Kyle, from Annie's Court."

"Spoken like a true runner. Hey, Raffy, how come none of you kids got last names? It's always Mikey from Calgary and Jamie from Portland or Nikki from New York. No last names. Don't you know, kid? Your last name is where your roots begin. From there, you only deepen the connection to your ancestors and once you find them, you always belong. That's what kids want, ain't Raffy, to belong?"

Jamison lit a cigar. The smoke swam into Kyle's head, taking him back to a night in Montana, a night Kyle had spent a year trying to forget. A night he would revisit when he turned eighteen in November.

The night his sister died.

Kyle struggled to stay focused. "I'm looking for someone," he said.

"Hear that Raffy, he's looking for someone."

Raffy looked up from the pool table. "We got no one here."

"You heard him," Jamison said. "We got no one here."

"A girl his age, probably. Twyla. Used to have long red hair. She recently cut it and now it's short. She's just over five feet tall. You know her?"

Jamison snuffed out the cigar and shook his head. He walked around a corner into a room filled with stacks of dusty books, behind another window, and flipped through a green ledger. Kyle tried to read the upside-down print through the window. New Orleans. Mississippi. North Dakota. Jamison's finger stopped in Washington. Seattle.

Kyle knocked on the window. He just needed information so he could reach Twyla's mother and get back to Arnie and his truck before nightfall. He missed the comfort of his own tent already, the ease of his warm sleeping bag, his own well-read books, and a lantern. Plus, if he didn't leave soon, he'd miss the market in the morning, the one place he could still count on seeing Twyla if she was still in Annie's Court. Juliet said she was pale and had a nasty cough when she saw her, probably running a fever.

If he got back up north tonight, he'd also see Juliet at the market. He couldn't stop thinking about her, her sharp gray eyes, her dark hair with cowlicks sticking up in all directions, a smile that could pull a kid right off the streets. Stop it, he warned. He couldn't pull her into his mess of a life. It wasn't fair. People he loved died. His sister had died. And it was his fault.

He knocked on the window again.

Jamison glared at him and went back to flipping pages.

"He'll let you know when he's ready," Raffy said. "He don't like people rushing him. The more you rush him, the more he'll find to do back there. I've known him to stay busy back there for days. That's how I got to be manager."

"He's irresponsible to give the job to you."

"Oh, I took it. No crime in a man claiming his territory."

A man. Maybe thirteen. Kyle scanned the room. Photos and dartboards lined the walls. An empty coffee pot sat on a table next to a roll of gauze and several dirty cups. The dirty linoleum floor cracked away from the walls. Particleboard separated a small room in the corner, a bathroom maybe, or possibly a storeroom.

Jamison opened the window and tossed a paper on the counter. He took off his glasses and ran a cloth across his nose before putting them back on. "Here she is," he said. "Twyla Anderson. Twelve years old last October, hometown girl. Got a birthday coming up. What do you want with her?"

"She's from Seattle," Kyle said. "Does it say where her mother lives?"

"What business is she of yours?"

Kyle thought before he spoke. What could he tell Jamison? She claimed Tony LeCrosse as her father and then recanted it; she lived in a landlocked ship from the 1800s with a cottonwood growing through the deck directly above where she slept; rats scurried around in the hull beneath her bed; the mold spores living in the rotten wood of the ship were probably making her sick; she refused all help.

Kyle had even gone against tent camp code and called social services. Nothing came of it.

Twyla had turned into a ghost, when the social worker arrived, and disappeared.

After three attempts, the worker gave up.

Now, neither Kyle nor Juliet could find the girl.

Kyle hoped she'd somehow made it home safe or would reappear for her mother.

"You don't talk, I don't talk." Jamison closed the window. The screeching sound of it sliding shut hurt Kyle's ears.

"Told you," Raffy said, leaning on the pool stick. "Come back tomorrow. He don't come out once he's closed the window."

"Can you convince him to come back?"

Raffy shook his head. "That's how I became manager."

"Oh, yeah. Manager." Kyle walked over to the photos and looked closely at them. Twyla's picture stared out at him, her red hair still long and curly, pinned back from her face. "This girl," he said. "Do you know her?"

"Sure," Raffy said. "We all know her."

"Why'd she run?"

Raffy shrugged.

Kyle had asked the wrong question. "Do you know where her mother lives?"

Raffy shrugged and scratched his nose. A telltale sign of a lie.

Kyle dug into his pocket. He came out with sixteen one-dollar bills, the bundle he'd gotten from the tent kids before he left Annie's Court that morning. "Just show me the house and I'll take it from there."

Raffy put the pool cue down, pocketed the money, and motioned for Kyle to follow him.

. . .

Raffy led Kyle to a city bus that took them to a dingy apartment building miles from the youth center. Kyle knocked. A tall, shirtless man with three days' growth on his chin answered the door, muscles bulging from his arms. "Can I help you?" he asked, slurring his words.

"Is this Twyla's home?" Kyle said.

"Who's asking?" The man towered over him, folding his hand into a fist, and unfolding it. A mean, no business look crossed his face. Laundry littered the floor behind him, and the smell of smoke and beer wafted out. A hole was in the hallway wall. Kyle wondered what mix of alcohol and arrogance created that. He looked behind him. Raffy had disappeared.

"My name's Kyle. Twyla's very sick. I'm hoping to find her mother."

"So, she roped in another fool, pretending to be all sweet and good. I've seen that one, pretending to be sick, pretending to be hurt, pretending to be hungry. All so you'll feel sorry for her. Well, no, the girl's mother is not here. But the girl, you bring her back anytime. I'll take care of her sickness. In fact, I'll come and get her."

"Are you her father?"

"That asshole ran off and left a load of bills. I told Raylene I'm not paying 'em. She can pay them. Hey, speaking of assholes, what an asshole I am. I didn't even offer you a beer. You want a beer?"

"No thanks," Kyle said. "I'm not of age." Like it mattered. Like the man didn't know it already. It was nothing, but Kyle felt like he was standing up for himself and for Twyla. Follow some rules, asshole. At least the man had that part right.

"Hell, you got a long ride back to… Where'd you say you drove from today?"

"California," Kyle said. "Do you know where I can find Twyla's mother?"

"Probably with the girl's father. Fickle bitch."

• • •

Kyle made it back to Arnie at his truck parked in the lumber yard parking lot an hour before dark. They made it back to Annie's Court just after dark. He climbed into the warmth of his sleeping bag with thoughts of Juliet. Did she find Twyla? Would she be at the market in the morning? Could he keep her safe? Did she like him?

Outside, a fire crackled and burned. Soft voices floated in as he fell asleep.

CHAPTER SEVEN

Saturday morning Juliet pulled jeans over her leggings for the extra warmth. She tucked her pocketknife and a five-dollar bill into her front pocket, pulled on a tan t-shirt and her mother's oversized ivory cable-knit sweater. She slipped on her knee-high boots and opened the door to the shed to bathe her face in the sun. The cool fall air filled her lungs. Across the street a town park provided running water and an indoor bathroom where Juliet took sponge baths.

The shed sat huddled inside a fence with two covered carports, without the cars. Instead, a treasure trove of seemingly abandoned storage items filled the ports. She had pulled the mattress and three camp chairs out of there, and the small table for her camp stove.

Before going to the Farmers' Market, she headed back to the rat-infested ship. She'd smelled and seen the rat droppings. If Twyla was back at the ship and continued to stay there, she'd be lucky not to get the Hantavirus. And Hantavirus could kill her.

Juliet knew a woman, a housecleaner, who died of it. The woman was in her early forties and doing just fine until she cleaned the wrong house, and without the right precautions. She was in the hospital for weeks before the doctors figured out what was making her sick. By that time, it was too late. She passed away, leaving her family shocked and baffled. No. Rat and mouse droppings were no good. Juliet had to get Twyla off that boat.

A loud clank stopped her at the stairs of the ship. A man's voice growled obscenities, and Juliet thought she heard a child whimper. She picked up a broken oar from the ship's floor. The sounds moved away from her, and she followed. At the top of the stairs, near the mast, Georgy My Boy had a firm hold on Twyla's wrist and was pulling her. She dragged her legs behind and stalled the momentum of whatever he pulled her toward.

Jumping in here could get Juliet into so much trouble. She knew she didn't stand a chance against George. But if she didn't stand a chance, how was Twyla supposed to defend herself? The girl weighed at least twenty pounds less than Juliet. And Twyla was sick.

"Stop now. Or I call the police," Juliet said.

She held the oar in one hand and the phone Picard had given her in the other. She dialed 9-1, holding off on the other 1 to see if George would let Twyla go. Juliet didn't want to make the call. They were all trespassing. She'd go to jail until Picard could vouch for her. Social Services would take Twyla. Or she'd end up in juvenile detention.

George, she hoped, would go to jail. Which wouldn't be bad.

He stopped, stared, and dropped the girl's wrist. He looked gray and pale in the humid light, his wrinkles abundant, his eyes under his glasses heavily hooded, on the verge of sleep. She didn't need a tarot reading to know that this man had been in trouble for a long time.

"She's coming with me," Juliet said.

"Finish the call," Twyla said with a dull stare. Her red hair was flattened on one side. She wore a windbreaker and boys' athletic shorts.

Juliet had this terrible ability to smell sickness. A bitter, nauseating odor assaulted her. Sometimes the smell had a sweetness over the stench. She smelled that odor now on Twyla. The girl needed medical care, or at least a warm bed for several days. What she did not need was a dark hole in a hundred-year-old ship, with a grown man dragging her God knows where.

She punched the off button and put the phone back in her pocket. "Kyle went to Seattle to find your mother so you can go home. You are way too young to be on the streets. We can convince her that her boyfriend is bad news."

"Call 911," Twyla said again, her voice fading.

Juliet looked at her, confused.

Twyla shook her head, stood up, and dusted herself off. "Well then, come on George. Let's go. Maybe you can tell me why another person who won't listen to me is interfering in my life."

•   •   •

Juliet got to the Farmer's Market just in time to set up her camp table before they closed it to vendors. She felt uneasy, obsessing over Twyla's response. *Maybe you can tell me why another person who won't listen to me is interfering in my life.* She couldn't make sense of it. And Juliet was good at making sense of things, even the nonsensical. Especially the nonsensical! She wanted to bring Twyla to safety. And, somehow, according to Twyla, trying to get her somewhere safe was wrong. Juliet couldn't figure it out.

The market's red brick courtyard filled with fall tourists and locals. Bikers on their way to the Oyster Run, which was like a Sturgis of the Northwest, slowed their motorcycles through Annie's Court. People bought fresh apples and home baked cinnamon rolls. Above the din, Juliet could hear shouts from the old railroad station where the martial arts students moved in unison. She pulled her sleeves over her fists and smelled the cookies, bread, fried noodles, peanut chicken, and barbecue. She would love one of those cheeseburgers grilling two booths down. Two readings, she'd promised herself, and she could take a break and buy one.

"Could you help me find someone?" Kyle pulled up the blue camp chair and sat in front of her table, acting like a customer. He pushed his hair back from his sharp-featured face. He looked more like a man and less like a boy every day. Juliet felt an unfamiliar sensation inside, something warm and good.

She liked Kyle. Really liked him.

You've got no business loving someone and bringing him into the mess of your life, she told herself. Think of others, her mother had told her a hundred times. Juliet held her breath, but that didn't stop the warmth crawling up her thighs to her chest, into her heart. She exhaled.

"You didn't find her mother," she said.

"I found her house and her mother's boyfriend, or ex. It's hard to tell which. I can see why Twyla doesn't want to live there." His brown hair fell into his eyes, and he pushed it aside, a gesture that caught Juliet right in the weakest part of her being. Her knees went soft.

"It's bad?" She hoped he didn't notice the effect he had on her. Did he always have this effect on girls?

"Very bad. The man was drunk, and it was early afternoon. Mean too."

"His reaction explains some things."

"You're such a genius." Kyle smiled at her.

"Smart guy. Sometimes kids with drinking parents stay. They watch over the drinking parent, make sure they get to bed at night. Call them in sick for work. No. It's his meanness and the absence of her mother. That's why Twyla wanted me to call 911. She wants the police involved. Smart kid."

"Whoa. Back up. When did she want you to call 911? And why wouldn't she just call them herself? And why did she hide from social services?"

"Earlier today, George was about to drag her off the old ship when I showed up. That's when she wanted me to call 911, which surprised me."

"It's a good thing you showed up when you did."

"So, you'd think. But then, she went with George." The conversation was helping her feel more in control of her feelings toward Kyle, and, thus, more in control of her life. "It was weird. There's something bad going on at LeCrosse's. I'm not sure what. I felt creepy when I first walked into that condo. And again, when I woke up with that headache, realizing someone had drugged me. And seeing my tape recorder in Tony's hands when I don't remember losing track of it. It all gives me a bad feeling. I have no memory of what happened later that night. Twyla can't possibly be safe there."

Kyle nodded and his hair fell forward over his brown eyes, making him look sultry, sexy, mysterious even. She took a deep breath and let it out.

"Will you talk to the tent people?" Juliet asked, redirecting her thoughts to the task at hand. "See if she can stay with your group?"

"Stephan will never let her."

"I thought he sent you looking for her."

"I shouldn't have told you that. He just wanted me to stop her from stealing. Now he doesn't want to have anything to do with her, says she'd make trouble for the tent camp. Says she'll bring the police down on everyone. He's a stickler for rule number one."

"No one under sixteen allowed," Juliet said. She remembered. She wondered what rule she had fit under. *No one over eighteen camps near the tent town.* They ran her off and that, the unfairness of it and the pure heartlessness of it, still hurt her feelings. Never mind. The shed suited her. She felt much safer and warmer there. And she had Wilma, the calico kitten.

"He even said to just call social services, breaking rule number four."

"But you already did that, and they didn't help."

"Right. They didn't find her on the boat."

"Maybe Stephan will make an exception for her," Juliet said. "She's in danger."

"He won't. He's hanging tight to the controls. Why doesn't she call the police herself?"

"Good question. I have no idea."

"Maybe I can pressure Stephan," Kyle said, "tell him if we break a rule for her, we can break a rule for him when he turns eighteen. Let her stay until we figure out how to keep her safe. And we'll let him stay after he turns into an adult. First though, we must find her again."

Juliet nodded. "She's probably with Tony LeCrosse."

"But where?"

She shrugged and shook her head. Lacking a better option, she put the tarot deck in front of Kyle. "Here. Shuffle the cards."

He looked at her.

"No cost. It's good for business to have the crowd see a reading. They get curious, voyeuristic, and soon they want to know what their futures hold."

Just like me, she thought, and smiled sweetly at Kyle despite herself.

• • •

Tucked into her shed that evening, Juliet sat cross-legged on the bed and pulled the army blanket up over her legs, thinking about Kyle's reading. She ate her cinnamon roll, feeding tiny bits to Wilma, who batted them around like toy mice. The room seemed expansive and empty for all its one hundred square feet. She had a towel, a couple of changes of clothing, a bed with bedding, a few dishes and silverware, a small propane stove, a lamp to read by, and a box to set the lamp on. It was simple, but warm. Perfect for her. Who cared if she was alone? She didn't. Of course, she didn't, she tried to convince herself, feeling the dull pain of the lie.

She mulled over Kyle's reading–the ten of swords in a prominent position, followed by the ace of swords. Some practitioners thought swords were danger signals. But Juliet thought of them as warrior symbols of caution and of strength. Kyle's eyes had gotten wide when she told him he was in for a challenge, probably with Stephan. He got quiet when Juliet related it to the trauma of his distant past, a past he felt responsible for. But there was nothing he could have done to change the course of another person's life. That person was a good friend, or a sibling, or maybe a parent.

After the reading, he'd mumbled something about his hometown in Montana, and said he'd see her later.

Almost immediately, like an omen, a woman from Missoula, Montana, who smelled like spiced tea, sat down to have her cards read. She wore a blue broomstick skirt and her blond hair spun wildly out of some semblance of a ponytail. She was Juliet's height and close to Juliet's age, only a little older. As she shuffled the cards, the woman looked around the market, distracted.

"Do you know that boy?" she asked, looking after Kyle, "the one who just had his cards read?"

Juliet felt her heart thudding in her chest. She shrugged, shook her head no. She wouldn't give out personal information. Instead, she asked, "How about a four-card spread?"

The woman looked back at Juliet. "Oh, okay."

Her first card came up reversed. The situation. Juliet expected a two of swords–denial, deception, something not to be trusted. Instead, the girl's first card was a six of cups. Even reversed, it was a good card. It promoted security, good fortune, and friends that bring stability.

The second card showed the obstacles. The nine of wands: a young man in boots and a tunic leaning on a wand, with eight other wands behind him. According to this card, there were no obstacles. The card pointed to a job well done. Juliet's suspicious mind began spinning its own tale. This woman seemed to be following Kyle. She might be a relative. Or a girlfriend.

Juliet's heart beat out of control.

The third card told Juliet she was not far off that mark. The world, upside down, indicated the girl was investigating something. Since the naked woman, inside of a green wreath, holding two sided wands, sat in the place of action, the girl from Missoula was likely looking for the truth. The truth about Kyle, Juliet thought. Does Kyle love her?

The last card was the infamous four of wands, signifying the outcome. Success. Whatever she wanted, she'd find. A sad wind had blown across Juliet's heart. Never mind bringing Kyle into her mess of a life. He was evidently already in someone else's life.

The girl had smiled at Juliet, paid for the reading, and took off in the same direction Kyle had gone.

Juliet petted Wilma and thought about her father. He had cared so little about Juliet that, once he left, he never contacted her mother again. Lila French thought something bad had happened to him, swore he wouldn't have left them alone, forcing Lila to search out work, finally finding a job at the convenience store on the corner.

Juliet had never told her mother what she knew in her three-year-old heart: Juliet was that something bad. She had made her father leave, just by her sheer presence and being alive, she had run her father off.

Juliet was a teenager when Harrison left and never returned. By then, she mostly understood it wasn't her fault. Yet, when the shadow of her young self, stood aside, arms crossed, watching, nodding her head, Juliet felt the twist of guilt in her gut.

She opened the shed door and heard the waves lapping against the shore. Picking up Wilma, she went out on the rocks near the old ship. She listened for sounds and heard nothing coming from the hull. Only the consistent sound of the waves crashing against the rocks filled the night.

And she thought, this consistency is what happens in my life. People leave me. Like the waves coming and going. Her father left, Harrison had left, her mother left. And now, with the woman from Missoula following Kyle, Kyle would likely leave her too.

Wilma purred against Juliet's chest. Juliet rubbed the little calico's chin. Cupping her belly, she pulled at the knotted fur on Wilma's legs. Wilma loves me, she thought, her heart hardening against Kyle, a strange anger brewing inside of her.

CHAPTER EIGHT

Kyle felt the storm come as he huddled in his tent Sunday afternoon, trying to calm the squall that Juliet's tarot reading had unleashed in his gut. Clouds grayed the sky, ready for the downpour. The rain would come hard and fast when it came. Wind pushed in at his tent walls, taunting him, trying to reach him, like the memories of the fire. He tried to contain them, force them away, get them out of his mind. The reading, that damn reading, hit too close to home, and he wanted nothing that close to home. Not now. Not yet.

As the sun disappeared, the tide rushed in. Tall waves thundered against the rocky shoreline where the runaways made their homes. The darkest storms had no mercy. They tore up everything not tied down. He'd seen Douglas Fir trees that had toppled in the coastal winds.

The wind dropped suddenly into a pervasive calm. He poked his head out at the camp. Oversized wall tents, colorful two-person tents, purple and blue family tents stretched down the shoreline. Some of them had two rooms and a kitchen table.

Runaways brought the tents with them from home or purchased them at the Red Door thrift shop. Two of the runaways stole their tents, although the camp leaders frowned on that. Tents came from dumpster diving at the campground just down the beach. Sometimes disgruntled campers tossed their tents into the trash, vowing to get an RV after a severe coastal storm.

The campground was a great resource for leftover stuff. They'd gotten pillows, fry pans, plastic glasses, insulated pants, and dozens of t-shirts. The t-shirts came from all over the United States. Kyle recognized some of them: The Lewis and Clark Caverns, Home of the Griz, Flathead Lake. Others inspired him to daydream about traveling: Chaco Canyon, Pawley's Island, Virginia Tech. Then, there were sweet shirts: Cats are people too. I strive to be the person my dog thinks I am. Giddy Up.

Kyle wondered if the campers had spotted the tent town and felt sorry for the kids and intentionally left things for them. Other times he figured it was just good old American consumerism: discarding something perfectly good for something supposedly better.

The wind picked up with a vengeance and rattled the metal roofs of the older RVs in the campground. The sound started out soft and low and built into a roar. The rain started and smelled like fresh cedar when it hit the trees. Ferns soaked up the water. Moss expanded on tree trunks. A bit of disintegrated plastic blew across his feet.

He needed to check on the tents, make sure loose flaps were tied down, make sure the ties held, see if anyone needed anything, water, food. It was going to be a long night. He pulled his hood up, and stepped outside of his tent, turned back to it, and zipped up the doorway. The wind pasted the sweatshirt to his back.

"Where are you going?" Stephan asked.

"I'm going to check on the tents. And make sure everyone is safely tucked in for the night." The wind blew his hair in front of his face. He pushed it back, tucked it into the hood. Hunching his shoulders up, he tried to keep the wind and rain out.

"Never mind," Stephan said. "I already took care of it."

"Got them water?"

"Done."

"Extra blankets?"

"Done. Go back inside and keep yourself safe." With that command, Stephan turned and walked off, the wind pushing against his sweater, helping him along.

"Okay, well I'll bring in chairs and cooking supplies," he yelled after Stephan.

Stephan stopped, his back to Kyle, a momentary lull in storm. He turned. "It's done," he said, snapping his voice shut, and turning on his heels.

Kyle stood for a moment, baffled. Normally, camp safety fell to Kyle. It was his job. A flood of rain fell from the sky, interrupting his thought and he rushed back to his tent. He struggled with the zipper, got the door open and dove inside, taking the rain with him. Spinning toward the door, he zipped the flap closed.

A shudder hit his chest. His muscles tensed. Something had changed. Stephan's words felt cold, like an admonishment. Had Stephan gotten word of his past, like Juliet's reading seemed to? She had seen right through him. If he didn't know better, he'd swear she saw the fire he'd started. If only he'd listened to his father and put out the lights when told, instead of lighting a candle to read by. Juliet must have seen the cowardice that kept him from going back into the trailer to get his sister, Katy.

He could have saved Katy. The wind slammed against his tent, yelling at him, seeming to agree. The thought tipped his stomach upside down. He missed Katy so much. The black smoke of that memory seeped into his heart, a blackness that would never go away.

Determined to ease his pain and try to do something right and good, he would help Twyla. She was the same age Katy had been when the flames hit. Twyla's fierce independence and stubborn will reminded Kyle so much of Katy. He fell asleep thinking of her.

The next morning, Kyle woke up early. He dressed and crawled out into the new day. The rain had passed and left the cedars and ferns drenched. White puffs of clouds hung in the sky. Garbage and feathers had washed up on the beach from the night's storm. Back in the trees fog looped the cedar and fir branches like lace. A fishing boat sounded its horn and the sound bounced off the cliffs. Seagulls squealed and circled the beach.

He walked the road to town and went to the old ship to check if Twyla had returned. He found her huddled in a dark room off the galley. A thin blanket sheltered her shoulders. It didn't take a doctor to diagnose sickness. A rotten smell oozed out into the room. A nasty red lump had swollen on her foot.

"You need medical care," Kyle said. Something scurried across the deck and Kyle cringed to think of the small creatures living there.

"No," she said, and pulled the blanket tighter.

"You can't stay here. You are sick."

She shook her head. Her eyes watered. Red skin drooped down her cheek, like she hadn't quite grown into her face. Kyle saw a vision out of a horror movie and thought that Twyla living in a century old ship while so sick was right out of a horror movie. He had to convince her.

If he'd gone back into the trailer to get Katy, he would have just picked her up and hauled her out of there. He had imagined himself doing that dozens of times. Dozens of times too late.

He couldn't pick Twyla up against her will and carry her off the ship.

"Please," he tried.

She pulled the blanket over her head and turned toward the wall. "Go away."

"I will bring help," he promised. "One of the town doctors."

"Everyone promises," Twyla said.

He went into town and stopped at Urgent Care. The doctors were all busy. Could he come back later? No, they didn't do house calls. They understood his concern, but he'd have to get the girl to them. Kyle did not know how he would do that.

. . .

When he got back to the tent camp, Stephan was busy. Kyle heard him loading wood into the firepit, and then the whoosh of the fire start. He ducked into his tent and pulled on a dry sweat-shirt. After zipping the tent up, he walked to the campfire and stared into the flame. He felt his shoulders tighten.

"Twyla is sick on the old ship," he said. "We need to get her help."

The wind blew Stephan's dark brown hair across his cheek-bones. He wore a black wool sweater and tan hiking pants tucked into work boots. He grimaced at the fire, like it had done something wrong. He sighed. Drew in a breath, let it out. The sound hung in the air, waiting for a word to be put to it. Finally, Stephan spoke.

"You brought the girl's mother to her?"

Kyle shook his head. "I couldn't find her. I think Twyla would come over here and stay with us if you'd let her. I'll ex-plain to her we can protect her if she is closer." Kyle didn't mention that the girl didn't want protection.

"She's too young to live in the tents. We'll all be in trouble if the police find her here." Stephan paced in front of the fire like a trapped cat. He looked toward the sea and down the beach, then squatted down on his haunches.

"They won't find her," Kyle said. "You are cautious. She'll be safe here."

"No one under sixteen. We've had three clean months. Don't you want that record to continue?"

Kyle had been a good partner, helping the runaways. He had worked hard for those three months, keeping everyone in line, making sure they kept alcohol and drugs out of the camp, and helping the oldest kids find jobs. Of course, he wanted it to con-tinue. But this girl was different: she was in danger, and she needed them. Even if she didn't know it. "We've hidden others and they were safe."

"Where would she stay? She's too young to work, and she's a thief."

Kyle tried playing on Stephan's sympathy. "Her cough is worse, and she's weak. I'm sure it's the wet cold from that old ship. She keeps going back there. Now her foot is swollen from a spider bite. She can't walk on it. It's too dangerous for her over there alone."

"Send her to the urgent care clinic." Stephan pushed the ashes around with a stick.

"She won't go."

"Get one of their doctors to go see her."

"I tried. They told me no. If we tell Dr. Roberts about her, he'll see her here."

"A sick twelve-year-old who can't walk." Stephan shook his head. "Roberts will go to the ship. Take him to her there."

"She's almost thirteen."

"And probably lying about that. It's too risky."

"It's a simple ride on your scooter. You can go get her."

"Why is she so important to you?"

For the first time, Kyle looked directly at Stephan. Shadows from the flickering flames danced on his face. He couldn't bring himself to tell Stephan that Twyla reminded him of his younger sister. Kyle couldn't reveal that Twyla was twelve years old, Katy's age when she died, and that Katy had pneumonia when she died in the fire–the fire that Kyle started. Juliet's cards were wrong. They said he wasn't to blame. But he was to blame. He could've prevented that fire. The campfire smoke made his head spin with the memory. "All the kids are important to me," he said, "and they all deserve a chance."

"No one under sixteen. We made that rule when the police took Jena, Elena, and Josh. Did you forget already?"

Kyle hadn't forgotten. It was horrible. Jena cried and cried, begging him to help her, saying she'd get beaten if she went home, even killed. "Just kill me now if you're going to send me back," she'd said. They did not know if she'd made it home, or if she'd survived.

The thing was, kids from happy families rarely run away.

Kyle only shook his head, to let Stephan know he hadn't forgotten. "You're nearly eighteen and you have gone nowhere. We break rules." Kyle bit his lip. He hadn't wanted to use that argument. Stephan would turn eighteen in a month. So would Kyle. At eighteen, they'd be free to walk the streets like any adult. Plus, then they could get in trouble for harboring runaways.

Stephan threw a rock into the fire. "So, it's true. You want me out of here. Mikey told me you'd always wanted to take my place. He told me you'd been planning behind my back."

So, that was it. Stephan thought Kyle wanted to sabotage his leadership and take over. And Mikey had fed him those lies. "Mikey likes to spread rumors," Kyle said, not wanting to give either of them the satisfaction of hurting him with it. He focused on Twyla. "She's a kid. She shouldn't die alone in a boat."

"A job for social services."

"They've been called." He pulled his hands in and caught the edges of his sleeves in fists. "When they couldn't find her, they gave up."

"Find her mother," Stephan said.

"I've looked."

"Look harder."

"No sign of her. What good are we if we let kids stay in dangerous situations? That's why we started this, for the runaways." Kyle ran a hand through his hair. "You were only fifteen when you started the camp."

Stephan stood up again, pacing in front of the fire. "We were in the caves then, and the police knew nothing. Any sign of trouble now and they'll come in here and flatten the camp. You know that."

Stephan had been a good leader, but he was wrong this time. "You turn eighteen and you're out too."

Stephan whipped around. "If you're going to challenge me, stand up and say it. Don't hide behind a kid to do it."

"I'm just saying that sometimes we make exceptions."

"Not this time," Stephan said.

Kyle stared into the fire and shook his head.

"We're done," Stephan said. He walked down the clearing to the largest tent tucked back from the water. The waves splashed, creeping toward the tents, the waves now like timid puppies, sneaking in and going out again.

"Yes, Stephan," Kyle said out loud, "we are done." He pushed the fire around with a stick. Under his breath, he mumbled, "You could leave." That would make room for Twyla.

Mikey stepped out of the shadows in his dark hooded sweatshirt and paced in front of the fire where Stephan had been.

Kyle wanted nothing to do with Mikey. "What lies are you telling Stephan?"

Mikey twisted a smile up at Kyle. "Lies?"

Kyle shook his head and walked away.

. . .

The next morning Kyle had barely opened his eyes and gotten dressed when Stephan and Mikey came to his tent. Mikey stood behind Stephan, probably trying to hide the smirk that showed his delight. Stephan stepped forward, confident, one hand on his hip, his hair blowing in the wind.

"I'm leaving next month," he said, "and I'm passing the leadership to Mikey."

"That's something we vote on." Kyle rubbed his chin.

"We voted," Stephan said.

"Without me," Kyle said. "So that's it. I'm out."

"It's better this way," Stephan said. "You've been unhappy. You'll be eighteen in a couple weeks. You'll be out, anyway."

"Why isn't Mikey telling me himself if he's the new leader?"

"He doesn't want trouble. He didn't know how angry you might get."

"Just like that? I've worked hard to keep everyone fed and out of trouble."

"Mikey has work at the lumber mill. I've got work out there too. We'll survive, like always."

"Doesn't sound like you're leaving," Kyle said.

"I am. But you leave tonight. You can set up your tent closer to town, and Twyla can stay with you."

"She's a kid. She can't stay with me."

"It's better this way. You'll see."

"Unbelievable," Kyle said, looking straight at Mikey. He wanted to say something mean, but Mikey already cowered behind Stephan. He knew Mikey had already faced a world of meanness before he ever ran away. Finally, he shrugged, tilting his palms up in surrender. "Good luck," he told them. Oddly, he meant it. Well, almost meant it. He was almost big enough to take this discard gracefully.

"That's not all." Stephan looked concerned. "A woman came here looking for you."

"What? What woman?"

Stephan shrugged. "Blond. About your height. Older than you."

Kyle shook his head. "No one I know."

"You can't stay any longer, it's too dangerous." Stephan and Mikey turned in unison and walked away.

Kyle watched them walk down the beach for a long while before he yanked his sleeping bag out of the tent. He stuffed it into a plastic bag and collapsed the tent poles, the nylon material flattening out like a grounded kite.

CHAPTER NINE

Juliet peeled a ten-dollar bill away from the thirty she'd made at the Farmer's Market that week, pulled a coffee tin from under her bed, and folded the ten in with the other bills there. After Monday's trip to the pet store for Wilma's food and stashing the money for a rainy day, as Lila French had been fond of saying, she now had nine dollars left–enough to buy milk, bread, and a small jar of peanut butter for Twyla.

It wasn't much, but at least the girl would have something to eat. That cough was not nothing. That's a double negative, Juliet thought. Who cared? She lived in a world of negatives: no food, no shelter, no family, no protection, no job, no safety, and nowhere to go. The negatives in Juliet's life compounded each other. Life as a runaway was one big negative. Not that she was a runaway anymore.

But Twyla was.

The rag boy that had tumbled out of the white van was.

She wanted to help them.

The tarot cards had been of little use. They'd gone blank and dark. That void was a clear message: the girl was none of Juliet's business.

But Juliet could not shake the feeling that Twyla's motives and her relationship with Tony LeCrosse were exactly her business. She was convinced that somehow the dark shadow over the tarot cards had come from LeCrosse. Juliet intended to find out how and why.

Meanwhile, she had found Twyla back on the old ship again. She now had a spider bite too. Dr. Roberts had agreed to trade a visit to Twyla on the ship for a tarot reading. The doctor wanted the reading for his granddaughter Amber, who was interested in metaphysics. He didn't understand her interest in magical gems, orbs, angels, and yoga when she could just as happily go to church. But if she wanted her tarot read, she would have it read. Juliet thought her interest might begin with her name: Amber, a healing stone known to balance emotions and clear the mind.

Juliet slid her rolled up camp table into the bag she'd made for it out of a pair of old jeans. The bag had a colorful pocket for her cards, with a picture of a lion–the symbol of strength–embroidered onto it. She loved the lion. It was her card.

Strength.

She packed the Angels' deck instead of the traditional tarot cards. Angels would speak for Amber, Juliet thought. She slung the table in its bag over her shoulder and headed for the ship. The fog had lifted, and fall's golden leaves sang in the wind. The morning sun warmed her and wove the radiant day into each slow breath she took.

The wet smell of a fall storm filled the air, and Juliet felt something like happiness. It was as close as she'd come since that day the officer showed up in his blue suit. Perfectly pressed, he stood tall and filled it out. He didn't have to say a word. She'd felt the wrongness of it all when her mother didn't return home after going out for a drive.

But the officer didn't know that. He looked too young to understand that she could know what had happened to her mother before he told her. Even though she was younger than the officer, she was Lila French's daughter. And being Lila French's daughter made all the difference.

Lila had taught her to summon knowledge, to trust her instincts. On that one occasion, Juliet had wished it wasn't so. The grief too heavy to hold by herself. She needed her mother.

The sun shifted behind a cloud and, as though she'd willed it, immediately returned. With a firm resolution, she pushed the memory aside. She'd been on the west coast since last spring, and it had been good. She'd missed the dry Arizona air at first, but only for a minute. Here, things grew in abundance, creating vibrant greens all summer and rich browns and golds in autumn. Even in the fall, life sprouted up all around her. Squirrels gathered nuts, deer came into town to munch on garden squash, and people invited her over for apple cider.

As she approached the ship, the wind suddenly picked up. It blasted Juliet's good mood as well as the old vessel. Potential mold spores flew across the deck as Juliet tucked her fists into her sweater and put an arm up to block the wind. Juliet saw no sign of the doctor and Amber, so she went looking for Twyla. She wanted to warn the girl that Dr. Roberts was coming so she wouldn't panic and hide.

"Hello," she called. "It's me, Juliet. I have some food for you."

No one answered.

"Hello, Twyla? Anyone here?"

A mouse scurried across the floor. Juliet made a mental note to get some mousetraps. The dark wood was wet and slippery as she moved across it. She knocked on the shabby door to the room where she'd previously found Twyla. No one answered, and she pushed the door aside. The girl wasn't there, and neither were her few belongings.

Juliet heard an empty can careen across the deck above her. Then, she heard footsteps. Following the sound, she found Dr. Roberts and Amber on board. The doctor was a thin man with a ruddy, shining face and a short gray beard. He was dressed in gray slacks and a blue fleece, dressed for an exam room rather than picking his way through the ruins of a long-abandoned ship.

Amber looked like a younger, feminine, version of Dr. Roberts. She was thin and ruddy, athletic, with a wisp of frailty mixed in. Her face radiated hope and laughter. Amber was too young and protected to have been disappointed much. Her cards would read like stars. Some people were like that, destined to experience only lovely lives.

The doctor introduced them.

Amber held her hand briefly, softly, and let it go.

"Twyla doesn't seem to be here," Juliet said. "The room she was staying in is empty."

"Maybe she went home," Amber said.

"Not likely. Her mother has also recently disappeared. All that awaits her at home is a mean alcoholic–her mother's boyfriend."

"It's no wonder she's sick, if she's been living here," Dr. Roberts said. "Can you get her to come in to see me? I'll give you a voucher for a check-up."

"I'll try to bring her."

"Try as hard as you can. This old boat cannot be good for her. Let's go to my office to get the voucher. You can ride with us and do Amber's reading there. It'll be much more comfortable than this moldy old ship."

"You smell it too?" Juliet liked to verify what she already knew.

*   *   *

"Of course, you can't find Twyla," Kyle said. "She reappears and then she disappears. It's scary. We don't know how much danger she is in." Kyle sat on a rock on the deserted mid-week beach and ate a large tomato he'd bought at the Farmer's Market that Sunday. Homegrown tomatoes held their own for a good while, he'd explained, offering half of it to Juliet. Juliet declined. She did not like tomatoes. Not even homegrown ones.

"She's sick and her stuff is gone." Juliet said. "She seemed pretty weak."

"Maybe she went home."

"Of course. Why didn't I think of that?" Juliet bit her lip. No need to be mean. Even if there was a young blond woman looking for Kyle. She took in a breath and let it go. "We know she didn't go home. I told her you found her mother's boyfriend drunk."

"I think all runaways just want a normal family life and a sense of security," Kyle said. "That's not possible when living with predators."

"We need to find her," she said. "Something isn't right."

"Now you're the genius."

Juliet winced, feeling the fool. She hated this tension between her and Kyle. She looked out at the waves that came in and retreated. The sea was so big, and they were so small. They were here for a moment and gone.

Sometimes she imagined that her mother lived in the beautiful night sky, forever looking down on her. That thought comforted her. But then, her mother was gone forever. Juliet could not touch her and hold her. She couldn't cry in her mother's arms.

What Juliet did have was this moment to do something good: help the twelve-year-old runaway to safety. And maybe she had Kyle, if he and the blond woman weren't lovers, if he liked Juliet, if she could let him in. That was a lot of ifs. She vacillated between feeling safe with him and feeling dull and terrified of loving him. She worried about his relationship with the woman from Montana.

"Did Twyla show up at the tents?" she asked.

"I don't think so." Kyle gazed out at the beach where the waves crashed. He bit his lip. "I'm not living there anymore."

"What? When did you leave?"

"A couple of days ago. Stephan kicked me out. I wanted Twyla to stay out there with us. We got into a fight."

"What was he upset about?"

"Mikey told him I'd been trying to take over." Kyle turned his face away from Juliet, grinding his boot heal into the rock. "Stephan believed him and, with my wanting Twyla there, he thought I was causing trouble."

"Why didn't you tell me?"

Kyle shrugged.

"Where are you living?" A sick feeling flopped over in Juliet's stomach.

Kyle shrugged again.

Maybe he didn't trust her. That thought made her feel ill. If he didn't trust her, she was alone again.

The pain crushed her chest, and she could barely breathe.

"I moved my tent to the other side of the campground," Kyle finally said. "No one is in those woods. It's easy access to the bathrooms, and a fire could be seen as part of the campground."

Juliet's shoulders relaxed. Like a wild animal waking up from a tranquilizer shot, she shook off the fear. She let go a sigh of relief, shook her head, and pulled the sleeves of her ivory sweater down over her knuckles. "I don't like it," she said, as if she was talking to the wind.

"It's okay." He touched her chin, pulling her face around to look at him. "I won't do anything stupid. I've been on the run for a long time. Someday I'll rent a small apartment."

"Why not now? You work."

"I still need to make sure the kids in the tent camp have food, and medical expenses covered, especially for the winter."

"They kicked you out!" Juliet understood that he'd make sure the kids would be taken care of. It was Kyle's nature. It was what she admired about him. Nevertheless, she was incensed.

"I know. It won't be for long." He lifted his hands as if to say 'what can I do' before looking away.

Maybe he didn't want her to see his grief or shame at being kicked out. Or maybe he didn't want to face her anger over it. Or maybe he just flat out didn't care about her opinion.

"Come to the shed and stay with me." As soon as the words were out of her mouth, she knew it was what she wanted. It would be safer for them both. "I have an extra sleeping mat and a palette. It's going to be cold soon, too cold for a tent in the woods. The campground will close for the season soon and a cook fire will be noticeable. The cops will come."

Kyle shook his head.

Juliet's chest tightened and the muscles hurt. But it didn't stop her. "It's a good idea," she said. "You can take money to the tent town. The shed is closer to work and convenient for errands."

Kyle kept shaking his head. "You're on private property."

"It's abandoned. No one's been around in forever."

"There was a padlock on the door."

"It was broken off. I cleaned it up and reattached it to keep others out."

"Still."

"I've been there two months with no trouble. If there's trouble, we'll leave."

He turned away and sighed.

She leaned in close to him so he could see her eyes and her smile. She felt an opening in the walls that protected her heart. The thought of him staying with her in the tiny shed made her unreasonably happy. "Just try it. For a night or two? There's plenty of space."

Kyle looked at her. "A hundred whole square feet," he said, and laughed.

"At least! So, you'll try it?"

"Not now. Maybe some time," he said.

"Sometime soon?"

He shook his head, but this time it wasn't a "no." This time it was more of a "what are you, crazy?"

And she knew the answer to that question. Deep in her heart of hearts, the part she shared with no one, the answer was a resounding "yes!" By most people's standards, she was very crazy.

CHAPTER TEN

Unable to convince Kyle to move in, Juliet went to see his camp in an isolated part of the forest. She didn't like him living in the damp woods any more than she had liked the idea of it the previous day. Dark things grew out there. Juliet could feel them crawling toward her. Her skin sweated under little bumps she imagined exploding across her chest from bug bites. Thinking of the dark things that could slither into Kyle's tent made her scared for him.

Kyle, apparently unconcerned, pulled her down a trail to the Northern Campground. Juliet said it again. She didn't like him sleeping alone in the woods like that. Again, he disregarded her concerns and let her know he was fine.

Fine, she thought.

Except for a couple of empty trailers and an old motorhome, the campground was empty. It made sense to Juliet. Kids had been back in school for almost a month, and summer was over.

"It's a ghost town," she said.

"Wait till the weekend." Kyle knocked on the door of the motorhome.

An athletic-looking older woman answered the door, sporting spandex tights with shorts over them and a rust-colored t-shirt that hung loosely on her shoulders. She had pulled her black hair back into a long ponytail.

A musky smell coming from the motorhome reminded Juliet of Harrison, her mother's cowboy, the stand in father who had raised Juliet and left without a word. How does a person do that? Raise a child and move on to something else without ever looking back? She didn't understand.

"Have you seen a girl with short red hair and blue-gray eyes, about thirteen? She should be in school, but she's not?" Kyle asked.

"Was she living on the old ship?" the woman asked. "The one with a very clear 'No Trespassing' sign to keep intruders out?"

"Yes," Juliet said.

The woman narrowed her eyes and tilted her head. She squished her lips together and raised a finger to them, a tsking sound escaping. "I haven't seen her," she said. "I heard some screaming coming from that direction last night. I told my husband that quite a party must be going on over there. The racket made my head hurt. Lots of yelling. Then, suddenly it was like a poker game."

"Poker game?" Juliet had only known poker games at her aunt's house that ended in trouble, fights, accusations, and a lot of screaming. The idea made her stomach flip.

"Yeah, you know, very quiet deliberation. I was about to call the police on them. Damn partiers." From the wrinkles in her face, Juliet thought the woman could have been a damn partier herself at one time.

"You didn't call the police?" Kyle asked.

"No. It started and ended just as quickly. The shortest bash in history."

"Thank you," Juliet said. She wanted to get out of there and away from anything that reminded her of Aunt Gloria and her freakish boyfriend, Layne.

•   •   •

After visiting the campground, and with no real hint of where to go next, Juliet and Kyle set out on a random, half hazard search for Twyla. Water crashed below the rocks that Juliet and Kyle climbed. In the hypnotic come and go of the sea, smooth sticks, polished by the water's constant motion, piled up in the crevasses between the rocks. Bits of shellfish stuck to the rock surfaces.

Juliet felt the desperation grow in her chest. Her throat tightened and she squished her eyes so that it wouldn't burst out. She wanted to find Twyla, and they searched for any hidden place that the girl might have set up camp. They crashed through cedar trees and the tall Douglas firs. Moisture from the ferns soaked their pant legs. They made their way through the ferns and into the woods, looking for remnants of a fire or any other sign.

They found nothing, no remnants of a campfire, no broken branches, no left-over candy wrappers. Only the things that belong, Juliet thought, as she pulled a spider web off her face, adding spiders to the list of small creatures that could join Kyle in his bed at night.

"She'd have to be crazy to live in these woods," she said, hoping he'd take her double meaning. "And without a shelter."

"A tent is missing from our camp," Kyle said.

"Their camp." Juliet bit her lip, wishing she'd let it alone. The image of the woman from Missoula gnawed at her. Was she his girlfriend? It put Juliet closer to the edge than she cared to be. Still, it was cruel to remind Kyle that Stephan had kicked him out of the camp.

Kyle stopped, whipped around. He pulled her to him. Her heart tumbled as he wrapped his arms around her and kissed her. "A tent is missing from their camp," he whispered in her ear. "And I don't like it."

Over his shoulder, an intricate spider web sparkled, iridescent in the sun that had just come out. Tiny raindrops clung to the web. The spider climbed off a leaf and went to work, his agile legs moving from one strand to the next.

Juliet tucked her head into Kyle's shoulder. "I'm sorry."

"It's true, it's not my camp anymore. I just need to get used to the idea. For a while, I had a family. I belonged, and it felt good. It felt good to be of use. It made me forget things I didn't want to think about."

"And now?"

"Time for me to face my life, my fears." He pulled her closer.

She leaned into his body, feeling a bit of the despair slip away. His warmth comforted her. A thousand feathered wings lifted her up and set her free. She didn't know what it meant for him to face his fears. And she didn't know if she could face her fears. She only knew that, in his arms, it might be possible.

"I want you to stay in town with me," she said. She felt his breath on her neck. When he didn't acknowledge her desire, she pulled slightly away, still holding his arms, and went back to the subject of Twyla. "I don't like it that we can't find her. It's weird that both Twyla and the tent are missing. Do you think Stephan is telling us everything?"

"I do," Kyle said. He caressed her arm and let her go. "He'd tell us if she had been there."

"She probably snuck in when everyone was gone. What color was it?"

"Blue. Powder blue with a rain flap." He turned away from her and pushed through the brush, breaking branches, and moving them aside. Western hemlocks and Pacific firs leaned into each other, creating barriers to the deep woods. Water from the overgrowth of trees dripped onto Kyle's head.

"At least she knew to steal one with a rain flap." Juliet followed and stopped. "She will not be back in here. It would take a long knife and probably a large saw to cut her way through these branches. She'd go somewhere simpler, hidden but welcoming."

A wind rustled the leaves of a lone paper birch, dumping more raindrops onto Kyle, making his face shine when he turned back to Juliet. He brushed them off his face. "Let's try the homeless shelter."

"Right. Then, the police and social services. She wouldn't just run off without a good reason. She has nowhere to go."

"Not that we know of. Only as a last resort do we go to the police. Asking the police for help should be her call. We don't know for certain she's in trouble."

"She's in trouble and she's looking for safety. We can talk to the police," Juliet said, thinking of Harrison. He'd been the detective working on her father's disappearance, searching for clues about what had happened to him. After two years, her mother had gotten very close to Harrison, and he moved in. Juliet was five. According to her mother, Harrison never gave up looking for Juliet's father.

When Harrison disappeared, other police searched for him. By then, Juliet was a teenager, old enough to grieve, old enough to be mad as hell, old enough to wonder if Harrison had given up on them. But Juliet's mother said no, he wouldn't do that. He was not a quitter. He loved them. Juliet thought about the police who helped her when her mother died. She thought about Detective Benson Picard. He wanted safety for the runaways.

"The police will help us," she said, "and they'll help Twyla. You saw her stepfather. Even the mother ran away from him. Twyla's in trouble, I'm sure of it, Kyle. I say we give it to the end of the day, then we go to the police."

Kyle shrugged. "Okay."

Before they went to the shelter, they checked with Stephan. No one in the tent town had seen her. "And we better not," Stephan warned Kyle.

As they left, Kyle said, "Stephan is such an asshole. I gotta brush it off. I could care less about his warnings."

But Juliet thought he did care. Kyle had a heart. A good heart.

. . .

The homeless shelter yielded no better results. Girls and boys moved through there all the time, they said, but they'd remember a girl with short red hair, age twelve or thirteen.

Juliet tugged Kyle's sleeve as they left the shelter. "We file a missing person's report," she said.

"Yeah," he agreed, "the one her mother didn't file."

"Maybe she figured it was the best way to keep Twyla safe from the boyfriend. When her mother gets settled, she might look for her daughter."

"Maybe," Kyle said. "But I doubt it."

Juliet braced herself to go into the red brick police station. Kyle was no help. He hemmed and hawed and dragged his feet. Juliet went in first, leading the way. The woman behind the Plexiglas slid it open. Her blond hair puffed up on top. A glittering red band held long bangs off her face and showed off her beautiful high cheekbones. "Can I help you?"

"Is Detective Picard in?" Juliet asked.

"He's not. Would you like to leave a message for him?"

Juliet shook her head. She didn't want to wait. "We'd like to file a missing person's report," she said.

"Name?"

"Twyla."

"Last name?"

"I don't know."

"Anderson," Kyle said.

The woman raised a dark eyebrow. "Where is she missing from?"

Juliet looked at her foot and pushed her toe into the linoleum like she might turn over a tile and find the answer there. She felt Kyle tugging on the back of her shirt, wanting to leave. He'd hated this idea from the beginning. The police brought too many kids back to bad homes. She hated herself for her next words, turning in a kid who'd been trying to find a safe place to belong. "She's a runaway."

"From Seattle," Kyle said.

The woman nodded. "How old?"

"About twelve. Or thirteen."

The woman held the pen against her cheek. "How well do you know this girl?"

Juliet didn't really know her. But she knew the sounds that had surrounded Twyla, and they were the sounds of danger.

"At first she had said Tony LeCrosse was her father, then she said she'd lied," Juliet said. "So, I don't think he is."

She put down her pen. "Have you checked with her father? You can't file a missing person's report on a kid you don't even know is missing."

But Juliet did know Twyla was missing. She felt the wrongness of it crawl across her skin and fill her blood. Every muscle in her body went tense. She had felt that same dark shadow seep into her veins when Harrison disappeared, when her mother died, and again when she moved in with Aunt Gloria.

The image of the death card popped into Juliet's mind: the armored skeleton riding his horse, carrying the flag of the mystic rose, death carrying a symbol of life. It rarely meant an actual death. It meant strife, worry, extreme difficulties. If the card was right, Twyla was alive and facing serious danger.

She said as much to Kyle when they left the police station. They leaned against a brick wall shoulder to shoulder.

"What now?" Kyle asked.

"I'm cold. I want to go back to the shed and warm up. Will you come with me?"

"I have just enough time for a cup of tea before work."

"I have tea," she said, suppressing her glee, and reached out and took Kyle's hand.

CHAPTER ELEVEN

Saturday came on fast, and Juliet pushed the week's useless search for Twyla out of her mind. If she wanted to eat that week, she needed to concentrate on reading tarot cards for the Farmer's Market crowd. Maybe the girl would show up. She had an affinity for the Market, albeit a criminal one. Juliet knew from her time spent on the streets from Arizona to the Washington coast a runaway thief never does well.

Juliet set up her table, took a seat in a camp chair, and placed the tarot deck out in front of her. Acorn squash, potatoes, beets, and long carrots with their green leafy tops piled high at her neighbor's booth. The earthy smell of vegetables reminded her of the safety she had once felt at home. They made her long for that earlier time of working alongside her mother. Her mother had been a master gardener. During harvest season, they'd all pitched in to can beets and pickles. Even Harrison had rolled up his sleeves and pulled sterile jars from the hot water.

Laughter in the mall brought her back to the market. A man in a booth across the aisle from her sold flags from all over the world. The green, white, and orange stripes of Ireland flew in front of him. An Australian flag stretched out behind him. Next to it was a black and red one with a beautiful yellow moon in the middle. That, she knew, was an indigenous Australian flag. A dozen tiny American flags stood at attention in a sand tray.

Down the aisle, tables overflowed with jams and salts, hand-made potholders, and doll dresses. The crocheted pillows and tablecloths competed with purses made from old jeans and velvet dresses. Fresh baked cinnamon rolls, bread, and fruit pies filled the mall with seductive scents.

Across the market, just down from the flag booth, Tony LeCrosse was selling his wooden toys — elephants danced around their babies, giraffes looked out over palm trees, a miniature train made its way through the mountains. An angel fell into a little city filled with commuters and miniature newspapers. Building lights came on as the clouds darkened the sky. They were clever, intricate toys, hand crafted treasures, toys that came to life on the shelves in front the toymaker.

He wore a brown leather jacket and a rust-colored knit cap. Juliet noticed that his soul patch had grown into a sparse beard. The twins sat on either side of him, their long skirts blowing gently in the autumn breeze. They both wore leggings under their skirts, wool sweaters, and hiking boots, ready for any season.

LeCrosse smiled at her, and she felt something flutter in the wind. Beside her the candles quivered. The sky opened to a time when her mother called her home to dinner. The clouds smiled on her and carried with them the smell of her mother's roast beef cooking. The memory of it nearly dropped Juliet to her knees.

Get a grip, she scolded herself. It didn't work. The memory of her mother was crippling, but it was a trick. Somewhere in her mind she knew it was a trick that LeCrosse wove, a facade of brocade and glitter designed to catch fools like her in his nest.

"That last reading was so interesting. I'd like another," he called out. The twins watched askance from the toy booth as he crossed the aisle to stand in front of her.

His luminous green eyes scattered enchantment across the market and Juliet felt herself caught in the illusion he cast. Potholders danced with purses. The jam and salt held hands, ducking between loaves of bread, runaway lovers of the market.

Juliet steadied herself. This ground. This table. This street. He would not take her will. He would not take her secure hold on reality. This time, she'd beat him at his game of smoke and mirrors. She ruffled the cards. The darkest side of them floated to the top of the deck.

"Your cards," Juliet said, looking him right in the eye. "Where is Twyla?"

The cards halted in his hands, but for only a second. "I don't know, at her mother's house?" His voice was smooth, cool. "Her mother is always coming to take her home, only to find another boyfriend who doesn't like kids, or likes them too much. Then, she sends Twyla back to me."

"She said you're not her father."

"She lies." He put the cards in front of Juliet. "Work your magic."

"It's not magic," she said, defensive again. "You want a full spread or short and sweet?"

"Short and sweet," he said. "Like you." He turned those eyes on her.

She laid out three cards, attempting to calm the pull LeCrosse stirred in her.

"This four of wands represents your past," she said. "It was filled with harmony, a good home life, and someone who loved you. Your parents, most likely. This second card, The Fool, is not so kind. You've gone on a wrong track, your own doing, refusing to listen to those wiser than you. See him high stepping, with his dog following?"

Tony raised his eyebrows and nodded.

"He's looking to the skies, chasing a dream, not caring that he's about to step off a cliff and drag his beloved dog with him. Be careful what you focus on. It'll hurt not only you, but those you love. You must consider the ground under your feet."

Tony shook his head. "Go on," he said.

"This third card, the five of cups, this dark cloaked figure looks sideways at three fallen cups. Two remain standing. This is a card of loss. But it's not too late. You can still salvage something if you pay attention and stop acting the fool."

"Do you always insult people?"

"You shuffled the cards. I'm trying to help you find some wisdom. Blame me if you want, but you should change your course now and come out of the wreckage with something good." A surprising thought popped into Juliet's head: At one time this man had a heart. "Drop the mask. Find your goodness again, Mr. LeCrosse. You'll be glad you did."

He shook his head. "I'm having another party. Can you come?" He lifted his bushy brown and gray eyebrows. The gray hairs twinkled in the sun.

Juliet shrugged. She shook her head at her own lack of wisdom.

"Bring your cards," he said.

"A hundred and fifty dollars and I bring my own drinks."

"You drive a hard bargain."

. . .

That Monday Juliet met Picard by the dog park. They sat on the sidewalk curb across the street from the brick mall and the martial arts studio, both empty at this time of day. The weather had cooled, moving toward winter. Juliet wore two thick sweaters, and her tall boots over her leggings, and still her muscles tensed at the cold.

Picard handed her a ham sandwich and a cup of coffee. "When's the party?" he asked.

"Saturday night." She took a bite of the sandwich. She was starving.

"I'll pick you up," Picard said.

"I don't want to go back there. It's weird, like the air glitters with an altered reality and I lose my good sense of things."

"You're susceptible to his charm. Maybe I shouldn't subject you to this case."

She nodded. "He's dangerous."

"Margo said a girl asked for me at the police station. I assume that girl was you."

Juliet nodded. "Twyla is missing. We haven't been able to find her. We've checked the old ship, the tent town, the shelter, and back in the dark, wet woods. Not that any fool would be back in there."

Picard took a drink of his coffee. "No sign of her?"

"I don't know if LeCrosse has anything to do with Twyla's disappearance, or any of the missing kids. I get the sense somewhere inside him there's a good guy."

"There's always a good guy somewhere. But the good guys don't stop the scumbags from doing damage."

"Can you find out if he's really Twyla's father?" Juliet asked. "He said she probably went back to her mother, that she has a habit of doing that, that she lies."

"It's not just Twyla. He's had other kids claim he's their father or uncle."

"Maybe they are," Juliet said.

"Big family. And the kids come and go."

"Maybe they all go home."

The wind gusted down the street. Picard put his coffee on the sidewalk and pushed his hands deeper into his wool coat. "New kids arrive. Others disappear. I'm certain he's in it somehow."

Juliet shook her head and took another bite of her sandwich.

Picard unwrapped his sandwich, looked at it, and took a bite. He wrapped it again and took a drink of his coffee. "Maybe you could rent a room somewhere," he said. "Wherever you're staying, it can't be good."

She watched his eyes soften. He looked tired and worried, almost fatherly. Juliet hadn't dreamed that he'd be concerned about her in that way. "Maybe. But I'd need a steady income to pay for the room next month and the month after that."

"You could attend the academy. Become a real detective." Picard picked up his sandwich and studied it, as if it fueled his thoughts.

She drank her coffee and wondered what it would be like to take a hot shower in her own home again. Then, she banished the thought to the furthest corner of her mind.

. . .

The week went by slowly. When Saturday finally arrived, Twyla was not at the party. Georgy My Boy had a beer in hand and was drooling over Juliet. He smelled like moth balls, as if he'd just taken his tweed suit out of storage. To get rid of him, she bumped into him, making him spill beer down his front. He looked like he'd peed his beautiful tweed pants.

"I'm so sorry," she said behind a stilted smile. Be nice, she told herself. That move was not nice. "Let me get something to clean that up with." She left him standing in the middle of the room while she went into the kitchen to retrieve a roll of paper towels. When she returned, she noticed the perfect view of the bay out the large glass window. A small boat out on the water moved toward the docks. She tossed the towels at Georgy My Boy.

"I thought you'd clean it up, since you spilled it," he said.

"You can do it," she said matter-of-factly, enjoying his misery.

The small boat docked, and a man got out. He looked familiar, but Juliet couldn't place him. A few minutes later, he knocked on the door. He was tall and burly, like a northern lumberjack.

"Arnold, my friend," Tony said. Tony wore an Italian suit that fit perfectly, a perfect contrast to the lumberjack. "We've got drinks and food. This is Juliet. But don't talk to her unless you want to know the good, the bad, and the ugly."

"I recognize you," Arnold said, "from the Farmer's Market."

Juliet nodded. A lot of people came through the Market. "I've never done a reading for you," she said.

"I'm too busy selling toys." He put a small wooden horse on the table.

"You're the toymaker." She looked at Tony. "You've been selling his toys at your booth?"

"Just the opposite," Arnold said. "Tony makes them, and I sometimes sell them. I watch the booth and find good homes for the toys." He pulled a tiny girl from the pocket of his red flannel shirt and placed it on top of the horse. "You can have that little gem for a reading."

The detail was amazing. The girl's face was an exact replica, the hair autumn red, the eyes gray blue. "Twyla," Juliet said.

"Tony's daughter. You know her then."

"She's gone," Juliet was still looking at the tiny carving.

"So, I heard," Arnold said. "That girl is a mystery, like her father, both always disappearing and reappearing. I guess that's why he's got me to watch the booth. Sometimes I drive toys into Seattle for him."

Juliet tilted her head in a question.

"When he's here, I deliver toys to the Seattle Market. When his other shops need him, I watch the toy booth here."

"He has other shops?"

"Yes, around the U.S." Arnold gave her a look that said, 'Been living in a cave somewhere? Everyone knows that.'

"But how does he make so many toys?" Juliet was astounded. One person was hardly enough manpower to fill several shops.

"He sells to select shops, for a high price. That little gem might go for a thousand dollars. Look at the details: the mane, the tail, all matching the girl's hair. These toys are special. They live tiny lives. Unspoken words float out of their mouths. Love grows in them."

A reading by Juliet could never be a fair trade for this intricate workmanship. She nodded in agreement. The toys were special. Then, she handed Arnold the cards. "Your shuffle."

CHAPTER TWELVE

While Juliet held court at LeCrosse's party, a protective urge came over Kyle. He intended to crash the party to guard her and keep her safe. The evening wind off the water whistled by as he approached LeCrosse's condo. A wooden boat he'd never seen before hugged the dock. He loved old wooden boats, so he walked over to look at it. Under a zippered canvas awning, an Oriental rug covered the maple floor of the living area. Three stairs led down into the galley. Kyle felt certain it was a Lake Union Dream Boat, built in 1928.

Focus, he scolded himself, his curiosity about the boat distracting him from his mission to check on Juliet. He turned and looked at the bright lights beaming from the condo's wide picture windows. LeCrosse stood near Juliet. A large burly man sat at the card table with her. Kyle recognized him. Arnie had given Kyle a ride into Seattle. He'd waited for Kyle to haul him back up to Annie's Court at the end of the day.

Through the windows, Kyle watched Juliet. He thought she liked Arnie. She was smiling. He was smiling, enjoying the interaction, more interested in Juliet than the cards or his own fate.

Alice LeCrosse looked on as the reading proceeded. Her auburn hair waved and curled. An elegant azure top clung to her chest. She was dressed in tall cowboy boots and a short party skirt that glittered with silver sequins. She was beautiful, and in LeCrosse's clutches. Or was he in hers?

A sullen mood had settled on Kyle. As if sensing his presence, Alice walked to the window, her gaze falling on him. He held her stare and, though he couldn't see them from that distance, he felt those green eyes digging for a deeper understanding of his needs, as though only she could see his true self. He shook off the feeling, wondering how much he'd made up. It was unlikely she even saw him.

Yet, Alice was a woman who got what she wanted through charm and practical intelligence. She was a perfect wife for LeCrosse–entertaining, but like Tony, not to be trusted. Kyle remembered the first party when she'd turned her charm on him. He'd forgotten about his attraction to Juliet and followed Alice around like a sick puppy. He'd done her bidding, getting her water, closing the curtains, cleaning a room. He hated himself for who he'd become in her presence.

By the time he remembered Juliet, she was passed out in the bedroom with George looming over her. He'd do better this time.

. . .

LeCrosse acted like he'd been expecting Kyle. His eyes were cool, his smile stilted. He might have been drunk or high or both, but in control. Alice hung on her husband's arm. "You remember my wife, don't you?"

He didn't miss a beat. "Alice."

Alice cooed as if she didn't remember Kyle. Maybe she didn't. She turned her brilliant green eyes on him, and he felt a dark wind fill his blood, mesmerized by her charm, just like last time.

She offered him a drink and he declined. Scooting out from under those eyes, he excused himself.

"It's a busy crowd," Kyle said when he found Juliet out on the deck. He wanted to put his arms around her and hold her close, protecting her. As if she needed that. As if she wouldn't bristle at the mere idea of someone protecting her. He could smell her lavender soap. Her gray eyes were angry, apprehensive.

"I just threw a spread for Arnold, that big burly man in the flannel shirt," Juliet said. "He runs Tony's toy booth sometimes. He tried to push himself on me."

"What?" Kyle felt his face heat up.

"Not a true assault. Just too fresh. What is it with these guys?"

"Let's get out of here. You don't need this kind of job." Kyle fumed. He felt the skin tighten on his bones, felt himself stand up straighter. Arnie had better not be forcing himself on Juliet. "He's just an old truck driver. I'll take care of him."

Juliet flipped her hand up. "No need. I put him off. I'm okay. We can't leave." She leaned out over on the deck railing. Grass stretched down a long hill to a paved walking path and on to the water. Wind blew her dark cowlicks to and fro. A powerful gust pressed her ivory-colored sweater against her belly, and she wrapped her arms around herself.

When she turned and embraced him, his dazed heart danced with delight. His mind cleared, and he felt strong. Kyle was warm in the cold breezes, and good in the midst of this dark party. The full moon illuminated his life, and he knew he belonged in this beautiful, radiant world, in Juliet's beautiful embrace.

"I'm surprised you came back to another one of his parties," he said, taking her hand.

"Something's going on here. Picard thinks LeCrosse might know something about the runaways, why they come to Annie's Court and why they disappear. Maybe we can find out where Twyla went."

"Who is Picard?"

Juliet halted, pulled her hand out of his. "Forget him," she said.

"You asked for him at the police station."

Juliet shrugged.

"OK," he said. "It's a secret. I see. Have you learned anything?"

Juliet looked out at the bay. The wind against her skin, blowing her hair back, gave her a wild, adorable look. She ran her fingers through the dark cowlicks, and looked up at him, revealing soft gray eyes and a smile that sent him reeling.

"That woman from Missoula was looking for you," she said.

The woman from Missoula? There it was. A second time. What the hell? "I don't know any woman from Missoula. My parents live north of there."

"Ok," she said and looked back toward the sea.

He moved close to her. "Need a date tonight?" he asked.

She shook her head.

For a moment, he couldn't breathe.

"I already have one." Juliet took his hand in hers. "Let's go in."

. . .

Alice wanted a reading. Kyle watched Juliet shuffle the cards.

"Do you have a question in mind?" She asked Alice.

"I'm just curious about this little pastime of yours," Alice said. "I'm wondering why on earth my husband hired you."

Juliet grimaced and stopped shuffling. She put the cards out on the table in front of Alice. "It's not wise to ask the questions if you don't want to know the answers."

"I'm sure I'll be fine." The woman glared.

Juliet shrugged. "It's your life. Go ahead and shuffle the cards."

Alice reorganized the cards and handed them back. Juliet laid out a four-card spread: The Magician, the four of swords, The Hanged Man, and The Tower. All upside down. Kyle was pretty sure these cards were downright ornery.

"The Magician here depicts the situation," Juliet said. "It implies it's time for a change. You have undeveloped powers at your fingertips if you decide to focus on them. They can get you into trouble, or they can lead you to the life of your dreams. Everything you've ever wanted is before you. You need to pay attention and choose the right time, place, and person."

Alice smiled and straightened her board-like back. "What about the next card?"

"This card shows a loss you've not given yourself the time to grieve. It's driving you further into exhaustion, further away from what is important to you."

A shadow crossed Alice's face. Her smile dropped for a second. When it lifted again, her face had become a blank mask. She pointed her chin and nodded for Juliet to go on.

"The Hanged Man," Juliet said, "is in the position of action. It's reversed, and shows you're stuck in a material world, neglecting your spiritual development. You are at a crossroads–a time to choose what path you want to follow. Deceit and lies, or a quest for truth. When the Hanged Man is upside down, he looks to be standing right side up, but if you look closely, you can see the deception. He is on thin air. Nothing there for you to stand on."

A look of disgust crossed Alice's face. "Tony actually pays you to come in here and predict demise? To insult our household?"

"If you've heard enough, I'll stop now," Juliet said. "You shuffled the cards. You asked the questions. All I do is lay the cards out and relay their potential meaning."

Alice rubbed her fingers against her thumbs, as if summoning a magic genie, and gave a sly smile. "OK, give me the last card. I'm sure it's my life in ruins."

From what Kyle could see, she wasn't far off. The card looked bad. Lightning destroyed a medieval tower, its inhabitants falling out of the tall windows with their mouths open in silent screams.

"This card shows that not much is going to change until you change your mind. Failure after failure will plague you until you alter your beliefs and fix what you've broken." Juliet looked at Alice, a sadness in her eyes. "Do you have a child?"

The woman looked like she'd been hit by a brick. "What business is it of yours?"

Juliet shook her head. "None. It's just a guess."

"Tell me this guess. No sense in leaving me hanging in the tower's dark mess."

"I'm guessing your child needs you. Going to him might be the change needed."

Kyle stared at Juliet. What was she up to? It was one thing to talk in generalities, but a whole other thing to bring the personal lives of real people onto the floor. And where did that wild card of a child come from? And why, oh why did she say it out loud?

Alice's face contorted. She moved close to Juliet and hissed something to her, laughed again, and walked into the middle of a group of young men, adorning them with her favors.

Kyle turned and saw Arnold watching. Arnold raised his eyebrows. "You pissed off the wrong woman this time," he said to Juliet with a shrug, and went after Alice.

• • •

After the party, the night was cool and wet from the sea mist. Kyle felt the cold in his bones as he walked with Juliet toward her shed. The party had been a waste as far as finding Twyla went. He wanted to see Juliet home safely, even though she'd been getting herself home safely all year, as she'd not so artfully reminded him. They strolled down the walking path that went along the water. Each time the path wandered close to a street; Kyle noticed the same car following them.

"Someone you know?" he asked.

Juliet looked over. "Wait here a minute."

His nerves were on fire as he waited, ready to jump in if anyone tried anything with her. One girl he knew had already disappeared. With Twyla gone, he had reason to worry when she leaned into the window of an unknown car.

"Juliet, let's go," he said, to let the driver know she wasn't alone.

She ignored him and continued leaning into the car window.

He walked over. "Come on. I'm freezing." He recognized the man in the car, from the streets. Her Picard, maybe. The name she'd let slip and then avoided.

"I'll be there in a minute," she said.

Kyle stepped back and shifted from foot to foot, shoving his hands into his pockets.

When she finished, she turned and walked down the path ahead of him.

He went after her, catching up. "Is everything ok?"

"Fine," she said. "No worries at all."

"Who was that?"

"A friend."

Kyle shook his head. "Oohkay," he said, drawing out the O. "Are you mad at me for being concerned about your safety? With Twyla missing? And some strange voodoo going on at Tony LeCrosse's place?" A part of him wanted to march off in the other direction, leaving her alone in the dark. But he'd be damned if he'd leave her anywhere in danger.

Juliet stopped. "I'll tell you who that was in the car, if you tell me who the woman from Missoula is. Why is she looking for you?"

"The woman from Missoula? I told you I don't know a woman from Missoula."

"The pretty blonde. Is she your girlfriend?"

"You are jealous of someone I don't know? Is that why you're mad at me." Suddenly it hit him. His heart exploded. If a woman from Missoula was looking for him, the police had sent someone to bring him back to Montana to face charges for the fire.

"Oh, I'm not mad at you," Juliet said. Her voice had softened, and he heard something close to fear in it. She started walking again, this time at a slower pace.

He followed. He couldn't tell her about the fire and his fear of the police, his fear that they had sent someone after him. He could tell Juliet how he felt about her and that's what he did. "I care about you," he said. "I don't have a mysterious girlfriend from Montana or anywhere. I don't even know this woman."

Juliet looked straight ahead and sighed. She shook her head, turned to him, and looped her arm through his. "Okay, I'm sorry."

He heard the relief in her voice. "It's okay. Let's not fight."

"You're right, I should have told you I knew that driver. But I can't tell you how I know him. You're just going to have to trust me."

"Picard," Kyle said, feeling that he'd just been made the fool.

• • •

When Kyle visited the tent town the next day, the wind had kicked up several notches. It sounded like thunder rolling across the canvas and nylon roofs. A fire burned in the pit down by the water. The flames lashed the air and Kyle saw it as an omen of things to come. He feared for the runaways hiding there. A lone figure huddled into his hood, stirring the ashes.

"The police were here," Stephan said.

"What did they want?" Kyle sat down on a rock. The cold granite made his muscles tense. So did the idea of police at the tent town.

"Seems someone from out here filed a missing person's report on a girl. That someone, I'm guessing, was you?" Stephan looked up from under his hood, his eyelids at half-mast. His navy sweatshirt had dots of bleached out tears down one sleeve, an indicator of the sad and resourceful lives they lived.

Kyle nodded. They hadn't finished the report, so he'd thought nothing would come of it. And why would the police come out *here*? The runaway camp had nothing to do with Twyla's disappearance. "Did they ask for me?"

"Just the girl. They went through every tent, trying to find her. We might have to move. We're camped in a no camping zone, and they don't like vagrants."

"I'm sorry."

Stephan kicked a rock toward the water. "We didn't build this sanctuary just to have you blow it for us."

A knot tightened in Kyle's stomach. "What are you saying?"

"You've been careless, Kyle. You can't come around here anymore."

Kyle sucked his lower lip between his teeth and bit down just enough to feel the pain. It was something he did when he felt anxious. Or angry. He hadn't been careless. In fact, he had been careful. He cared about the tent kids. He'd been caring. For the past year, he'd given most of his time and all his money to the tent camp.

"Stephan, you have little authority here," Kyle said in a deadly, calm voice. "Once you're eighteen, you could be arrested for harboring runaways."

"Is that the best you can do? Threatening me? Mikey, who'll be taking over for me, agrees with me. You're gone. We, me and you, we're done."

Kyle looked at the angry waves crashing against the rocks and rolling hard onto the beach. He hadn't thought Stephan could break his heart any more than he had the day he kicked him out of the camp. Even then, Kyle had thought they'd remain friends somehow. But he was wrong. Stephan's cruelty pushed Kyle into a stunned void, an abyss he'd worked hard to avoid. Unprepared to leave this place forever, he pulled his hands out of his sleeves and warmed them over the dancing fire for what was supposed to be the very last time.

CHAPTER THIRTEEN

After the party, Juliet dropped into a deep despair. She'd lost her home, her mother, her Aunt Gloria, and any sense of security. She'd been sexually assaulted by that creep Layne and told her aunt, only to be accused of lying. She ran away from the warm dry air of Arizona to live in an abandoned shed along the cold, wet Washington coast. Other than Kyle, and maybe Picard, she had no friends.

How did her life turn so wrong? Why did her mother die? Why her? Of all the good people in the world, why did it have to be her mother who hit that power pole? Who was Juliet to want to help Twyla and the other runaways? Her own life was a mess.

Rain pelted the tin roof and the plywood walls of the shed, and she snuggled under a blanket. Wilma came through the small opening in the back of the shed where Juliet had nailed a piece of towel over it to make it a cat door. The kitten jumped up on the mattress Juliet had pulled from one of the lean-tos, and rubbed her wet fur against Juliet, purring her "I'm hungry" purr. Purred into submission, Juliet put a handful of dry cat food in a dish and set it on the floor near the small table that held Juliet's cook stove.

She had hooked a small propane tank up to a camp stove. On cold nights, she put three large rocks in the frying pan, put it on the burner, and turned it on low. The rocks held the heat and made heating with a cook stove almost efficient. She was proud of herself for thinking up that strategy. The shed wouldn't hold the heat for long, but it would warm up soon enough. She and Wilma were alike that way: they both loved the warmth.

She thought of Kyle and felt the regret run through her. She felt terrible for going cold on him, and wished she could live that night again, do things differently. She'd apologized, but still felt rotten. Things might be ok, but she wasn't sure. Maybe he held a grudge. Unlike Juliet, some people held onto things and punished people later. She'd seen it with Layne and Aunt Gloria. Layne had a whole list of wrongs he felt Aunt Gloria had done to him. Part of his revenge, he took out on Juliet.

If Kyle ever decided to stay in the shed with her, she needed to be honest with him about Detective Picard. It was time to tell him, anyway. The thought of telling him she worked unofficially for Picard sent her stomach tumbling.

Juliet pushed the troubling thoughts away and focused on the warmth of the fire. She'd always been that way, blessed with a great imagination and able to use it to calm down. She could see something in her mind and watch it materialize before her eyes.

Her mother had given her that gift when she was young. Juliet had benefited from her mother's daily meditation. That example was part of how her mother had taught her to stay relaxed and alert while taking tests in school. She'd also taught Juliet the art of arguing with a calm voice. And how to run fast by envisioning herself in a natural, relaxed flow. To know things by remembering details.

When Juliet was young, she enjoyed running. She moved through the world with her back straight and her limbs relaxed, following her body like an afterthought. It comforted her one day, when she was watching the martial arts class, to hear her mother's concept repeated: "Relax. Stand tall. And the rest will come easily." It was as if her mother was speaking to her from the grave.

She missed her mother. Lila French. If she'd married the cowboy, Harrison Love, her name could have become Lila Love. Such a poetic name. But she'd wanted to keep Juliet's father's name because it told everyone Juliet was her family.

Juliet was six years old when her mother first sat her down to remember her father. It surprised Juliet, because by then, she had thought of Harrison as her father. Lila sat Juliet in the brown overstuffed chair. The chair felt like a large teddy bear holding her in its lap. She folded her legs up and sat with her back straight.

"Close your eyes," her mother had said. "Think of your father. Tell me every detail you remember."

Before long, his dark hair parted in a cowlick over his right eye. The hair in the eyebrow over that same eye pointed out in all directions, as if it couldn't remember which way to go. Juliet wondered if that was what had happened to her father. He had lost his way.

A smell of oil and grease came up out of the chair and she saw the yellow station wagon he had worked on, and later, the salve he had rubbed on his hands to wash the grease off.

She remembered the shower soap of her father's freshly washed face, and his deep, rich voice when putting her to bed. The laughter that rose out of the kitchen that night, and the soft sounds of her parents murmuring as they moved toward their bedroom. In the morning, he'd made them eggs and pancakes. Sitting in that brown overstuffed chair, Juliet had remembered it all.

When she opened her eyes, her mother's tears ran down her cheeks.

"Good," her mother had said.

A couple years later, her mother gave her a deck of tarot cards. She told her she had an intuitive gift. The cards would help her use the gift. They were not the source of it. She made Juliet repeat that. The cards were simply a vehicle to capture what she already knew, a way to communicate her knowing to others, a way to help, a way to soften the world. Dreams could be a guide in the same way as the cards, as could the earth and sky, and Juliet's own feelings.

"You have the skill," her mother had said. "But to use it, you must learn to harness it. You must sit quietly and clear your mind, let the images come to you."

Juliet had wanted to go outside and play. Outside, she heard the neighbor girls giggle and splash in their pool. Through the window she saw a blue truck pull up in front of their door. "Trouble," she thought. The thought stopped her.

She looked at her mother and said, "Sally should not go out with Joey tonight." The thought surprised her. She didn't know Joey.

Later that night they'd heard that Joey had gotten into a wreck. He'd be okay. As luck would have it, he'd had no passengers. A passenger would have been killed. Sally's parents had kept her home. That early knowing was Juliet's first time understanding the powerful gift she had been given. And she wanted nothing to do with it. The cards sat on her bedside table, until Lila French brought them and Juliet out into the living room where they sat across from each other on the floor.

Her mother's brown hair curled around her chin and her blue-print dress fell away from her knees. The sound of her mother shuffling the cards calmed Juliet and set her mind at ease. Her mother looked gently into Juliet's eyes, and she felt something stir. Eyes locked, Lila French reached out and touched Juliet. The skin-to-skin touch brought a jolt of understanding, a knowing beyond words.

That knowing was small at first but grew each time they sat on the floor with the tarot deck between them. Little by little Juliet absorbed her mother's teachings. Her mother told stories of how her own mother had taught her to pay attention, to listen. Anyone could read a book about how to read the cards but letting them be a way toward her own seeing required trust and surrender to the gift.

Little by little Juliet let the cards help her. She learned their signs. Let them talk. With Lila French by her side, she had learned to trust her own wisdom.

"There is downside to working with tarot cards, or any gift," her mother had said. "You can get lost in the thoughts and feelings of others. You must take great care not to take on their troubles."

Juliet had nodded, thinking she did understand, wondering why her mother felt compelled to warn her. Hadn't she already guided Juliet in the right way of the cards?

"Worse," her mother had continued, "You might use your gift as a power to sway others, a power over them. You must never do this."

Her mother had barely begun teaching her the dangers of the gift when she ran Harrison's truck into a power pole. It was so wrong. Her mother still had so much to teach her, but she had died and left Juliet with a smidgen of the knowledge she needed.

Juliet felt so sad about her mother. She wondered if she'd ever stop needing her. The fire in Juliet's cook stove burned steady and warmed the shed. At least she had this shelter and this warmth. Her mother had taught her that too: find something good to focus on and more goodness will follow.

Outside, something crashed against the wall, and she wondered if it was Kyle. But no, Kyle would just knock. The wind picked up, and Wilma ran and hid under the bed. Juliet wondered what was crashing against her wall, but not enough to stick her head out in that weather.

Soon, a knock came at the door. She looked out her little peek-hole and saw the rag boy, the blond boy who escaped the van, standing there completely drenched, his hair pasted to his head, his ragged shorts hugging his quivering knees. He appeared to be alone.

She opened the door. She looked around for whatever had slammed against the shed and saw nothing. The boy stepped inside, and steam rolled off his sweatshirt.

"You've got to be freezing," she said, tossing him a towel. "Take off that sweatshirt and let it dry by the stove."

He nodded, his face wise. Too wise for his ten or eleven years.

"How did you know I was here?" she asked.

He shrugged.

"Do you talk?"

He shrugged.

Juliet was baffled. She hoped she was right to let him in.

The boy pulled off his sweatshirt and handed it to Juliet. Underneath it he wore a navy blue, short-sleeved t-shirt. His arms were covered in bruises.

She took his arm, but he quickly pulled it away. "Who did this to you?" Juliet thought of Twyla's bruised arms.

He didn't answer. Instead, he looked at the fire and rubbed his hands in the heat lifting from the rocks.

"We must call someone. No one should hit you." Although she knew it was part of street life, she didn't like it.

The boy shrank away from her and pulled his sweatshirt into his lap. "No," he said. "They'll send me home. And I don't want to go."

"It can't be worse than that." Juliet pointed to his bruises, feeling a vague sense of déjà vu. "Are you hungry?"

The boy didn't answer but didn't leave.

She dumped the rocks out of the frying pan, washed it out, put clean water in it, and added a handful of broken Ramen noodles. The boiling water made the room smell homey, like chicken soup. Once the noodles were cooked, she handed the frying pan and a spoon to the boy.

"No police," he said.

"Eat."

"No police," he said again.

"Okay."

"Thank you."

She smiled. He was not too hungry and bruised to be polite.

"Thank you," he said again. "For trying to help me that day they caught me and put me in the van."

Juliet nodded, afraid to ask the obvious question. "You're welcome."

"Outside," he said, "Just now? The wind threw a broken branch against your shed."

Juliet lifted her eyebrows to that.

"That loud noise was the wind. Nothing bad."

She felt his explanation and reassurance as a sense of relief she hadn't known she needed. It was good to know when loud noises were nothing bad. "I'm glad you told me," she said.

The boy didn't put the sweatshirt back on but kept it next to him, as if wanting to be ready for a quick getaway. He ravished the noodles and broth and handed the frying pan back to Juliet with a wide smile, the smile reaching his eyes. She wiped it out with an old cloth and put the rocks back in it, hoping she hadn't poisoned the boy with some mysterious bacteria growing in the pan from the rocks.

"You can stay here tonight," she said, pulling the extra sleeping mat off her bed and putting it on the plywood floor. Then, she threw the extra blanket on it. "Tomorrow, we talk with Detective Benson Picard. I don't like those bruises. Picard is a good guy. He'll help you."

His eyes dropped; the brief joy gone out of them. The boy reached for his sweatshirt. "You said no police."

"Okay, okay. Just stay the night. We can talk about it in the morning."

The rag boy sat on the mat and wrapped the blanket around his shoulders, keeping his ever trust-worthy sweatshirt nearby.

The little calico poked her head out from under the bed, watching, evidently deciding if he was friend or foe.

"What's your name?" she asked.

"Roy."

"Juliet." She broached the next subject carefully. "That day with the van? Who took you?"

He shook his head. "I don't know. He wore a mask."

"How did you escape?"

"I think I was thrown out. A lumberjack threw me against the back of the van. I heard the latch on the back door click open, and next thing I knew, I hit the street and rolled."

"And took off running."

"Yeah, I didn't wait around to see if they'd made a mistake."

"A mistake?"

"Unlatching the door. I think the guy, the lumberjack, did it on purpose. Without his help, I'd have been in real trouble."

Juliet nodded to his arms. "Looks like you're still in trouble. I can buy a bus ticket for you if you want to go home. I've been saving money for something like this. The streets are too dangerous for kids your age. Do you have somewhere safe to go?"

Roy shook his head.

She put a thick stick into the door lock to hold the latch shut. "You'll be safe here tonight. No one's coming in without our permission."

Roy, the rag boy, had already slumped over on the sleeping pad where Wilma joined him. He sank into his bed, a hand on her furry back, and fell sound asleep.

By morning, the wind had died down, the rain had stopped, and the boy was gone.

•   •   •

Before Juliet could get her bearings that morning, with Roy gone as mysteriously as he'd arrived, someone knocked.

Wilma scurried out the cat door.

Hoping it was Kyle, she looked out the peek-hole and saw a blue-uniformed policeman. She froze. Maybe if she stayed quiet, he would just go away. But all he had to do was push the plywood forward and poke his head inside. There was nowhere to hide in her little ten-by-ten shed. She pulled on a sweater and opened the door.

The officer stood back, his right hand, gun ready. He looked around the room, apparently saw that she was no danger, and motioned her outside. "Are you living here?" he asked.

Looking back at her makeshift home, she could see the mattress and the cook stove through the doorway. Lying would be futile. "Yes."

"Do you have permission?"

Another chance to lie. "Yes," she said.

He spoke into his radio, asking for an owner's name and number for the property at 204 Mission Street. He drummed his fingers on the radio while he waited for his answer. Once he got it, he made the call on his cell phone. "Care to change your answer?" he asked as he waited for someone to pick up.

Juliet took in a breath and let it go, ready to tell the truth.

Right then, he held up a finger. "Yes, sorry to bother you, Ma'am. A young woman lives in a shed on your property. We wanted to know if you were aware of this?" He looked at Juliet and raised his eyebrows. "I see. Yes, Ma'am, you're right, I shouldn't be bothering your guests this early in the morning. Yes, Ma'am, I'll tell her." He clicked off the phone and put it in his pocket. "Sorry to have bothered you. We got an anonymous call that you were trespassing. I should have called the landowner first."

"It was time for me to get up anyway," Juliet said, pushing the hair out of her face – a gesture designed to hide her dismay. Who owned this property and why had she protected her? Who had reported that she was trespassing? She'd thought only Kyle and Twyla had known she was there. But as it turned out, at least four other people knew: the officer, the rag boy, the owner of the shed, and the anonymous caller.

· · ·

Later that day, a ruffling wind puffed across the rocks where Juliet found Kyle. He sat facing the waves. Fog rolled into the bay, and Juliet felt the cold through her whole body. She sat down next to him.

He looked over at her. "Are you still mad at me?"

"I wasn't mad," she said. "I was confused about the woman from Montana."

He nodded. "Understandable."

She fought the urge to push him away. If she wanted too much he'd leave anyway. Juliet didn't know if she could just get to know him without running or clinging.

"Can we try again?" She asked. "Only this time I won't go all sullen and mysterious on you."

"Sullen and mysterious is interesting." He laughed. "You're okay. Nothing to do over."

She let out the breath she'd been holding and felt the relief fill her chest. "Last night the rag boy came to my shed. I told you about him. His name is Roy."

"He just showed up?"

"Yeah. In the storm."

"Why didn't you bring him with you?"

"He was there and by morning he was gone," she said. "He had bruises up and down his arms, just like Twyla. That boy is in trouble too."

Kyle nodded, tucking his knees up under a yellow sweatshirt and pulling the sleeves down over his fists. "I have a feeling they're in the same trouble. Why didn't he stay, though?"

Juliet looked at the ground. Shame filled her chest. The boy had left because he didn't trust her. "I told him I'd call the authorities."

Kyle nodded.

"The police showed up this morning."

"What?"

"At the shed. Did Roy call the police to get back at me?" Juliet asked.

"Doubtful. None of the runaways want anything to do with the police."

"A revenge call?"

"You fed him and gave him a place to sleep for the night. He's on his way in the morning. No need to rat you out."

"The owner didn't have me arrested for trespassing."

Kyle tilted his head in a question.

"Why not?" She asked. "None of it makes sense."

"You are right. It doesn't make sense."

"Maybe we can go to the plat room at city hall to see who owns that property. That person knows something. She's a silent watcher."

"She? A silent watcher? Poetic. Creepy."

Juliet smiled at Kyle. It was the first time she'd smiled all morning, and it felt good. "The cop kept saying 'yes, Ma'am' in a very apologetic tone of voice. I'm sure it's against code to use a shed for living quarters. I wonder what she said to him. She had no good reason to protect me."

"And yet she did."

* * *

The plat room showed an Antonia L. Corrales as owner of the shed property. Ms. Corrales lived nearby on Church Street. Juliet and Kyle watched her unload groceries from her Subaru Legacy, an older car with rusted side-rails. She wore a purple print skirt that flowed to low-heeled leather boots. Gray streaked her dark hair, which she had pulled into a half-hearted bun. A white picket fence lined a neatly mowed lawn edged with beds of mums, sunflowers, and leftover pansies.

"May we help?" Juliet asked. In jeans and a white long-sleeved t-shirt, her hair combed flat, she hoped she looked like an upstanding citizen. "I'm Juliet. I live in the shed on your property."

The woman looked at her blankly.

"You helped me this morning by not turning me over to the police for sleeping in your shed. This is my friend Kyle." He too wore jeans that fit and a t-shirt, his hair combed out of his eyes.

Ms. Corrales nodded. "Grab a bag and come on in."

She unpacked her groceries, opened two plastic containers of chicken tortilla soup, and put the soup on the stove to heat. The range looked like it hadn't been replaced since before Juliet was born. Everything was spotless. The comforting scent of rich spices filled the air, mixing with the aroma of the chicken soup.

Juliet felt oddly at home in the small kitchen.

"I've known you were down there for the last couple of weeks," Ms. Corrales said. "I brought some stuff to store in the shed and found your mattress in there. I parked and waited for you." She looked at Juliet with sad eyes. "I was going to confront you, but when you arrived wet and cold, I felt sorry for you. No harm done. Storing old clothes is not much of a job for that shed. Better that it makes a home for someone."

Kyle and Juliet looked at each other.

"Thank you, Ms. Corrales," they said in unison.

She laughed a hearty belly laugh.

Juliet liked her.

"Call me Antonia," she said. "You can stay there, but it's not a good situation for a young woman. You should get a job and a little apartment or a room." She poured the hot soup into white bowls decorated with colorful wildflowers, put the bowls on the table, and motioned for them to sit and eat.

Kyle dove right in.

"Things happen here," Antonia continued. "Things young people shouldn't have to experience."

"What kind of things?" Kyle held his spoon halfway to his mouth.

"Kids go missing. It was in the paper last week. Several out of state parents have contacted the police. Someone put it out on the internet that Annie's Court is a safe place for runaways. The paper said that kids are coming from all over the country. But it's not safe. Not now. The kids are showing up in droves and some of their parents never hear from them again."

"It was in the paper?" Juliet asked.

"Yes. The article said that a parent found the invitation to kids on the internet and contacted Annie's Court's Police Department."

"Are parents showing up?" Kyle asked.

Antonia shrugged. Strands of her hair had escaped the bun and softly framed her face. "According to the article, a woman and a man showed up last month. Their twelve-year-old daughter, Gabriella, had disappeared from a schoolyard in Boise, Idaho. They swore she would not have run away. The police had been looking for her. She was on an Amber alert. And nothing, until the parents found the website about Annie's Court."

"Did they find her?" Juliet asked.

"By some miracle, they did." Antonia looked at Juliet with soft hazel eyes that had seen plenty, eyes that were full of earned wisdom. The woman reminded Juliet of her mother, breaking her heart a little. "The paper said they found the girl on the roadside. She had a disease that sent her into frequent seizures. Someone had evidently picked Gabriella up, found her lacking, and discarded her."

Juliet nodded.

"I have too much time on my hands," Antonia said. "I'm a retired middle school teacher and I couldn't stop thinking about that girl. I've seen kids with disabilities kicked to the fences. I got the feeling that whoever took her decided she didn't measure up."

"Did the girl, Gabriella, tell the police who took her?" Kyle asked.

"The paper didn't say." Antonia twisted the edge of the blue tablecloth around her index finger.

"My bet?" Juliet said. "She won't talk about it."

Antonia poured tea into their cups. "More soup?"

Juliet declined, but Kyle? Kyle, she thought, ate to his heart's content.

CHAPTER FOURTEEN

After visiting with Antonia, Juliet and Kyle returned to Antonia's tiny shed. Juliet no longer feared being evicted, but something else was off. A terrible smell came from inside the shed, and smoke spilled out from between pieces of the wood siding. She scrambled to open the door. When she finally got in, they found a smoking object. A smell wafted off the pile of embers, putrid and animal like.

Her heart seized up when she saw the orange fur. "No!"

"Shhhh," Kyle said. "It's okay. Looks like deer hide."

"Deer hide?" Not Wilma?

Just then, Wilma came in and stared at the strange, putrid object.

"Wilma," Juliet said with a soft breath and pulled the kitten into her arms. "Baby. Sweet Baby. You're safe." She held her close and kissed her a dozen times on her head, petting her warm body over and over. "You're here. You're alive." The shock slowly left her bones as she whimpered, "It's not you."

She continued to caress Wilma as she looked more closely at the burned lump that was emitting such a stench. She could see the fur came from a fresh kill, and the only hunter she knew was George.

Kyle took the smoking thing outside and put it on the graveled ground.

Inside, a creeping, foreboding feeling spread across Juliet's entire body as her eyes took in another object that did not belong in her living space. Sprawled out at the end of her mattress was a tiny wooden doll, one leg torn off and flailed aside, the other leg twisted up toward where the head should have been. She spotted the head on the floor near the bed, got down on her knees, and retrieved it. Juliet swallowed hard as she stared at a distorted replica of her own head, cowlicks sticking out in every direction and deranged red eyes glaring back at her.

Kyle came back in, his eyes falling on the dismembered doll.

"Tony LeCrosse," she said. "He sent George to do his dirty work."

"Warning you off."

"From what? How could he think I'm a threat?" She didn't think LeCrosse knew anything about her work with Picard. He'd have no reason to see Juliet as a danger to him. But then, she thought, maybe this threat wasn't about her work with Picard. "I have been asking a lot of questions about Twyla. If he's involved in her disappearance, he'd want to stop me.'

"What about Alice?" Kyle asked. "She didn't look happy about her tarot reading. She gave you some very dirty looks."

An icy shard shot straight through her. Maybe she had made an enemy. "She was angry with me at that party," she said. "The tarot cards hit too close to home."

Juliet thought about how Alice had flamed up and dampened her anger in seconds. Not liking how Alice had treated her from the beginning, Juliet had given Alice the worst version of the cards' meaning. It was unethical and cruel, Juliet thought. And childish. Now someone had upped the ante.

"Creepy," Kyle said. "But why? It's such an overreaction."

Placing the head on top of the body, Juliet laid the doll on the bed. It looked wild and scared, ready to run. They even dressed it in running shorts and a tank top. The workmanship was immaculate. They had crafted running shoes from light canvas material, with tiny Rs on the side. Were the Rs another warning? "R" for "run?" Her mind raced crazily, grasping for meanings. Her head hurt as she sat on the bed.

With that doll in the shed, she was sure of this: the LeCrosses had threatened her. She thought of the police arriving the morning after Roy arrived and left. When that police visit didn't scare her off, they burned the deer hide and sent the doll. The message seemed clear: Go and don't look back.

Wind picked up through the open door of the shed and blew the rancid smell of the burnt deer hide toward her. She drew in a sharp breath as she thought about the LeCrosses. They were after her. They meant to harm her. The icy wind ran hard through Juliet's blood as she realized given the chance, they might even kill her.

She struggled with herself. It would be so easy to go and forget everything in Annie's Court. She'd left Arizona. The ease of that departure had surprised her. This one, with no real connections other than Kyle, would be even easier.

But she wouldn't leave now. She wouldn't leave Kyle or their mission to find Twyla. And maybe now, Roy. If she looked deeply enough, if she could quiet her mind, go into that intuitive knowing, the gift that her mother had taught her, and receive the hints rumbling around in the air, in her mind-if she could only catch their meanings, she'd find Twyla and Roy. And most likely Tony and Alice LeCrosse would lead her right to them.

Wilma squirmed in her arms; her fur roughed up from Juliet squeezing her. The movement brought Juliet back to the shed. She put down the kitten. "Glad you're okay, Little One."

Leaving the door open, she and Kyle went outside. Wilma followed. Come on, wind, Juliet thought, clean up that disgusting smell. Dread replaced the relief she'd felt about no longer being evicted from the shed.

"Will you stay here tonight?" she asked Kyle, her heart throbbing in her chest.

He nodded. "I'll gather my stuff this afternoon."

"Where were you last night?"

"Out by the campground. I wasn't quite ready to move into town."

"Now you are?"

"Well," he said with a mischievous smile, "it looks like you need me."

She looked back toward the shed and the Juliet doll and then at the smoldering hide. "It would be safer with the two of us here." She sounded so practical, betraying none of the desire she felt to stay close to Kyle, betraying none of the fear she felt about that desire.

Kyle poked the smoking thing with a stick. "They are definitely trying to scare you," he said.

"Tony's doll is doing the trick."

"The LeCrosses don't live at that condo. It's mostly empty. The lights are on only when they entertain. They are there when they have parties, and I heard George mention business lunches. We'll be closer to solving this puzzle if we find out where they live. Picard must know where they live. You work for him, right?"

Juliet nodded. Now was as good a time as any to admit it. "Why wouldn't he tell me, though? If Picard knows, why keep it a secret from me?"

"Maybe he wants to solve this mystery himself. He wants information, but he holds his cards close."

"Well, if they're tarot cards," Juliet said with a smile, "I'll sort them out."

. . .

That night Juliet dreamed of the boy dressed in black. He stood outside of the shed looking in through the open door, his mouth open. He was ready to tell her something, but she woke up too soon to hear his message. It was the second time that week she'd had the dream; the boy appearing sullen and dark and poised to tell her something, Juliet waking up just as he was about to speak.

She looked over at Kyle sleeping peacefully on his makeshift bed on the floor. A pale morning light shone through the small, shed window and fell on his face, making him look young and innocent. A pang of grief shot through Juliet. He should be home with his family, finishing school, and making plans for the future, not sleeping in some cold, damp shed. He'd be finishing his last year of high school if he'd stayed in Montana with his parents.

Juliet had been camping in Montana with her mother, on vacation, sheltering from some unknown storm in her mother's life. When things got rough, they packed up their Arizona home and headed for the mountains. They stayed until the land froze and the winter snow covered the mountaintops before heading for the desert again.

Maybe Kyle was the boy in the dream. She thought Kyle had a darkness that haunted him. She saw it in his eyes when they turned distant and sad. Juliet shook off the dream and walked outside. Soft pink clouds hung over the buildings. The sun came up just over the bay. She took out Picard's cell phone to call Gabriella. She dialed the number she'd found in an old newspaper where the girl's parents had run a "missing persons" ad. Before the phone could ring, she hung up. It was too early.

Grateful for its convenient location across from her shed, she walked to the park's indoor bathroom. After completing her business, she washed her hands and face and brushed her teeth. She tucked the washrag and toothbrush into a shoulder bag she'd made from an old pair of jeans. Sun warmed her face as she walked down the beach to the old ship. Approaching it, she listened for noises, heard nothing, climbed aboard, and went down to the galley. This old ship must harbor clues to Twyla's disappearance, she thought. The musky hull assaulted her. Go, it said, echoing LeCrosse's message. But no. She would not go. She'd stay and find Twyla. Once she found her, she'd secure her safety.

With that determination Juliet riffled through candy wrappers and pop cans littered on the floor. In among them, she found a pocket-sized notebook. Help me, one page read. Leave me alone on the next page. Juliet understood the contradiction. She had felt herself walking that edge with Kyle. Love me. No, don't love me. But this writing wasn't love or the avoidance of love in the notebook. This writing was danger.

The sun climbed higher in the sky and the clouds opened. She sat on deck, took out the phone, and called Gabriella again.

Victoria Daily, the girl's mother, answered. Juliet explained she worked with the police to locate the missing runaways. She wondered if Gabriella might have information about them. Victoria said Gabriella was at school. Her experience in Annie's Court troubled her, but she wouldn't talk about it.

Her daughter brooded more now than before she ran away. She spent hours alone in her room, often not coming out to eat, saying her stomach hurt. She snapped at her parents when they tried to comfort her and clammed up tight when they asked questions. They'd hired a counselor, but Gabriella refused to talk to her. Victoria said she'd take Juliet's number, but doubted her daughter would call, and she didn't want to push her.

Juliet hung up, feeling dismal and useless. There was nothing she could do about Gabriella, but there was something she could do about this phone. Back in the shed, Kyle was still asleep. She stashed the cell phone in a small cardboard box in a corner as far away from her bed as possible. She was sure she'd felt the phone vibrate in her hand without it ringing, without a call coming in. Phones bothered her, especially cell phones. They could find someone through the air, with no connection to the earth. What kind of dark magic was that?

Plus, what would the thing do to her brain if she used it regularly? Juliet needed all her brainpower. All that electromagnetic energy, her mother used to say, was bad for you. No one else she knew gave that theory much credence. But Juliet and her mother were both convinced it was only a matter of time before science proved a need for caution with cell phones. Juliet was probably allergic to cell phones. They made her tremble. Electromagnetic sensitivity, she decided, as she waited for Kyle to wake up.

When he didn't wake up and seemed as sound asleep as anyone she'd ever seen, she left him to it and went to find Picard. They had filed a report about the burned hide and the doll, but so far, an officer hadn't come by. Picard would help.

. . .

Picard met her outside of the Hungry Bear Café. He arrived in a wrinkled suit, looking tired. Without saying a word, he lifted a hand toward the door indicating for her to go inside. She led the way, and they sat in a booth.

"Did I interrupt something," Juliet asked.

"Nothing important. Bureaucratic red tape is all," he said. "I'm trying to get you paid with a weekly check so you can get an apartment somewhere."

She nodded at that. "It would be good. Did you read the report we filed yesterday?"

Picard's eyebrows went up.

"I had a visit from Tony LeCrosse," she said. "Or at least I'm pretty certain it was LeCrosse, or someone associated with, or representing him.

"Can I get you some coffee?" The waitress skidded to a stop in front of their booth. The place was busy, and she was running from table to table.

"Two ham and cheese sandwiches," Picard said. "And a chocolate shake."

That order made Juliet happy. Food made her happy. A chocolate shake made her especially happy. She nodded approvingly. "Food is good," she said.

"This visit? What did LeCrosse say?"

"Leave town. Although not in words. He left this at the shed where I'm staying." She slid the Juliet doll across the table to him.

He picked it up, turned it around. "You are staying in a shed."

"That doll is LeCrosse's handy work," she said, ignoring his apparent dismay. She knew she should have told him sooner about living in Antonia's shed. But she hadn't wanted to tell him while it was a secret, and she was trespassing. Now that she had permission and the whole world seemed to know, he might as well know too. "And yes, I live in a shed."

"A shed," he said.

"A shed."

Picard rubbed his bald head and slid the doll back across the table.

"Why would he threaten you? He wouldn't know I've asked you to watch him."

"That's not all," Juliet said. "Someone set fire to a piece of deer hide in the shed. I think they know I suspect them of something illegal, even though I don't know what it is yet. My guess? They want to keep their secrets. That's why they are trying to scare me off. I filed a police report yesterday, but so far, we've heard from no one."

"I'll find the report and make sure someone gets over there today. I'm assuming the report includes your mysterious address."

"It does." Juliet felt funny, like she was in trouble for hiding the truth. But how could she be in trouble? Since she ran away, she hadn't been responsible to anyone but herself. This, she thought, this sense of duty is what entanglements get you. She didn't want Picard to worry for her. But she knew she had no control over his worry. Still, she worried about his worry. Entanglements.

· · ·

Kyle was gone when Juliet returned to the shed. He left a note saying he'd gone to run an errand. When he didn't come back by late afternoon, Juliet went looking for him. She pulled a bike from its hiding place in one of the tin lean-tos on the far end of the lot and rode toward the campground. She didn't find him where he had last camped, so she went to the tent town.

She parked the bike and climbed through thick foliage to a bluff where she looked down on the little city. Blue and orange roofs wavered in the wind like grounded kites. Smoke from a campfire filled her nose. It burned in a pit in front of the tents. Two older teens stoked the blaze. Sparks flew over their heads, settling in the cold gray.

Juliet walked toward the teens and had almost reached the fire when a boy intercepted her. He was tall and lanky, with dirty brown hair and brilliant green eyes. Stephan. She knew him from when they asked her to move her tent away from the camp.

"Who are you?" he asked.

"Juliet. You don't remember me. I was camped over by the campground, wasn't there very long. You asked me to leave. I'm a friend of Kyle's. Is he here?"

The boy glared at her, turned, and stomped off. He came back with Kyle in tow. "This recklessness is why I told you not to come back," he said.

Kyle shrugged, offered Juliet a big smile that made her feel warm despite the cold wind blowing off the sea. "I had to get a couple things," he said.

"Get them and leave." The boy's chin jutted out.

"Juliet, this is Stephan. Stephan, Juliet."

"Cut the crap. I know who she is. Now others will find us. The police have already been here. You've ruined everything. I knew we couldn't trust you."

"Everyone knows where the tent town is," Juliet said. She bristled at Stephan's abruptness. She wanted to take Kyle away from this mean-hearted boy, protect him, and keep him close. Drawing in a sharp breath, she surprised herself at her protectiveness and her heart opening to… to what? Love? Not love. Love hurt. Love left.

Still. Something fluttered in her chest and broke free.

"She's trustworthy, Stephan," Kyle said. "She's trying to find out what's happened to the kids who have gone missing around here. At first, remember, we thought they just went home. But it's happened so many times, it's concerning. We are trying to find Twyla."

"Yes. I know. The girl the police came looking for." Stephan nodded his head at Juliet without looking at her. "She's over eighteen."

Kyle raised his eyebrows to that.

"I've been here long enough to prove myself," Stephan said.

"Next week, after you turn, you'll get slammed into jail if they catch you here contributing to the runaway problem."

"That's precious. You telling me how to live is precious," Stephan said. He did another about-face and stormed off again.

"He's pretty good at that," Juliet said, stepping closer to Kyle. The sun came through the clouds in a rainbow of ocean spray. The sea washed everything clean, and she felt it now, that sense of everything being pure and good, like something good could happen here with Kyle.

"Being a hypocrite?" He asked.

"That too. I meant the one-eighty. He should be in the military."

Kyle pursed his lips and nodded. "Maybe so."

CHAPTER FIFTEEN

A surprise greeted Kyle and Juliet when they returned to the shed. Police had been there and encircled it in yellow tape that warned "Crime Scene Do Not Cross." He was with Juliet the previous day when she had filed a report about the doll and burnt deer hide. They had waited most of that previous day for an officer to stop by.

By the time Kyle woke up that morning, he had given up on the police. In the comfort of the warm shed, he had pulled the blanket up over his shoulders and gone back to sleep. When he woke up the next time, Juliet was gone.

She had found him out at the tent camp. When they got back to the shed, yellow police tape spoke loud and clear. The police had finally arrived and left again. Kyle watched Juliet tear the yellow tape down, go inside, and sulk. "I don't trust the police," she said. "Two days! It took them two days to show up. It took me going to Picard for them to show up."

"Detective Picard is an in for us," Kyle said. He wanted Juliet to tell him more about Picard. But she seemed resistant to his gentle persuasion. He laughed at himself. Can't even get a girl who likes to talk to talk to him!

"Can't you please get me Tony LeCrosse's phone number? Please?" Juliet was asking. Her wide-open eyes pleaded with him.

"Can't you just get it from Picard?"

She went quiet, chewed on her bottom lip, and turned toward the door.

Wind swirled through the opening, bringing the sense of a new danger. It reminded Kyle of the day in Montana when an escaped herd of thundering horses had stampeded over Katy's yarn pictures, scrambling the yarn, and leaving dust in their midst. He had rushed to her and lifted her out of the way just before the hooves crushed the dirt where she'd been playing. His stomach rumbled. He had saved Katy's life that time.

But this time, here now, what could he do for Juliet that the police hadn't done? He had the sinking feeling the police had found nothing to incriminate the LeCrosses. Kyle knew LeCrosse made the doll. It was his work. Yet, anyone could have placed it in Juliet's shed.

"I shouldn't need Detective Picard to be taken seriously when someone is threatening me," she said. "I filed the report, and they acted like it was nothing. I was just another kid complaining about some prank."

Juliet, who never asked for anything, sounded young, almost whiny. He felt her new vulnerability touch a tender spot in him, a spot he wasn't sure he still had. It was his heart. She trusted him and Kyle knew trust wasn't easy for her. But still, he was reluctant. "How can I get their number?"

"Just try," she said. Those gray eyes opened wide, and he felt their spell working on him.

"I'll go down to the station and see what I can find," he said.

· · ·

Sure enough, Kyle ended up standing in front of Officer McCormick, trying to get the LeCrosses' phone numbers. Girls. And the world of things he would do for them. Well, for the right girl.

Officer McCormick stood six feet tall. His pants hung loosely in folds around his legs. He had a kindly face but was all business.

Kyle looked up at him, wishing he'd sit down. "Are you sure you don't have their number?" he asked. "We can't find Roy or Twyla, and we're worried."

"They probably just went home, like the others." McCormick lifted an eyebrow. "Who exactly is 'we' and where would you expect to find them?"

Kyle shrugged. "Alice LeCrosse seems fond of children. Twyla said Tony was her father, but later denied it. We think they might have gone home with the LeCrosses. That'd be great as long as they're safe. We just want to know. I tried Alice's number."

"And?" He lifted that eyebrow again.

"It's disconnected. But you know how that is, an unpaid bill and you get a disconnect message. Then, a week later, the bill is paid and someone answers. They must have another number. Tony probably has a number. Can you try it? I've got these things of Roy's." He held up a plastic bag.

The officer ignored the bag. "I don't have the number."

The officer's hand went to his ear each time he said he didn't have the number. He's lying, Kyle thought.

"You can look it up for yourself." The cop pushed the phone book over.

"That'll help," Kyle said, knowing it wouldn't. They'd already looked. Alice and Tony LeCrosse were unlisted. Untraceable. Probably had only cell phones. At least the officer had softened toward him and his cause. Kyle flipped through the phone book, and of course, found nothing. "They are not in here," he said finally.

"Uh, did you look in the yellow pages?" A clever smile creased the man's face.

"Under?"

"Toys."

Under toymakers, there was one phone number for Talented Toys in Annie's Court. Kyle wrote the number on his hand.

"Gee, I would have given you a piece of paper," Officer McCormick said, pulling out a business card and offering it.

The cop knew more than he revealed. No matter. Officer McCormick had already shown his allegiance and it was to Kyle and the missing kids. He'd just walked around the regulations, doing it without putting himself in trouble. "Here you go."

"Thanks." Kyle took the card, looked at it, and wrote the toy store number next to the officer's number.

"What is it?" McCormick asked, picking up the phone.

Kyle told him, and he punched in the numbers. "Disconnected," he said, "please check the number and try again."

"Let me try." Kyle got the same disconnect message. He wanted to slam the phone but didn't. He was afraid Alice and Tony LeCrosse would disappear, just like Twyla and Roy had. "Do you have an address for them?"

"No," McCormick said, shaking his head. "That information I cannot divulge." The man sank into the chair by his desk, crossed his arms over his chest, and straightened his long legs out in front of him.

Kyle pulled the teddy bear from the bag he'd been carrying. Its gray fur was matted down on its head and its blue eyes stared at the officer, pleading. "Please help me find the boy," Kyle said. "This little guy belongs to him. He said he slept with it every night to remember his mother. At least we should file a missing person's report. Don't you have an obligation to go look for him at the LeCrosses' place?"

McCormick pulled his legs in and leaned toward Kyle. "Let's file that report, and we'll go looking for him. But I'm not sending you out there. All I need is another missing kid. It'd be on my head, something I couldn't live with."

"I'm almost eighteen."

"No matter."

"You'll look for him?"

The officer nodded. "I'll see what I can find out."

Kyle put the teddy bear on McCormick's desk. It sat looking at the cop with those pleading eyes. The teddy bear did belong to Roy now, even though Kyle had bought it earlier that day at the secondhand store, for twenty-five cents.

CHAPTER SIXTEEN

Juliet woke in the middle of the night to thunder and wind, until rain crashed down on the shed roof. Lightning lit up the tiny, shed window, revealing Kyle sound asleep on a cot at the end of her bed, his sleeping bag pulled up over his shoulders. They had bought the cot for Kyle earlier that day at the Red Door Thrift Store and it barely fit along the side wall. Her bed tucked into the back wall.

When the lightning brightened the window, Juliet counted the seconds until the thunder arrived, judging the distance of the flash-three seconds, two seconds-feeling the electric closeness of the strike. She wanted to wake Kyle and climb into his sleeping bag along the far wall with him. Instead, she huddled in fear under her blanket, wondering where Wilma hid.

The next morning, she woke early and sat on her bed listening to the wind and waves and wondered if any docks had gotten torn up in the storm. She'd heard it had happened in past winters-chunks of concrete torn from foundations, flying toward the houses. She thought of these things to keep herself from constantly thinking of kissing Kyle. Having him in her shed made her want to sit next to him and hold him close.

She knew what she felt should come with a warning label. She couldn't trust love. Too often it disappeared. Death robbed her of her mother's love. Aunt Gloria might have loved her, but given the choice, she'd chosen Layne, her boyfriend with roaming hands, and a violent tendency toward her only niece. Her dad left before she knew him.

No, Juliet knew love could not be counted on. For her, it had been one disappearing act after another. Now, she feared Kyle would jump aboard that vanishing ship and sail away on a new adventure, without her. What, oh what, was she doing inviting this boy with the mussed-up hair and some secret past into her life?

Enough thinking. She did not want to think about kissing Kyle. Thinking of all the complications was no better. It all sent her into a fit of despair.

Juliet climbed out of bed and took the frying pan off the stove, opened the door fast and wide, letting the hinges squeak, and threw the rocks out in front of the shed. She shut the door, banged around on the pan shelf, and pulled the coffee pot out.

By then, Kyle had poked his head out from under his sleeping bag. She met him with a morning smile, and a not so sincere apology for waking him. "I'm making coffee," she said, as if it wasn't obvious. Kyle sleeping tenderly in her shed had been too much for her and she wanted to wake herself out of this new-found vulnerability, and that meant waking Kyle.

He threw the sleeping bag off, swung his legs around, and placed his stocking feet on the plywood floor. Wilma jumped up on his cot and he petted her. He rubbed a hand through his messy hair, messing it even more.

"What's the plan for today?" Juliet asked. Not thinking about kissing him.

"We can try the LeCrosse phone number again." Kyle's soft lips moved gently. His eyes brightened when he looked at her, drawing her close, weakening her will.

Kyle had been good about trying to help. Too good. Relying on him scared her. He didn't seem to notice or care that she felt scared, and that thought really frightened her. What if he didn't want to kiss her?

"Maybe the phone will get turned back on," he continued. "Few people live without a phone these days, especially where business and drugs are concerned."

"We don't know what part drugs play," she said, trying to shake her desire, but inching closer. The cups sat innocently on a shelf just beyond his cot. She leaned over to get them, kneeling on his bag, touching his shoulder with her arm.

"It's just a guess." Kyle reached over and caressed her arm. He rubbed a hand through her hair, catching his fingers in the cowlicks, and pulled her to sitting on the cot beside him. She let out the breath she'd been holding and leaned into his palm. His touch felt so good. How long had it been? She knew the answer. It had been a lifetime ago, before she ran, before her mother died. She felt the tears spring into her eyes.

She took his hand in hers and leaned her whole body into him, putting her head on his chest so he wouldn't see her tears, talking now about anything but her affection for him.

"Running drugs is a stereotype," she said. "They could be breaking the law in other ways."

"Not much illegal in running a toy business." He pulled her hand to his lips and kissed it.

Juliet felt her eyes and heart go soft at the same time. Fending off love had made her tired. She needed a rest and Kyle's presence soothed her broken heart; a heart shattered too young from too much loss. She lifted her head and kissed him, losing the fight to keep her distance, a fight she was glad to lose.

• • •

When they disentangled, Juliet poured coffee for them. She felt light-headed and slightly off balance. She sat crossed legged on the bed facing Kyle while they drank their coffee, smelling the fresh air from last night's storm.

"You and me," she said, wondering what it meant.

Kyle put a finger on her lips, balanced his coffee cup on his knee, and leaned over and kissed her. His touch was so tender she felt her bruised heart start to heal. She wondered if it could last. She wanted to cherish this moment. She wanted it to last into the next moment. And the next.

Then, she felt the fear swarm her. It filled up her ears, fogged her brain, made a mashed-up mess of her heart. Kyle had a birthday coming up. Did he have plans for the winter? Would he stay here in the shed with Juliet? Or would he return to Montana? And who was that woman with the blond hair from Missoula? If he didn't know her, why was she asking about him?

And then, like some dark demon the fear let in, LeCrosse's face reached across town and loomed in front of her, stealing the kiss between her and Kyle, shaming her for… for what? Kissing Kyle instead of him? He was twice her age, dark and dangerous. Kyle was light, beautiful, and kind.

Go away, LeCrosse. You are not welcome here, she said to his image, trying to push the fear away. "What is our plan for today?" She asked again, glad to be making plans with Kyle.

"They sell toys at the Farmer's Market," Kyle said, rubbing her shin with two fingers, tugging gently at the bottom of her leggings.

"We could follow them home. They live somewhere. They take credit cards, so they must have a verifiable physical address."

"Okay. They're registered somewhere. We just need to find out where."

Suddenly, Juliet felt the fear again. That woman from Montana plagued her. Kyle had denied knowing anything about her, but was he telling the truth? Could she trust him?

People lied.

All runaways lied.

"Hey," Kyle said. "You disappeared on me."

"Just like the runaways," she said without a hint of a smile. A sudden morose darkness invaded her. "Just like my father and my stepfather." Even though her mother had never married Harrison, Harrison had been the only father she'd ever known.

"Sounds like a sad western," Kyle said. He gazed at her. "What happened?"

"Harrison was my mother's cowboy, and she loved him. I loved him. He took me riding, taught me to rope a calf. Let me help load firewood. Bought me a kitten. He was a good guy. But he broke my mother's heart."

"That doesn't sound like a good guy."

"After thirteen years, he just disappeared." Juliet knew her tone was flat, holding old emotions at bay. "He was the detective who investigated my father's disappearance. His investigation never found my father, or anything that explained what had happened to him. He was around so much, a natural friendship developed between him and my mom." Her legs were numb, the old floating feeling suspending her. Nothing was real.

"Your father disappeared and then your stepfather disappeared? What are the odds of those two things happening and being unrelated?"

"My mother thought Harrison had finally found out what had happened to my dad." And that someone had shut him up to keep from being exposed.

Juliet hesitated before continuing. "My mother didn't believe Harrison would leave without saying something, without saying goodbye. It drove her crazy. She started drinking, drove into a telephone pole, and died."

"I'm sorry." Kyle put his arms around her, drawing her close again and gently pressing her head to his chest. "I am really sorry."

For the second time that morning, hot tears coursed down her cheeks.

. . .

Juliet didn't want the LeCrosses' caller ID to pick up Picard's cell phone number, so she and Kyle tried the number from one of the last standing pay phones in Annie's Court.

This time someone answered. "Shello?" a woman slurred.

"Yes, is Alice in?" Juliet asked.

The line went dead.

She shook her head and looked at Kyle.

"Try again," he said.

Again, a woman answered the phone. "No one's sheer." The slurring could have been alcohol or drugs or lack of sleep or a disorder of some sort. If this was Alice, it was not the put together, composed woman Juliet had met at the parties.

"Is Alice LeCrosse in?" Juliet asked.

The phone line went dead again.

She tried the number a third time. A loud voice boomed clearly through the phone, with no hesitation. "You've got the wrong number. Stop calling."

After that, when she dialed the number, the phone just rang and rang.

. . .

That Saturday, Juliet set up her table at the Farmer's Market. Kyle put out three camp chairs and sat down in one. He shuffled the cards. Juliet watched, wondering if he felt as aimless as he looked. She wondered what the cards would say if he pulled one right now, after having rifled through them with no apparent intention. Would they tell of his secret life in Montana? Would they tell the future after their kiss?

She turned away and watched Alice, who stood behind the tiny dolls, toy trucks, and wooden train sets at the toy booth. Miniature children played on miniature teeter-totters and swing sets. A little circus troupe included acrobats on a high wire and a glittery woman riding an elephant.

A child who looked about seven stood in front of the toys, fascinated. The twin girls stood behind the toy table in warm sweaters and pointed at different toys as they talked to him. Juliet thought they might be explaining the best toys to him in case his parents wanted to buy one.

She looked for the boy's parents but saw no one who seemed concerned about him.

Alice handed the boy a cinnamon roll and one of the circus toys. He took the roll and the toy and sat in a folding chair behind the toy table, between the twins, eating contentedly. When he finished eating, the twins each took him by an arm and walked him over to a moving truck. They let go of him and went back to the toy table with Alice. The boy cheerfully slipped into the back of the truck with Tony LeCrosse.

To make sure the boy was safe, Juliet waited for him to come back out.

He didn't.

The moving truck pulled out while Juliet was in the middle of a reading. "See this inverted queen of pentacles?" she asked the man in front of her. "It means someone may try to block you from accomplishing your purpose. You should be very careful who you trust."

The man nodded.

As the truck disappeared down the street, Juliet wondered if she hadn't just pulled the inverted queen for herself.

She looked helplessly at Kyle.

He shook his head, grabbed his coat, and was gone.

CHAPTER SEVENTEEN

Kyle chased the moving truck on his bicycle. Traffic was light, so he could see the vehicle for long stretches. He pedaled hard and fast; the wind stinging his face. No way did he want to lose sight of that truck. After two miles on the highway, it exited onto a side street. Kyle followed. It had stopped in front of an old warehouse with tall windows in solid brick walls. He cruised toward the old building, hit a patch of gravel, and almost wrecked, shifted his weight, righted the bicycle, and kept his eyes on the truck.

Its back door opened, and the boy got out, with Tony at his side. Now the youngster's face looked dazed and frightened as Tony fiddled with the warehouse door.

"Hey," Kyle yelled, against his better judgment.

"Over here," the boy yelled.

LeCrosse started at the sound. His hair and sunglasses reflected the sudden sunlight as he turned toward Kyle. He shoved the boy back inside of the moving truck and climbed into the driver's seat. The truck took off again, spinning up dirt as it turned and sped past Kyle. Kyle pedaled as hard as he could, as fast as he had ever pedaled, until the truck faded from sight, down the long stretch of highway.

He turned back, cycled to the warehouse, and knocked on the door.

No one answered.

Kyle looked around for a window or door lock he could pick. Then, he tried the door handle. It opened. Kyle figured it must be a trick. Maybe someone waited inside to jump him. Maybe an alarm had already gone off. He hid his bicycle in some bushes, his mind racing. With rapid speed, his thoughts turned to the police. Let them come. He'll go with them and maybe have a warm cell for the night and learn something about the LeCrosses and their toy business. He'd solve this thing from the inside and hope like crazy he'd be able to get out again.

Sliding through the doorway, he halted and listened. The giant room seemed to hum quietly, like something large and breathing lived beneath its floor. Other than the soft humming, no sound came. Kyle figured the place was uninhabited, but a heater rumbled on a distant wall. In the dim light, he saw shelves and shelves of wooden toys. At least five thousand square feet of toys filled the warehouse. This building was clearly a storage unit, and maybe a place for shipments. Rows of tables had flat cardboard boxes stacked up behind them. He tripped over a wooden doll and picked it up.

It fit neatly in his palm. The doll wore a red swimsuit and a finely constructed straw hat with a shiny red ribbon. Amazed at the intricate workmanship, Kyle lifted the hat to get a closer look. A cascade of red hair fell out. Dark air filled his chest. A chill crawled across his skin. He'd seen that hair before. The color matched Twyla's exactly. According to Juliet, Twyla had gotten her hair cut and taken away at the Farmer's Market. Kyle didn't know for sure, but he'd bet money this red cascade had come from Twyla's head.

He turned the doll over and pushed the thick hair aside. On the doll's back, in barely perceptible scratches, someone had carved the words "help me." Black gloom descended on him, clouded his brain, and threatened to pull him into a never-ending abyss. Twyla was in trouble, and he didn't know how to help her.

Just then, a car pulled up outside. He slipped the doll into his pocket, looked around, and crawled under a worktable. He pushed his body up against the wall as far as he could. A ray of light spread across the floor. Kyle heard Alice LeCrosse's voice.

From under the table he could see tall black boots that came within inches of the hem of her black lace miniskirt. She disappeared behind a shelf of toys and came out at the other end. When she disappeared again, Kyle could hear her boots clicking up and down the aisles.

She came out of the final row and sat on the front counter, where Kyle could now see her. "Yes, it's unlocked. I'm looking," she said into the phone she held. "Everything seems in order. I doubt he even tried the door."

Kyle's leg cramped. Pain seared up his hamstring. His mind ran to thoughts of drugs, kidnapping, and the possible torture he'd face if they found him there. Maybe he exaggerated. He didn't know. He did know he did not want to be on the wrong side of Alice LeCrosse. He waited for her to talk before he moved his leg, to soothe the cramp.

"Calm down. You don't know he followed you. We can't get sloppy now. Everything's okay here. You're being a little paranoid." Alice stopped talking for a moment and listened. "I know, I know."

Alice crossed her legs. She held the phone in one hand and held her other hand close to her face, looking down at the nails. With a quick shake of her head, her hair bounced at her ears. Her chest raised and fell as she heaved a sigh. "That little party trick was a lapse in judgment on my part. Scaring her just drew the police in our direction, but you heard them. So apologetic. I had to leave the room to keep from laughing."

The room went quiet, and she nodded. "No one knows. The kid on the bicycle, he's been to a couple of our parties." She tilted her chin toward the ceiling, now sending her auburn hair back away from her face. "Even if he opened the door, all he saw was a warehouse full of toys. We have a toy business!"

She ran a hand through her hair. "Listen." She sat up straight, jumped off the counter. "We know how to deal with snoops. And we just shut that new kid up. He'll know who's boss soon enough. Hold his food. Once he realizes who will feed him, he'll comply."

For a minute, she went quiet, leaning against the counter. Waiting for her message to be heard, Kyle thought. His leg cramped again. He needed to get out of there. But he couldn't go anywhere with Alice LeCrosse standing straight and strong at the counter of the toy warehouse, threatening to withhold food from a child.

"Yes," she said. "The feisty ones are all defiant in the beginning. Remember Twyla?" She stretched her back into a catlike arch as she listened. "Well, if you must. Make sure the shot isn't too strong for his size. If you kill his appetite, you kill his motivation to work. The parents don't like them drugged out. They like the lively, vivacious ones."

She paused, as if listening, and said, "And yes, compliant. You know the drill."

The sun moved through a window as she turned away from it. "Yes. I'll keep an eye out for the kid on the bicycle. You're right, but he's too old, too strong." She laughed, her green eyes glistening with a strange brightness. "Right, they all get a little weaker with a shot or two. Still. He's a bad bet on our part."

Alice clicked off and put the phone in her pocket. She opened the register, took cash out, wrote a note, and left it in place of the cash. She took one last look around, heaved another sigh, and left the way she'd come in.

Kyle heard the door click closed.

An electric fear vibrated through his whole body. Adrenaline cleared his head. He wanted to run. He wanted to ride his bike as far away from the warehouse as he could go. Foreboding about his safety set in. He cocked his head and listened. Once he heard the car pull away and was certain Alice was gone, he scooted out and went to the door. She had locked it.

From the outside.

He needed a key to open it. Kyle searched for the back door and found it. He turned the dead bolt, only to discover that it, too, was locked from the outside. The windows hovered ten feet above the floor like taunting watchmen, out of reach.

Trapped in the warehouse, Kyle's heart drummed a fast beat, his chest ready to explode. He felt his face turn clammy. Down one aisle, he found a sliding ladder with rollers on the bottom. He feared they might also lock the windows from the outside. Kyle knew he had to work fast. He could feel the sharp talons of panic begin to pierce his skin.

He had to get out of there before his chest seized up and his lungs collapsed. He'd felt it before, when his parents' trailer caught fire in Montana and smoke filled his lungs. The heat seared his skin, and he ran. Now, regret hit him hard. He ran without Katy, his sister. And Katy had died in that fire.

He knew he had to get out of that warehouse to help any of the others, to find the courage he had lacked when he ran out of that trailer without taking Katy with him.

If it meant breaking a window, leaving evidence of his invasion, so be it. They'd know someone had been in there listening to Alice's end of the conversation. Something told Kyle they didn't take too kindly to breakouts.

Touching the doll in his pocket to make sure it was secure, Kyle drew a deep breath, grabbed a hammer off a bench, slid the ladder into place, and set his sights on finding an exit. As he suspected, they had locked the window from the outside. He braced himself and swung the hammer hard. He broke the glass with the first try, setting off a loud alarm. The sound hurt his ears. He swung again. Glass crashed to the ground as he knocked a man-sized hole in the window, big enough for him to get through.

It was a good fifteen feet to the ground. Jumping was going to hurt, but not as much as getting caught would. He leaped, landed on his feet, and rolled, hurting his ankle. Kyle limped to his bike and was out of there.

154

CHAPTER EIGHTEEN

A shudder went through Juliet when she saw the doll with the words "help me" scratched across her back. She insisted they bring it to Picard. Kyle didn't argue.

"It looks like human hair," Detective Picard said when he saw the doll. He sat on the street curb near the deserted Farmer's Market mall. "You say it's the same color hair belonging to the girl you've been trying to find?"

Juliet nodded. "Twyla."

"I looked for her mother," Kyle said, "but my search was a lost cause. If we can find her mother, we can test her DNA."

Picard rubbed his beard. "I see you've been watching crime shows."

"Before I ran, I had a home." Kyle blushed.

Juliet liked seeing him blush. She'd never seen this shy side of him before.

"Well?" she asked. "Can you find her mother and see about testing Twyla's hair?"

"Not on this. Even if I could, it would mean nothing. She could have sold her hair to LeCrosse. Runaways are clever about getting money for food."

"What about the 'help me' scratched into the doll's back? That's got to mean something."

Picard shook his head. "It's nothing. A teacher might make a referral to a school counselor. But not law enforcement. Nothing illegal here."

"Something scared Twyla," Kyle said. "She just disappeared."

"Something scared someone," Picard said. "We don't know if it was Twyla."

Juliet sucked her lower lip in. "Whether or not Twyla wrote those words," she said. "She is scared and running. We haven't seen her for over a week. Last we saw her; she was sick and had bruises on her arms."

"Or she could be hurt somewhere waiting for help." Kyle brushed his hair away from his face, making Juliet's heart jump a little.

"It's really a job for social services," Picard said. "I'll go by the warehouse, and look around the outside, knock on the door, and ask some questions if anyone is there."

"If that's the best you can do," Kyle said.

Juliet watched Picard as he gave Kyle a hard look. "You say you found the doll outside the building? And you were never inside?"

Kyle nodded, his face solemn and sincere.

• • •

Juliet walked around to the back of the warehouse with Kyle and Picard. Someone had already replaced the window Kyle had damaged on his escape and cleaned up the broken glass. It was open, as if to let in a cool breeze.

"Nothing here," Picard said.

"Nothing," Juliet said.

"Anyone could have left that doll out there," Picard said. "I'll see if anyone is working in the warehouse. Maybe they have answers."

Juliet waited with Kyle while Picard first knocked on the door, and then let himself in. He came out, the corners of his mouth turned down. He looked at Juliet and Kyle and shook his head. "Nothing."

"What did you find out?" she asked.

"Not much. The janitor was inside, and he didn't know much. He'd just started working there, said they were cleaning it up to sell the building."

"Did he let you look around? Did you look at the other toys? Maybe there's another doll with red hair." Juliet felt the disappoint rise in her throat.

"No. I mean nothing. The warehouse is empty," Picard said.

Juliet looked at Kyle, who shook his head.

"It wasn't empty yesterday," he told the detective.

Picard raised his eyebrows. "How would you know that?"

"I saw through the open door before LeCrosse left."

Juliet wondered at Kyle's ability to lie so quickly. He hadn't missed a beat. It was a runaway trait, for sure. She just didn't know how it translated to her and an honest relationship between them, if they had an honest relationship, if they had a relationship. The memory of the mystery woman from Missoula nagged at her. Kyle had said he knew nothing about her.

Truth or lie? Juliet didn't know.

"Can't we find Twyla's mother," Kyle was asking, "and get a sample of the girl's hair? And send the doll in to be tested, see if it's a match?"

"We've been over this. Even if it is, that's not a crime," Picard said. "It tells us nothing about anything."

The ocean wind blew inland and past Juliet, taking her glimmer of hope with it.

• • •

The next day, Juliet rode her bicycle out to the tent town to meet Kyle. She passed a line of cars heading toward Annie's Court, the last few tourists coming out for the weekend. Fall had arrived in earnest and a cool breeze froze her ears. Shivering, she reached up and pulled her hat to cover her earlobes. She turned at the campground, rode her bike through the campsites and down the beach, and stopped at the edge of the tents.

Kyle came to meet her. He wore an army coat—maybe his grandfather's—making him look like a 1960s rebel. The camp was quiet and mostly empty. Only the seagulls swooped in and out on the wind.

"Come on," he said, opening the door of an old green wall tent. The wall tent looked like it could have come from the same era as his coat. Inside, a sleeping pad lay along one wall. A purple backpack with clothes spilling out of it lay against the other wall. Kyle pulled a cell phone out of the pack.

"How'd you get a cell phone?" Juliet asked. Eager to get out of there, she stood by the door flap. The green canvas smelled old and musty.

"It belongs to the camp. Stephan wouldn't be happy if he knew I was using it."

"Whose name is the bill under?"

"The less you know, the better. That way you're not implicated."

"Implicated," she said out loud, annoyed with him for acting like he was above her. "You have Twyla's mother's phone number?"

Kyle nodded. "I also have the number for the Phoenix Center. I'll call there first. Could be she's back in the Seattle area again, safe from anything here." He dialed the phone.

Juliet felt edgy. She wanted out of there before Stephan found them. She'd seen the anger in his eyes when they were there before. He made her nervous.

Someone answered and Kyle identified himself, then asked for Jamison. "Did Twyla ever show up there?" he asked. After a brief pause, he said, "I did. I found her stepfather, but not her mother." He listened again and then said, "Okay. I will. Thanks anyway."

"Well?"

"No sign of her. He said try her mother's number." Kyle dialed and put it on speakerphone. The phone rang until a recorded message came on, saying the number was no longer in service. Kyle dialed another number, putting the phone on speaker again.

"King County Social Services." The woman's voice lilted up at the end as if she was asking a question.

"This is Detective Benson Picard." Kyle turned away from Juliet as he reported Twyla as a missing person. He gave the woman Twyla's last known address and asked that she do a welfare check on her, in case she'd gone home by now. "This is my private cell phone. Please leave a confidential message if the girl is home safe. Thank you."

He put the phone in his back pocket and left the tent.

She shook her head and followed. A thief and a liar. Kyle's runaway skills were considerable. "Stephan will know, and you'll be in so much trouble," she said.

He shook his head and shrugged.

Juliet couldn't believe his nonchalance as she followed him down the beach. Far from the camp, a group of teens surrounded a large campfire. She felt great relief, like a soft light settling on her, to see that Stephan wasn't among them. One of the younger boys wore a white scarf with peach-colored circles dotting it. It was the same scarf Twyla had worn at the Farmer's Market the day she'd had her hair cut.

"Where did you get that scarf?" Juliet asked.

"I found it. It's mine." He put his hands to his throat, protecting his possession.

"Where did you find it?" Juliet stood tall, hoping to seem like a giant authority figure, someone the boy would want to answer honestly.

Kyle moved in closer to her, which helped.

"Is it yours?" The boy asked and removed the scarf. A cloud passed overhead, the shadow of it falling on the boy's face.

"No. And you're not in trouble." She'd scared him. He had, no doubt, seen that authoritarian look before. Clearly, it hadn't ended well for him. "I just want to know where you found it. Someone might be in trouble. That's her scarf."

A look of recognition came over him as he held it out to Juliet. "I found it out at the caves," he said. "It was just lying on the rocks, damp and muddy. I washed it up."

"You keep it," she said, and turned to Kyle. "Let's go."

When they got to the caves, the tide was in and they were locked out by high water.

CHAPTER NINETEEN

After work, Kyle rode his bicycle down the walking path and stumbled upon a moving truck. The truck sat next to a white van in an RV park. Sunshine slanted through the autumn clouds, illuminating George's pale face as he paced near a picnic table. He drank from a ceramic cup and wind blew the thin strands of his hair around. The RV Park was about an eighth of a mile down the path from LeCrosse's party condo. George being there in the RV Park struck Kyle as odd. He stopped, sat on his bike, and considered George, the van, and the truck.

When George left in the van, Kyle followed from a discreet distance, watching as he pulled in front of LeCrosse's condo. He saw no movement through the large picture windows. George never appeared to be on the main floor. No one did.

Kyle got closer and noticed the basement windows had been boarded up. He heard a child's cry come from the basement floor.

"Hush up. I won't tell you again." George's voice was loud. "You'll work harder when we get back, won't you?"

The child mumbled something between sobs. Seagulls squealed a warning to the bay, swooshing across the sky, nearly drowning out the child's pleas.

"I thought so." George's voice turned calm.

The cry settled into a low whimper.

. . .

Kyle strained his legs, driving the pedals hard as he hurried to Juliet's shed. He still thought of it as hers, not theirs. He found her sitting on her bed, wrapped in an army blanket, the door propped open, an icy wind blowing into the shed.

"Why don't you shut the door?" Kyle asked.

"I burned some soup," she said. "Did you find anything?"

"I don't know." He shook his head. "George was at the RV Park. I followed him over to LeCrosse's condo. Did you know they boarded the windows on the basement?"

"No crime there."

"How about a kid crying inside, and George threatening him?"

Juliet's eyes got wide. She dropped the blanket and pulled on her coat. "Now that's worth a closer look. Let's go talk to Picard."

Together they went to Picard's office. Books that looked like they'd never been opened sat on a dusty shelf. A gray throw rug ran in front of a large wooden desk. Juliet pulled a chair up on top of the rug and folded her hands on the desk. She nodded her head toward Kyle. He pulled up another chair and told the detective what he'd heard.

Picard rubbed his chin. "Kids cry all the time. They throw fits because they're asked to do chores, or they don't get what they want. We can't enter a home on those grounds."

"But Kyle heard George threaten him," Juliet said. "That's a welfare concern, if nothing else."

"What exactly did he say?"

"He said the kid would work harder when they got back." Kyle's voice fell. He pulled his fists into the sleeves of his sweatshirt, feeling suddenly feeble.

"Sorry," Picard said, rubbing a hand across his baldhead.

. . .

In the dark of that fall night, the moon hid behind the clouds. A sea mist crept ashore and gave Kyle and Juliet a cold blanket of cover. Kyle watched for LeCrosse, or anyone associated with him, while Juliet pried a painted board off one of the windows. Wind blew cedar branches where tiny animals once crawled. The soft whooshing sounded like coastal phantoms. Things lived in the rocks and trees at the edge of the water. Although innocent in the daytime, they turned treacherous at night.

That night, the sounds mimicked the fear Kyle felt. He knew that he, Juliet, and the children would all be in danger if LeCrosse caught them snooping around his condo.

Kyle's trepidation expanded with the sound of that wind. He lost his footing along with his courage and tripped over the grass. "I changed my mind," he said, "let's get out of here. If we can hear them, they can hear us."

"I don't think anyone is in there now. If a child is in danger, we can't just stand by and do nothing." Her voice sounded strained. Panicked. From everything he knew about Juliet, she didn't scare easily.

The clouds moved. The wind blew the mist back to the sea. A sliver of moon shone on her face. Her soft gray eyes filled with something that looked like determination. A fierce longing rushed up inside of Kyle and out toward Juliet. He wanted to put all this snooping aside and kiss her, a magical kiss, a kiss that would ensure her safety. Did she feel it too? Even a little bit? If they weren't tearing the boards off LeCrosse's condo, looking for clues to a possible missing child, would she move toward him?

Juliet put a hand on his face, stepped close, and put her lips to his ear. She took a deep breath, as if consoling herself, and then him. "We'll be safe. The first sign of someone coming, we're gone."

He pulled her close. Her cowlicks tickled his nose. A primal smell drifted off her and pulled at the wild desire he felt in her presence. She buried her head in his neck, cupped the back of his head with her palm, weaving her fingers in his hair. Kyle felt secure and safe with Juliet. An owl hooted in a nearby tree, breaking the spell. She let go of him and he let her go.

The place was eerily still. "I'll go in," he said, feeling the protectiveness he felt toward her surge. "You stand watch. You'll be no good to Picard if you're in jail. And at least I'll get three meals a day."

"Maybe I want three a day." She tilted a crooked smile toward him. The cowlicks had grown into short curls, and they bounced like tiny springs close to her head, nodding their agreement.

"You don't," Kyle said. "I'll go."

"If you get caught, you'll lose your job," she said. "I'm smaller and I can get through these little windows."

Against everything he knew to be right, he relented, and Juliet went in.

Kyle waited, pushing his foot against the lawn, and staining his tennis shoes. A real Nervous Nelly. Scared Juliet would wind up trapped inside the condo. The sound of car tires crunching the gravel traveled west. After that, the dense silence nearly smothered him. Fear lodged in his chest and crawled up his throat. This panic was the same feeling he'd had the night of the trailer fire, the night his sister died.

"You tried," his mother had said in a half-hearted, heartbroken way. But he hadn't tried, and they both knew it. He was sure she blamed him for his sister's death. Why wouldn't she? He blamed himself. He could have pulled her from the rubbish, and the medics would have saved her. If only he hadn't lit the candle that night. If only he had done as his father said and gone to sleep.

Juliet came out, carrying the teddy bear Kyle had given to Officer McCormick for Roy.

"At least he delivered it," Kyle said.

She nodded. "Yeah, to someone."

"He knows more than he's told us." He thought about the boy crying. Had he made more of it than was there? Maybe he was just in trouble for not doing his chores. Kyle felt struck by the idea that maybe it didn't concern them, that they'd made up the whole danger thing. That Officer McCormick knew lots more than he told Kyle. But if it was true, that was McCormick's choice. He didn't need to tell Kyle police business.

He heard the lapping of the waves hitting the shoreline as he followed Juliet back over to the walking path. Out on the bay, he saw the light from a small boat making its way back to Annie's Court. What kept it so long into the evening, he wondered.

"Do you think McCormick is in on it?" Juliet asked.

"Not really," Kyle said. "Whatever it is, he seemed genuinely concerned."

"OK," she said. "We must be careful about assuming things. It can distract us from the truth."

"Did you get that bit of wisdom from a tarot book?" Kyle laughed.

"You, my friend, are beginning to understand me." Juliet smiled and his heart went wild with hope from that simple acknowledgement.

A streetlight designed for the walking path illuminated Juliet's gray eyes, her black curls, and the sweater and leggings encasing her small, athletic body. Kyle stalled a minute and took it in. She seemed like a mystical woodland creature, something washed in from another time. He felt certain her simple beauty stopped his heart. He hit his chest with his fist to start it again.

Under the light, Juliet broke open the stuffed bear Kyle had bought at the secondhand store and given to Officer McCormick. A plastic bag full of a white powder appeared.

Kyle raised his eyebrows. Now this substance was something. "They're using the toys to ship drugs? That can't be right. Most of their toys are made of wood."

"What is it?"

Kyle shrugged.

"I guess that's a good question for Detective Benson Picard," she said.

"But how will we tell him we found it? Breaking and entering is a crime."

"I'll think of something."

Back at the shed, she pulled her grandmother's small sewing kit from a box under the bed. "I took it when I left home," she said. "I wanted something to remind me of her. She was a talented seamstress, made my school dresses and coats."

"You never told me why you left your aunt's house." Kyle was fishing carefully for information, not wanting to scare her into silence.

"That's a story for another time," Juliet said. "But it's probably similar to why you left home." She took the lid off the sewing kit, revealing about twenty spools of thread in an assortment of colors.

"No, my situation was different," Kyle said. He drew in a breath, trying to clear the smoke stuck in his brain from the fire.

"Someone blamed you for something you didn't do. You were confused and full of regret and shame. You ran on the heels of a lot of grief."

Kyle looked at her, stunned. Was she that good a detective? "Good guess. But not quite. You are right, though," he said, shifting the topic away from his life, "a lot of runaways leave home for the same reasons. Someone hurt them, blamed them, and discarded them. When we find Twyla and Roy, we'll learn their stories. Once they are safe, you can tell me your story, and I'll tell you mine."

Juliet laughed. "It's a deal." She tucked the bag of white powder back into the secondhand bear's stomach cavity. With matching thread, she stitched up the little bear.

"Leave it loose enough so the bag will show through the thread but not fall out." Kyle said, guiding her to do what she was apparently already doing.

"So, Picard sees it when he sees the bear and has a reason to question LeCrosse."

"But I still don't get how we are going to get them all in the same place at the same time."

"I'm still thinking up that part," Juliet said. "We'll figure it out. Maybe we'll just invite Detective Picard to walk past the condo with us, looking at the boarded-up basement windows."

"That's sweet, inviting the detective to go for a walk with us. But it doesn't get us anywhere near the bear and LeCrosse."

Juliet squished up her nose at him. A soft breath escaped her lips. "I'm still thinking."

Wilma came in through a hole in the wall. She sniffed around her food bowl, got a drink of water, and jumped up into Kyle's lap. He petted her, pushing the black fur into the orange fur and back into the black fur. When he stopped, she pushed her head into his palm, and he started again.

Once the kitten slept on the cot and the bag of white powder filled the bear's belly, Kyle and Juliet walked back down the paved path to LeCrosse's condo. The fall air felt cool and crisp on Kyle's skin as he walked beside Juliet. She cradled the little bear in the crook of her arm.

In the dim light of the walking path, he saw a tender look on her face and thought, this kindness filled her eyes when she held Wilma the day the deer hide had been burned in her shed. That day she had been so careful and full of love for the tiny creature. He didn't think she'd ever let go. And he'd known he'd stand there with her for as long as she wanted to hold the little calico.

At the condominium, Kyle waited outside as Juliet climbed back through the basement window and put the stuffed bear back where she'd found it. Partway out of the window, her sweater caught on a nail bent around the wood to keep the window boarded up. She stopped, half in half out of the building, to free it.

"Let me," Kyle said. He unhooked it and she slid the rest of the way out.

. . .

The next day, with plenty of light and all the nearby condominiums seemingly empty, including LeCrosse's condo, Kyle helped Juliet search the grounds for signs of drugs. The condos were summertime affairs and many of them seemed to be vacated for the winter.

They walked up and down the long lawn, over into the bushes, across the walking path and back again. Seagulls circled and squealed out their warnings. The sky lit up brilliantly, then went dark with clouds. Gray patches moved over the cedar branches and big leaf maple trees. Waves lapped continuously at the shore.

Back in a small grove of maples, a sickly, bitter smell hit Kyle's nose. He finally found something. A mess of yellowed coffee filters and punctured antifreeze containers packed a tiny homemade landfill. Kyle traced the smell back to the condo, where burn spots littered the lawn. Someone had dumped chemicals into the grass. All of it pointed to cooking meth.

Although he'd never seen one, he'd heard the older teens in the tent town talk about their parents' meth labs. One girl said she found boxes of her parents' "shake and bake" lab under her bed when she was eleven. Once social services moved her to a new home, other troubles began, but her headaches stopped. Another teen talked about the sores on her father's face. One teen said how grateful he was when his father went into recovery, and how disappointed when the center put his father out when the insurance stopped paying.

They all agreed on the cat urine smell. More than that, they all agreed that meth meant a hard life, and as badly as their parents wanted to be free of the drug, the drug had a strangle hold on them.

Kyle touched nothing.

"Picard gave me a cell phone," Juliet told him. "Time to call him."

"You've had a cell phone all this time?"

"I don't like to use it."

He shook his head, wondering about Juliet's other untold secrets. "What will you tell him? This stuff could belong to anyone. Or are you still thinking?"

"Smarty pants."

"Well?"

"I've heard LeCrosse talking at the parties. They come over here for lunch some days. When they do, they usually bring the twins and a younger child with them." Juliet furrowed her brow. "You said at least Officer McCormick delivered the stuffed bear to Roy."

"What are you getting at?"

"Maybe McCormick didn't give it to Roy. Maybe he just gave it to LeCrosse, and LeCrosse did what he wanted with it. Since it was here after George threatened the young boy, LeCrosse might have given the stuffed bear to that child."

"And?"

"He could have been the boy you chased in the moving van with Tony. Maybe they brought him and his teddy bear to lunch at the condo."

"But why?"

"You know how a realtor shows houses?"

Kyle cocked his head. "I am not following you."

"I overheard George at their toy booth at the Farmer's Market."

"You mean you eavesdropped on their conversation," Kyle said, not knowing if he should admire Juliet for her deviousness or run far away from it.

"He talked about their guests. They come from out of town and go to lunch at the condo with them. It sounded like they were going to introduce the boy to the adults."

A sick feeling hit Kyle in the stomach and nearly dropped him to his knees. Introducing a young boy to adults at a condo lunch can't be good. He picked a piece of lint off his sweatshirt and let the wind toss it across the lawn.

The words popped into his head and out his mouth. "For what reason?"

"I don't know. It sounded like couples come to lunch at the condo." Juliet pursed her lips. "George said something about a silent auction, maybe they have the children present the toys, and sell them to high end buyers?"

"Where do people bid on this silent auction?"

"Once they see the toys, they go online and bid?"

"Still nothing illegal that we know of."

"Do you really think the boy who disappeared into the moving van is legitimately in the care of the LeCrosses?"

"I don't know, Juliet. We seem to be chasing our tales."

• • •

Kyle stood next to Juliet and listened as she told Detective Picard about the signs of cooking meth in the yard. She told him about her theory on the boy from the moving van. And she told him she thought LeCrosse was using young children to present the toys for the silent auctions, hoping to get a high price for each toy. Picard agreed to look at the condo and what they had found.

Kyle listened as Juliet suggested what he thought was strategic timing. Lunch time. He also felt his hopes dwindle as there was no guarantee either the young boy or the stuffed bear with the bag of drugs sewn inside would make an appearance. In fact, the bag of drugs might not even be drugs. In the end, it all seemed like a fool's errand. And the closer they got to LeCrosse's condo, the sicker and more hopeless Kyle felt.

They sat on a bench along the walking path. A dog and his person strolled by. The sea crashed against the rocks behind them. A ferry sounded its horn.

Before long, LeCrosse came through the door with a young boy who was carrying the stuffed bear. The boy was the same child Kyle had chased to the warehouse where he'd broken a window to get free.

A very different type of broken glass played a part that day. Kyle had hit a taillight on LeCrosse's car, knocking the bulb right out of the socket. LeCrosse left the complex and pulled onto a city street. Kyle heard sirens blare short and sweet, the sound of pulling LeCrosse over. Picard had suggested the patrol car hang out in the vicinity. Just in case something came up and they needed them.

Nothing was on the up and up, Kyle thought. He felt nervous about it all. "We should check the bear," he said to Picard, feigning an innocence he didn't feel. "I've heard that's one way people transport drugs."

"We have no reason," Picard said, his voice calm, in control. He gave Kyle a sideways look and then looked at Juliet.

Juliet shrugged.

He put his mouth to the radio. "Check the kid's bear," he told the officer.

Sounds from the officer's radio came through loud and clear. LeCrosse went from a calm voice to yelling and finally threatened to sue the city.

The officer found nothing but cotton stuffing in the teddy bear.

The boy, no older than seven, jumped out of the vehicle and ran for the woods, right toward the grove of maple trees where the makeshift landfill sat ready to engulf him. Kyle went after him. He didn't want the boy falling into that pit. Anything in the manmade hole of discarded drug paraphernalia could hurt him.

He wasn't there. The forested area beyond the landfill had swallowed him up.

Juliet joined Kyle and he stayed close to her as they searched for the boy. Seagulls circled in the gray sky above them. Small creatures slithered away from them. Juliet held her hair out of her eyes with a knit cap. She wore a light blue sweater and black leggings. On another day, Kyle might have imagined taking her hand and walking her home to the shed. Forget this police stuff. Forget Picard and LeCrosse. He wanted to go home with Juliet, where they belonged.

Together.

But with a young boy running for shelter in the direction of danger, he couldn't go home with Juliet. Home had to wait. They had a child to find. The boy had disappeared without a coat. The cool fall air already bit Kyle's skin. In a few hours it would be dark and much colder.

"Here," Kyle said to Juliet. "Take my coat."

She shook her head and shivered. Her gray eyes softened. On an apparent second thought, she took it. "If we find the boy, I'll give it to him."

"When we find the boy," Kyle said.

They scanned the woods, circling through cedars and western hemlock, traversing the neighborhoods along the walking path and down by the RV park. They even went as far as the Farmer's Market mall, the dog park, and the Red Door Thrift store. They found no trace of him. No, no one had seen him wander through the grocery store or past a gas station, or anywhere near the fast-food restaurants. The tent town was too far south. Kyle didn't think he would go that far.

They didn't go out to the cave where the teen had found Twyla's pink polka dot scarf. The tide would be too high this time of evening. Plus, it was a long way for a maybe seven-year-old to travel by himself.

They were about to skip the old boat when Juliet said, "But on the other hand, all runaways seem to gravitate toward the ancient ship."

Kyle sucked in his lips, thought about it, and nodded. "Let's go."

The setting sun and mist off the sea made the old ship feel cold and clammy. Kyle slipped on the deck where the constant moisture rotted the wood. They had no light, no food, and, having given his coat to Juliet, Kyle had no coat.

"He's not here," she said.

"Doesn't look like it."

"Let's go back toward the condo and search along the walking path."

"We already looked there," Kyle said.

"He might have been hiding."

They found him on a rocky stretch of beach south of LeCrosse's condo. He hid between two boulders, just out of reach of the crashing waves. A short-sleeved t-shirt revealed two bruised arms. He was shaking, nearly mute, only his teeth chattering.

"So many bruises," Juliet said. "How did you get them?"

Wide-eyed, the boy looked at her and looked away.

She took off Kyle's coat and wrapped it around the boy. He seemed to fall into it and Juliet caught him in her arms. Kyle's heart broke for her tenderness toward the boy, and the boy's troubles.

"Come on," he said. "Let's get you home."

The boy shivered and shook his head, fear lighting his eyes.

"We can't take him back to LeCrosse," Juliet murmured.

Kyle agreed. The boy would be in more danger than ever if he went home with LeCrosse. "Call Picard. We can't take him anywhere near LeCrosse. It's too dangerous."

Kyle regretted his words as soon as he saw the terror in the boy's eyes, a wide-open startled look. As young as he was, he knew all about danger.

.   .   .

When Picard arrived, he said he'd called social services and they would help. They would also pay LeCrosse a visit. The boy went with Detective Benson Picard without argument. Kyle hoped he went willingly because he knew he'd be safe with Picard. The day had been long and had already turned into night. He was freezing and just wanted to go back to the shed and be warm.

Back at the shed, Juliet reached over and turned on a lamp. She lit the stove and put the frying pan and rocks on to heat the shed. She sat on the edge of her bed, pulled out a deck of tarot cards, and flipped them over, one by one. Wilma pawed each one as it landed, messing up the perfect rows.

Kyle wondered what it all meant.

Juliet looked up and smiled at him. Those soft, silken eyes warmed his whole chest. Much better than the fire. Under her gaze, he felt strong and tall, proud to be her partner in searching for the young boy, in searching for Twyla and Roy. He wondered if she thought of him as a partner in this way, and maybe more. He sat down next to her. She leaned into him, pressing her shoulder into his.

"See this card?" She asked. "The five of wands? It looks like all the young men are fighting, but the moves are all in sync with each other. It is more like a dance than a brawl. It's showing me all forces of nature are working together for good. That was my mother's motto: every person, every event, leads us to our best selves and the best lives we can live."

"Even if it's painful?"

"Especially then. If only we learn from it and open our hearts." She looked up at him with those deep, sultry gray eyes. "Just as we needed him, Picard arrived. Social Services took the boy into care."

Kyle shook his head. "The boy might have information when he decides to talk." He drew in a sharp breath. "Maybe the children work on the toys. They give the meth to the children to keep them working," he said, as if he knew. And he thought maybe he was on to something important. "They're addicted. No wonder they go back to LeCrosse. Once he gets them hooked, he has what they want."

"And he has complete control over them."

"Any word on Twyla or Roy?"

"No. But if we find them, we find some real answers." Juliet flipped over another card. A woman sitting blindfolded, with her back to the ocean, holding two swords in an x in front of her. "The two of swords," Juliet said. "What is it we're not seeing?"

Kyle shrugged his shoulders. Wilma batted the card to the floor.

"There's something else too," Juliet was saying. "Someone's been snooping around the shed. I saw footprints in the mud that aren't yours or mine. Nothing is missing, not that I have anything to steal." She tilted her head and smiled at him.

Juliet was so beautiful and in so much danger. The idea of someone skulking around her shed hit Kyle hard. Anger surged through him. "Do you still have that little tape recorder?" he asked.

Juliet nodded, looking bewildered.

"And a tape for it?"

"What are you thinking?"

"Let's set it up on voice activation." Kyle's brain was clear and focused now. "If the snoop says anything, we might recognize the voice. In that case, we can turn the tables on whoever it is and catch the person red-handed."

Juliet took his hand in hers. "We're in this mess together, aren't we?"

A glorious warmth filled Kyle's chest. "Yes," he said. "Yes we are."

CHAPTER TWENTY

The next morning, Juliet waited with Kyle for the tide to go out. The wait brought on Juliet's habit of biting her lip until she felt the pain, a habit her mother told her would ruin her smile and turn it upside down. It felt upside down now, even with Kyle's warm hand on her arm. They'd gotten up early, made their way just north of the tent town, sat on a cluster of rocks, and watched the water.

It was a gray, bitterly cold day. She pushed her hands into the pockets of the black down vest she wore over her cable-knit sweater and ran her fingers over the plastic of her trusty pocket-knife. Thanks to her mother, that pocketknife and a folded five-dollar bill were two things she never left home without. You never know when you might need a knife or money, her mother had said.

Watching the waves splash and swirl around the cave rocks, her mind turned to LeCrosse and the menace she feared he was to her and others. Looking for the boy for hours yesterday had been too much. She thought about how desperate the boy must have been to jump out of LeCrosse's car and run. And hide. Just the thought of LeCrosse off-centered Juliet. Dizziness overtook her. A sense of foreboding descended on her, as if the toymaker's influence disappeared her too, turning her frail and ghostlike.

The only real thing was Kyle's palm where he touched her arm. She warded LeCrosse off by taking Kyle's hand in hers and silently chanting, "Only this hand, this back, this voice, this laughter is real." Kyle's eyes, lips, and smile were more powerful than anything LeCrosse had. At one time, she might have thought LeCrosse could be good, but no. She was wrong. Now, she believed he was a dark demon who wanted to dissolve her, scatter her into the wind like a wave upon the sea. He was after her. He wanted her very essence, like a parasite, and he wouldn't rest until she had no sense of self left. Until she was completely gone. Until she was completely his.

Is this disorientation and loss of control what Alice LeCrosse had felt in the beginning? Or had she started dark and dangerous, a kindred spirit to Tony?

"Whoa, come back," Kyle said, jolting her out of her dark thoughts. "Sometimes you just go away." He hugged her hand close. "Don't worry, we'll find her."

Find her. Twyla.

Juliet reveled in Kyle's voice, a rich balm soothing her soul, his voice bringing her present—this rock, this wind, this man. Kyle touched a part of her that LeCrosse could never come close to, no matter his skill in the dark arts.

The tide went out and the mouth of the cave opened in front of them. The cave was a great hideout, but only accessible at low tide. If Twyla was in there, she couldn't stay much longer into the season. She couldn't stay warm in that kind of dampness.

"Ready?" Kyle asked.

"Yeah," she said, ready as she was ever going to be. The thought of going into a cave only accessible at low tide scared her. But she couldn't let Kyle go alone.

They walked through mud and seashells and climbed over rocks shaped by the constant flow of water charging in and receding. The cave felt eerie and again a rush of trepidation crawled across her skin. Half afraid of what she and Kyle might find, Juliet wanted to turn around and sprint out of there. But the thought of Twyla being in there alone stopped her. She picked up a candy wrapper.

"Could be anyone's," Kyle said.

"But look." She pointed to a fire pit and what looked like a leftover tub of potato salad. A blanket lay crumpled next to a curved wall. She looked at Kyle, glad he was there with her. "Let's go tell Picard."

"Wait," Kyle said, running his light across the walls and deep into the cave.

"This place is creeping me out." Juliet reacted to the new depth of cave Kyle's light now exposed. "Let's get out of here before the tide traps us. You don't think she's in here, do you?"

"Maybe. Twyla?" he yelled. A clear echo came back. "Twyla! We can help you if you're here."

Here, here, here, the cave answered.

"I don't think she's in there," Juliet said.

"You think she's back with the LeCrosses?" Kyle asked.

Juliet shrugged. "I don't know. It could be bad if she is. It scares me. They don't like troublemakers. If she was out here, I'm sure they wouldn't like it."

Kyle stood next to her as the water splashed against the stones. She felt the warmth from his body and gratitude welled up in her. Kyle took her hand again and, together, they turned to face the ocean. The waves crashed relentlessly against the rocks.

Juliet shivered, longing for consistency like the waves. They came and went on a rhythm, their timing counted on by sailors for eons. When was the last time Juliet had felt such good consistency in her life? When had she last known what she could count on from one day to the next? When was the last time she'd felt truly safe, or slept peacefully in a proper bed, without that gnawing feeling in her gut that something bad was going to happen?

She'd been running on adrenaline for so long and living with that deer-in-the-headlights feeling for so long, that she hadn't realized how it had consumed her. For Juliet, safety had died with her mother. She turned and hugged Kyle. Out of the corner of her eye, she saw the blue material.

"Kyle. Look."

They walked over to it and Kyle picked up a corner of the blue tent that had been missing from the runaway camp.

Twyla had been there and now, again, she was gone.

. . .

That night, Juliet had the dream again–the one about the boy dressed in black, lingering outside her shed. In the dream, he had something to tell her and when she went to talk to him, she saw his bright green eyes just before he turned and ran. She ran after him, but he vanished into the dark.

"It's got to mean something," she told Kyle in the morning. "I've got something gnawing at me, trying to get my attention. I wish the dream would just tell me what it is."

Kyle rubbed the sleep out of his eyes. "Dreams don't talk."

"They do if you know how to listen. Remember that first party at LeCrosse's condo? A boy dressed in black was there. That's the image in the dream." The boy in black could mean someone with secrets. A dark heart. A dark past. Or all of that, or any combination of those things.

Those images basically described every runaway she'd ever known. Even Kyle. No. The dream was about the boy at LeCrosse's party. He was there and then was gone, in an instant.

"I didn't see him," Kyle said. "He must have left by the time I showed up."

"Right."

"Are you sure he was at the party? You were drugged that night."

"I don't think I made him up," she said slowly, shaking her head. "I remember thinking he looked familiar but out of place and sullen. Like he could have been someone's rebellious son."

"Have you seen him since?"

"Only in my dreams." Juliet smiled.

"Well… have you ever dreamed about me?" Kyle looked like a little boy as he asked, rather than the young man she knew him to be.

. . .

On Saturday morning, Juliet got an early start, thinking it might be her last day of the year at The Farmer's Market. Most locals didn't want a reading. They were practical and wanted tangible things, things they could hold in their hands, things like pot-holders, candles, and root vegetables. The tourist trade had grown depressingly thin.

She set up her table, sat down, and shuffled the cards. To occupy herself, she put out a four-card spread. The first card was the two of swords. Another two of swords. It signaled she was blind to something right in front of her nose. Take off the blindfold and she'd see it.

The dream.

The boy in black meant something.

The second card was the inverted moon, the moon at the bottom of the card, an upside-down dog, and a wolf howling. That moon could mean that the obstacles had a strong feminine influence, something or someone calling for help, or oppressing the call for help. The third card was a woman with a lion. Strength. Juliet's card. It pointed to the need to act, if only she could figure out what action to take. The last card, the Chariot, said if she found a way, things would work out.

Not a bad reading. If she could find a way… to see what was right in front of her.

To find Twyla. And Roy.

She looked up. A young pregnant girl was watching her–a girl Juliet had never seen before. The girl had pulled her mousy brown hair back into a thin ponytail. Her T-shirt stretched out over her large belly. Juliet figured she was about fifteen and eight to nine months along. She motioned for her to come closer.

"Want a reading?" Juliet asked. "I'll buy."

The girl smiled but shook her head.

"Are you here with your parents or a friend?"

Again, the girl shook her head, but said nothing.

The girl seemed exceptionally timid to Juliet. "Do you need help?" She pointed to her stomach. "Are you by yourself with a child on the way?"

Before she could answer, LeCrosse showed up. He took Juliet's hand and shook it. "Glad to see you, Miss French." His green eyes glazed sleepily. He lifted the eyelids and looked at her. She went weak in the spine. He let go of her hand and the spell dissipated. Juliet stood on firm ground again.

"No," he said. "She doesn't need to mess with the cards. No telling what future you might worry her about." He took the girl by the hand, caressing it gently in his. "Come on, darling," he said. "You're way too young to know what's good for you and what is clearly bad for you." He looked at the girl's stomach.

Was he shaming her? Juliet held her breath.

Then, LeCrosse turned his eyes on her.

He was shaming Juliet too!

She'd fix that. "When are you going to hire me for another one of your parties?"

"I'm not sure," he replied, his voice sweet and full of kindness. "Halloween maybe."

"Maybe you could have the party at your toy warehouse."

LeCrosse lurched slightly toward Juliet. It wasn't aggressive exactly, but it was intimidating, and Juliet felt the fear rise in her chest like a dark, ghostly fog.

The pregnant girl took advantage of him being distracted. Snapping her hand free, she took off running across the mall, quickly putting distance between her and LeCrosse.

The fog in Juliet's brain dissipated as quickly as it had arrived, and she felt pleased with herself. She'd read the situation correctly: the girl didn't buy LeCrosse's sweet talk. She hadn't wanted to go with him.

"You don't want to make me angry," LeCrosse said. The clouds thickened. A light drizzle began. He shook his head with a haunting half-smile on his face. He narrowed his eyes and trained them on her for a long time. Neither of them spoke.

"Halloween," he said, finally, "you'll be there."

It wasn't a question. It was a command, a command that, against all her better judgment, Juliet felt compelled to follow.

•   •   •

Juliet needed to find Twyla before that party. She went to the ship the next morning, placing her feet carefully as she crept across the old planks. She found the pregnant girl sitting in a rotting canvas chair. "Hey," she called out. She should not be on the old boat with the mold. She realized how bad the mold would be for the girl and her baby. Just the thought of poisonous spores drifting into her lungs and making their way to the child, made Juliet jump into savior mode.

She could help the girl. Because she was pregnant, it would be easy to set her up with social services and a place to live. It wouldn't be long before she gave birth, and an infant would not do well living out in the weather with the runaways.

The girl threw a startled look at Juliet, then loped down the deck and disappeared through an open hatch.

It baffled Juliet. Why would she run from her? She wanted to help her.

Foolishly, Juliet had worn leather sandals with bottoms that slipped on the rungs. She had to creep to the lower deck to stay upright. Once down the ladder, she found herself in the room behind the galley. The girl, of course, was nowhere in sight.

"Hey," Juliet called again, wishing she knew the girl's name. "I mean no harm. I'm here to help." She listened for a minute. The ship was cold and dark as silence rose up and stopped time, the vessel's ghosts frozen for eons in the rooms, their secrets locked away, the musky spirits seeping out and smelling nearly alive. What had they seen? What could those ancient spirits tell her?

The rain started up and hit the deck above with a persistent patter. This girl was in trouble. She wouldn't be any safer on the old ship than Twyla had been. And now, she too, had vanished.

Juliet went back to the shed, but Kyle was nowhere to be found. Maybe he was at work. She put rocks in the frying pan and turned on the propane stove, then pulled on a pair of thrift store sweatpants and sat close to the fire. Her belly growled. She hadn't eaten that morning, and she'd eaten very little all week. She knew she should spend more of her savings on food. But what if a runaway needed something? What if an emergency hit? Her life insisted she somehow prepare for the worst.

She poured water into a teapot and set it on top of the rocks. She'd looked for, and found, rocks flat enough to balance pots on so she could heat the room and food or tea water at the same time. Now if only she had some food.

She'd have to get an actual job soon. The Farmer's Market would close for the season next week. Her mother would laugh at the idea that her simple curiosity about dreams, tarot, and psychology-a curiosity Lila French had ignited in Juliet-had turned into a little business for her daughter.

Her mother had been an artist. She'd even designed her own tarot deck. She'd insisted the images meant nothing on their own. It was only when they touched the heart and imagination of a person that they came to life. Each image affected each person differently. The tarot cards brought the questioner's internal conversation into a conscious light.

Juliet had nodded mindlessly when her mother had talked about the cards, thinking it was all too deep for her. Then, one day, the concept took hold. She suddenly understood what her mother had been saying. The cards were vehicles to explore hidden thoughts.

Lila French had had a passion for synchronicity. "There is no such thing as coincidence," she used to say. "Watch carefully and you'll see there is a rhythm to everything."

Why then, Mother, did you die when I was just sixteen? Juliet had asked that question a thousand times. The answer was always the same: for no good reason. Her mother's death had no rhythm to it. It wasn't fair. A girl needed her mother. She needed her mother.

And Aunt Gloria's house had been no good. When her boyfriend came into Juliet's room for the last time, Juliet fought him off with a wild violence. She had to bear her aunt's dirty looks in the morning. Aunt Gloria had no mothering instinct for Juliet. She was too busy standing by Layne, giving Juliet the silent treatment. As if *Juliet* had done something wrong. Juliet didn't think she'd done something wrong, but she knew deep down that she *was* something wrong.

She bought a bus ticket and left for the coast, hanging her head in shame.

Juliet snapped back to the present when someone knocked. It seemed like she'd abruptly gone from living invisibly to living in Grand Central Station. She unfolded her legs and took a deep breath. Like a cat–but not like Wilma, the cat, who had already scurried under the bed–she tiptoed to the door and looked through the peek-hole.

Antonia Corrales stood there with a mesh bag at her side, probably wondering how it had come to this–having to knock on her own shed door. She looked nice, in a brown sweater, and loose brown trousers, her hair in a long braid over her shoulder. Even through the peephole, Juliet could see the concern in her soft hazel eyes.

She opened the door. "Come in," she said, feeling awkward about inviting Antonia into her own shed.

"I brought some good soup." The woman handed her the bag. "And some rice and canned beans, too. I put the rice in a glass container, so the mice won't get it."

"Mice?" Juliet sounded more fearful than she liked. But the thought of tiny creatures populating her little home slid over her like wet gauze, making it hard to breathe. Funny how she was brave in so many areas, but the idea of mice made her knees tremble.

"Yes. I set up traps to get rid of them, but any open food and they'll be back." Antonia pointed to an empty yogurt container in the corner.

Juliet immediately tossed it into her thrift store garbage can. "I hate mice."

"They have their place in the world," Antonia said, her hazel eyes bright and alert.

"Just not here." Juliet poured the soup into a saucepan she had bought for fifty cents. "Thank you for the food. I'm hungry."

"I thought you might be. But that's not why I'm here."

Juliet lifted her eyebrows.

"The girl whose parents came to get her. Gabriella? They say she's talking. They called the reporter who first broke the story about Gabriella and told him what she said. I called him. I left a message that I was covering the story for a small Seattle paper. He called back with an update. She had been with Tony and Alice LeCrosse and remembers a farmhouse not too far out of town, maybe a mile, close to the campground. That's where they keep the kids, she said. It's gray with a red roof. Children come and stay for a while and then they leave, all different ages. She thinks they're all related to LeCrosse, but he's not nice to them."

"How could he have so many children?"

"The foster care system?"

"But I think the system would be on to him. And why would they stay awhile and leave?" She stirred the soup. The aroma made her belly growl.

"That's what happens in foster care homes," Antonia said. She looked down at her brown trousers and brushed some lint away. Wilma scooted over to her and jumped in her lap, replacing the lint with cat hair, purring a happy sound.

Juliet shook her head. "The runaways flock to him. He has something they want."

"Until they don't want it. Remember, I told you they tracked Gabriella here because teens were posting on the Internet about Annie's Court?"

"Yes."

"Shortly after the children posted they had arrived here, their posts stopped. Then their profiles disappeared altogether."

"Someone took their phones away."

"No phones would make it difficult for them to call out for help. She said an older boy fought with LeCrosse about limiting their access to the outside world. The boy asked him to at least let the younger kids call their parents. Tony would have nothing to do with it. He kicked the boy out, told him to never come back."

The dream image of the boy in black flashed into Juliet's mind. Was this the older boy LeCrosse had fought with? She took two cups off a shelf.

"Soup?" she asked, playing the perfect hostess.

• • •

Juliet leaned her bike against the café's brick wall across the street from the police station still thinking about what Antonia had told her the day before. She would wait here, underneath the awning, for Picard to come out and notice her. Bitter waves shattered the coast, the sound an assault to Juliet's ears. Cold raindrops pelted her face, chilling her to the bone. The weather had turned menacing.

Finally, Picard arrived and invited her into the café for coffee and breakfast. She smiled. She had hoped for coffee and breakfast.

"What's important enough to bring you out in this weather?" He took off a knit hat and rubbed his hand across his baldhead.

Juliet recognized that rub to his bald head as a nervous gesture. He was probably worried about her. Worried about her. The thought made her laugh. She'd been fending for herself the last two years, two years she should have been home finishing high school. Someone, Aunt Gloria, should have been worried about her then.

"Did you ever get permission to have me on the payroll?" she asked.

"Why?" He answered a question with a question, her mother's pet peeve.

"Why don't you answer me?" Juliet asked, returning the favor.

"No," he said, pushing a twenty across the table. "But I'll keep trying. It would be better to hire you in an official capacity."

She took the twenty and pocketed it. "Some things are better done outside of official channels," she said, feigning a nonchalance she didn't feel. With the market closing for the season, she wanted money she could count on.

"Yes, but it could get you into trouble, and you don't need more trouble."

Detective Picard was being fatherly again. It was sweet. She hadn't imagined it in the beginning but, now that it was here, she didn't mind it at all. If she ever was in serious trouble, she could go to him. He had a good heart and sharp enough mind, easy to fool, but not easy to fool for long. She respected that.

"You could maybe get hired as an administrative assistant," he was saying. "Learn about police work from the inside and leave this more dangerous work to those with less to lose. There are benefits–insurance, a paycheck, retirement."

"Detective Picard," she said, amazed that he thought she had something to lose. She had no real home, no family to speak of, and no career. She had lost her mother and two fathers, been molested, and been discarded by the only person who was supposed to care for her. What, exactly, did she have to lose? Juliet saw her life as a long black tunnel, leading to nowhere. Might as well be of use now. "I'm only eighteen. I'm not thinking of retirement."

"Not now. But it'll sneak up on you." He rubbed his hands together.

She felt the twenty in her pocket, which was damp from the rain. "I suppose. But I don't know how I'd work in an office. I'd rather wait tables than sit at a desk."

The waitress showed up and Picard told Juliet to get whatever she wanted.

Juliet smiled, her belly rumbling. She ordered a turkey and avocado omelet, a cup of hot coffee, and a glass of milk.

"I should make sure you always have food."

Juliet nodded gleefully, the thought of food making her giddy. "Food is good."

"Besides food, why are you here?"

"Antonia Corrales, who owns the shed I live in, said a girl named Gabriella used to be a runaway. She said Tony LeCrosse held her captive for a while, and then threw her out. Gabriella says they have kids, nine to ten-year-old kids, come and go all the time. They live in a farmhouse outside of town, gray with a red roof."

Picard raised his eyebrows at her. He furrowed his forehead into deep, thick rows.

"This Gabriella had a seizure disorder. We think they figured she'd be too much trouble and they cast her aside for it. Her parents came and got her. The girl wouldn't talk about it for a long time." Juliet slid a number across the table to him. "Here is Antonia's number and Gabriella's parents' names and numbers. They think she'll talk to the police now."

The waitress brought her coffee.

Juliet warmed her hands on the cup, relishing the dark smell of it and sipping carefully so she wouldn't burn her lips, waiting for the food to come. Finally, she thought, we are getting somewhere.

CHAPTER TWENTY-ONE

Several days later, Picard paid Juliet. She bee-lined for the super-market, happy to have money in her pocket. This money was all hers, to use in any way she saw fit. She could splurge on ice cream if she wanted, or a dozen cinnamon rolls. Be reasonable, she told herself, heading for the produce. In front of the baking potatoes, Juliet almost crashed into the pregnant girl from the Farmer's Market and the old ship.

The girl looked up blankly and blinked.

"Excuse me," Juliet said.

The girl smiled but said nothing. She wore the same clothes she'd been wearing at the Farmer's Market earlier that month. The t-shirt now hung loosely on her, like a worn blanket.

"You had your baby!" Juliet said. "Congratulations. What did you have?"

The girl shrugged her shoulders, her smile frozen in place.

"Boy or girl?"

Again, the girl shrugged, a vacant look in her eyes, shifting sideways.

Juliet followed her eyes to LeCrosse, who was standing by the lettuce staring at them. An intense protective urge welled up in her. She flew across the aisle toward him. "Where's her baby?" she demanded.

A smug, vengeful look filled LeCrosse's face and vanished, replaced by his soft green eyes and his charming smile. He shrugged, just like the girl had. He motioned the girl toward him, and, to Juliet's surprise, the girl moved closer.

"Where is her baby?" Juliet repeated.

"At home with her grandmother," he said. "An exquisite little girl. As you can see, Bernice here is incompetent. It's a good thing she has family to help her take care of the baby." His smile shifted so quickly from something she saw as wicked to something sweet and charming, full of care and watchfulness, catching Juliet right in the damn fool of her heart, knocking her senses sideways. She felt unreal, like her spirit lifted out of her body, starting the long ascent home.

Her knees trembled as she shook her head and called her spirit back to herself. Not yet, I am not done here yet, she said, talking to the disconnected part of herself.

Bernice's vacant smile remained, but her eyes got wide and wavered, her fingers twisting the hem of her blue t-shirt into a tiny rope.

Juliet struggled to find her voice and found it. "How'd she become incompetent?" she asked. "Did you help her out there too?"

"Now darling, you know that's just nonsense," he said. The green eyes. The charm.

Juliet shook her head and held her ground. LeCrosse was a dangerous man. He'd hurt the girl. Careful here, she could almost hear her mother's voice from beyond the ethers. Careful. Juliet knew something, felt it in every inch of her being. LeCrosse had taken this girl, twisted her will, and done something wrong with her child.

• • •

"We have to get Bernice and her baby out of there," Juliet said to Kyle and Detective Picard as they stood on the rocks at the edge of the sea. The last heat of the warm fall day glistened around them.

"Maybe the baby is with her real grandmother," Kyle said. "Right where she belongs."

"He didn't mean grandmother." She threw her hands up in frustration, the wind blowing her black sweater wide. Even the wind was angry. "He meant Alice! I'm telling you, that's where the baby is, with Alice and LeCrosse. Or..." Juliet hated to finish that statement. The child could be anywhere by now.

Picard rubbed his chin and took off his hat, looking back and forth between Juliet and Kyle. "Again," he said, "we don't have enough information. Just because you feel something bad is going on, doesn't mean it is bad. We need evidence."

"So, get some," she said. "You are the police!"

Picard nodded.

"For all we know, Bernice could be LeCrosse's daughter," Kyle said.

"She's not." Juliet shot daggers at Kyle and then at Picard. She knew she shouldn't be mean. She knew them not believing her wasn't personal. Picard had to consider every angle. And Kyle evidently thought he had to please Picard. Nevertheless, she felt distressed. Her mother used to say she always knew when Juliet was afraid because her face grimaced and her eyes hardened.

Grief ran through Juliet like a red-hot lava flow. In times of trouble, Juliet missed her mother so much it took her breath away and Juliet thought she might join her mother in that always and forever land. She worked hard to pull in a new breath. And let it go. She stretched her shoulders, pulled in another breath, and let it go, until the familiar sweet rhythm of calm breathing returned.

"Has social services talked to LeCrosse?"

"Not yet."

"We have to get them out of there," she said again.

"You mean kidnap them?" Picard asked. "It doesn't help anyone if we become criminals."

Kyle looked at him with a baffled look on his face, moving his mouth to say something and stopping.

She knew what Kyle was thinking. In Montana, there was a long history of criminals and cops banding together. He'd told Juliet the story of a thirty-year crime spree in his hometown, a criminal team of two cops and a civilian. He said he couldn't trust the corrupt system there.

Juliet didn't know all of it, and she tried to comfort him, convince him the police could help him if he was in trouble. Kyle had been too overwhelmed with something like guilt or shame to listen.

She understood Picard's hesitancy. Kidnapping was illegal. But if the law wouldn't protect an infant, who would? Social Services? They hadn't been helpful with Twyla. Still. They were their best bet to check on a child's welfare.

"Maybe we could call the Department of Family Protection," she said.

Picard nodded. "They won't do much without some complaint. You finding Bernice in the produce section of the grocery store, with a blank look on her face, is not a complaint. In fairness to you, I think you are probably right. There's something to it. LeCrosse has seemed shady from the beginning. Seeming shady, though unsettling, is not a crime. Find me evidence and I'll send someone to get the child."

"And get Bernice and the baby into a proper home," Juliet said.

"Check the condo first." He put his hat back on, signaling the end of the meeting. "See if there's any sign of activity."

"They seem to have an abundance of places to move the kids," Kyle said.

"It's child labor," Juliet said.

"And drugs," Kyle said.

"Get the evidence," Picard said. "In the meantime, I'll see what I can find."

. . .

The next day, Juliet waited behind a bush outside of LeCrosse's condo from eleven until two in the afternoon. Her legs ached and she felt the bitter cold freezing her hands and feet. She heard the ferry's arrival horn. And she watched the traffic pick up and diminish. Seagulls squawked overhead. The wind smelled like seaweed and driftwood washed ashore. A few stray tourists sauntered down the walking path in front of the condominiums, looking and pointing.

Juliet wondered if they thought of buying a place for themselves in Annie's Court. If so, she understood. After all, the small coastal town had captured Juliet with its charms. She cringed at the word "captured." Perhaps, it had captured others who felt imprisoned by its spell, by LeCrosse's spell. And just like that the sweet moment of the town was ruined. If she was to stay, she needed to figure out what secrets that condo held.

When nothing happened in those three hours, and all was for naught, she packed up her snack bag and water and started toward home, almost missing the out of state sedan, a red Chrysler, when it arrived. Nevada, the license plate read. A few minutes later, LeCrosse showed up with Alice. Alice opened the back door of the white van and the twins got out.

They wore pink skirts and white ruffled tops. Their hair was cut sharp at the chin, like Alice's. And Juliet couldn't be sure, but she thought they'd had blond hair when she first saw them at the Farmer's Market. Now, both heads of hair bobbed auburn red, like Alice's hair.

A boy, about nine years old, someone Juliet had never seen, slid across the back seat, and climbed out behind them. He wore khaki slacks and a navy-blue golf shirt. His eyes darted everywhere, like a wild animal taking in his surroundings. The twins waited for him and walked side by side with him, their shoulders touching his, urging him into the condo.

The doors on the Nevada car opened simultaneously. A young couple emerged. The woman leaned back in and brought out a large purse and shut the passenger side door. The man looked over the top of the sedan at her and shut the driver side door. Juliet heard the click and ring of the doors being locked. He carried a briefcase.

Everyone disappeared into the condo. Juliet edged up to the condo stepping carefully, silencing each step before it happened. At the edge of the big windows, she heard muffled greetings. They all sat at the large table just within view of the windows that looked out on the bay. Even the children sat at the table.

What sounded like introductions were made, and Juliet tried to make out the names. She could not. Marie, or maybe Mary, or even May. Ryan or Riley or Randy. The boy perked up at Lukas or Luke. He ducked under the table as all heads turned to him. LeCrosse vanished under the table and returned the boy to his seat.

"Fifty thousand," LeCrosse said. "He's fine."

The couple, seated across from the boy, nodded, and looked at each other. The man shrugged. The woman smiled. She pulled some papers out of her large purse. A bunch of ruffling and sharing of papers was done. Something that might have been signatures happened and the man put the papers in his briefcase.

Once that commotion wrapped up, Alice served up lunch. It looked like deli sandwiches all around. Certainly not a fifty-thousand-dollar meal, if that fifty thousand had referred to money, which Juliet assumed it had. Her belly grumbled as she watched them eat. The boy barely touched his sandwich, even after the twins seemed to encourage him.

When lunch was finished, and the twins had removed the garbage and plates from the table, they retrieved the boy from the table. The three of them sat on the floor, away from the adults, and played with a train set. Juliet could hear the whir of the electric train and see it go around and around on its tracks.

The train stopped. LeCrosse and Alice shook hands with the couple. Each of the twins took their turn hugging the boy before they left the condo. Outside, they each hugged him again before he climbed into the back seat of the red Chrysler sedan and drove off with the couple from Nevada.

• • •

On the walk back to her shed, Juliet tried to make sense of what she had seen. There was no sense to it. What was that fifty thousand statement? Maybe she had made it up, facing the simple fact that she couldn't hear well through the glass, no matter what her heightened senses told her.

She could throw the tarot, but she didn't trust herself not to interpret exactly what she wanted to interpret. Something her mother had adamantly warned her against. You can always read the cards in your favor, she had said. But then you miss their message, even if they are favorable. Some part of you will always know what is real and what you have manipulated to appear as real.

"What a rough night," Kyle said, when he got home from work. "It was so busy. I feel like I'm wearing the leftovers of every meal that went through the Hungry Bear tonight."

"I'll heat some water for you." Juliet took a pot from a shelf in the corner of the shed, near the hole where Wilma came and went. She placed it on top of the flat rocks in the frying pan on her cook stove. From a plastic jug she had filled over at the park, she poured water into it. With a long red ignitor, she lit the stove. The fire warmed the rocks and room, eventually heating the water.

Juliet enjoyed taking care of Kyle. She liked it when she could do one simple thing for him, like provide hot water to wash the workday off. That warm water would make him feel better. She had so little to offer. And this one thing felt like gold. She hoped he liked it too.

"I went over to LeCrosse's condo today," she said.

"Alone?" Kyle sounded startled.

"Yes, I'm a big girl now," she said. The air in the tiny shed shifted and, even though the water heated, the warm feeling from the stove evaporated.

"I just mean you should have waited for me. I would have helped. LeCrosse is not to be trifled with," Kyle said.

"Yet Detective Picard dismisses everything we bring to him, as if Tony LeCrosse is no threat at all to anyone, just an unpleasant wayward soul."

"But we know something is askew with him," Kyle held his hands over the stove where the heat lifted into the shed. "What do you think? He's dangerous, right?"

"I think so," Juliet said.

"What did you see?"

"Tony, Alice, the twins, and another young boy, this one about nine years old." She wasn't sure why she stalled on telling him about the couple from Nevada. She didn't want to be told it was nothing again. She couldn't stand to have one more of her perceptions tossed away like sad garbage, especially not by Kyle.

He nodded. He got a washcloth out of his pack and dipped it into the water. After running it over his face and hands he hung it on a nail and came back to the fire. "Nothing too suspicious there. They were having lunch?"

She cringed. She also hadn't given him all the information. "A couple from Nevada also showed up for lunch." Wilma came in and jumped up on the bed with Juliet. She picked her up and held her close. "The boy left with them."

"What did you make of it?"

"Nothing really. Well, a lot really. But I don't know if I'm making things up and assuming a whole hell of a lot of nothing. I thought I heard LeCrosse throw out the number fifty thousand."

"Dollars?"

"I don't know. Money is my assumption."

"I wonder what it was for."

"A toy order?"

"That's a pretty large order of toys," Kyle said.

Juliet thought about that. "Yeah. That's a lot of toys."

"Maybe it's for a down payment for one of their buildings. The warehouse is empty. The janitor said they are selling it."

Juliet took in a breath of relief. That explanation made perfect sense. Silly her. Of course, they were talking about the building. "That must be it. So, I waited in the cold with aching bones for nothing. I'm such a fool."

"Yes, but you're my fool, just the kind of fool I like," Kyle said, and moved around the fire and kissed her. His kiss warmed her aching muscles. His arms surrounded her and pulled her close, making the shed, their shed, a home.

CHAPTER TWENTY-TWO

Tourist activity had slowed down in the last few days, and Kyle felt grateful just to wash dishes and ponder a peaceful life. He rinsed a large chili pot in the kitchen of the Hungry Bear Café, his face enveloped in steam. Finished with the pots and pans, he wiped his hands on his stained white apron, loaded a tray with dirty glasses, and sent them through the dishwasher. When the silverware tray was full, he sent it through. Some people would complain about washing dishes–the heat, the grime, other people's leftovers. It wasn't dignified. Kyle didn't care. He liked it. It fed him, and it had helped feed the kids at the tent camp. Now it could feed Juliet if she wasn't too proud to accept the food.

He smiled. A big "if" with Juliet.

Washing dishes gave him time to think. Kyle liked how mindless it was, loading a dish tray with plates and cups, or scrubbing a stew pot. He just let his hands do the work. He'd worked there almost 100 days, and it soothed him.

Good dishwashers were scarce, the staff had told him. His boss said the kid before him had complained about having to stand. "Have you ever had to stand a whole hour?" the kid had asked the boss. After a stunned silence, the kitchen staff broke into a hard laughter. The kid walked out mid-shift, leaving the opening for Kyle.

Kyle should have money in his pocket, but he didn't. He made ten bucks an hour, and he'd spent it on the camp kids.

Fifteen teens lived in the camp. They needed milk, meat, and vegetables–healthy food. Last month Brody had a tooth go bad. The dentist cost two hundred and fifty dollars. Joshua needed insulin and Kyle had gotten social services to step in. They put him back with his mother, who left him with a neighbor who broke his jaw when he beat him. Joshua came back to the camp still needing his insulin and needing his jaw fixed. The tent kids needed shoes, coats, pants, and shirts. They needed blankets, pillows, soap, shampoo, toothpaste, toilet paper, and towels. And books to keep up with their studies.

Kyle didn't want to wash dishes for the rest of his life. He didn't want the tent kids to wash dishes for the rest of their lives, either. He wanted good homes for them. He wanted their parents to stop doing drugs, stop beating them, and stop falling in love with adults who had a thing for children.

Too many of the tent kids were angry. They didn't trust adults. In fact, they blamed all adults for their pain. Many of them were thieves and liars. Good people thought they could change the hard ones by loving them. Maybe they could, but they needed a realistic idea of what they were getting into. Some of the available foster parents had a romanticized view of saving a child.

It took work, self-evaluation, and specific knowledge. The seasoned foster parents understood that. They took their time, gave love, and set limits. They braced themselves for disappointment after disappointment, accepting the children as they were. Sometimes the kids recovered. Sometimes they didn't.

Kyle had learned a lot from living in the tent camp. He realized he was lucky he loved his parents, and he trusted most adults. It allowed him to work for honest pay. It allowed him to think about going home. But every time he got close to moving back to Montana, he stopped. He couldn't face his parents, not after the fire and his sister's death.

"Kyle," the cook yelled. "Are you floating in the South Pacific or washing dishes?"

Kyle smiled at him and shrugged, ready to get back to work.

"Never mind that. There's a girl to see you."

Kyle turned off the water and wiped his hands. He liked it that Juliet wanted to come to see him at work, but he'd have to warn her off. He'd get in trouble with too many interruptions and lose his job. His boss had made it clear: "No visitors while you're working."

But it wasn't Juliet. Bernice, the new mother Juliet had told him about, stood in the doorway. She had a large bruise on her left cheek, and she was shaking.

"What happened?" he asked, pulling her into the hallway.

"I couldn't find Juliet," she said. "She told me you worked here."

"Okay, tell me. What happened?" Kyle asked again.

"He hit me," she said.

"Who?" Kyle knew. But Picard kept saying they needed facts.

"LeCrosse. And he threatened to withhold food from the baby if I don't do what he says, which is to follow the plan."

"What plan? And where is your baby?"

"With her grandmother." The girl became robotic.

"Alice?"

She nodded.

"What's your real name?"

"Leah."

Kyle nodded. "And your baby's?"

"Princess."

"Princess Leah. What's your real name? Maybe we can get the baby's real grandmother to come and get you both."

Fear lit up her eyes, and she turned to go.

"Wait!" Kyle knew that feeling, going to someone for help and then running away in terror because they innocently suggested the unfathomable. "No real grandmother, promise. What did he want you to do?"

She stopped, her back to Kyle. "Get pregnant again."

"So soon?"

Bernice shrugged. She started walking.

"Kyle!" the cook called. "We got work to do."

"Do you know Twyla? You two can help each other."

Bernice turned to Kyle with a cringe. "Twyla is gone. She wouldn't follow Tony's plan, so he got rid of her."

"Got rid of her like killed her?"

"No. Just got rid of her."

"Kyle! Get your butt in here and get back to work."

He turned to the kitchen and yelled, "Just a minute."

When he turned back, Bernice was gone.

• • •

Kyle's face glittered with sweat and dirt from a night's work, and he wanted a good old-fashioned bath. Instead, he'd have to settle for a hot sponge bath. Maybe next week, when he got paid, he'd splurge on a shower at the RV Park. He pulled on the shed door, and it was locked from the inside. He knocked. A shadow crossed over the peephole and the lock slid open. Juliet opened the door four inches and the scent of spiced tea wafted out like a welcome mat.

She looked both ways. "You alone?"

"No, I have the boogie man with me. And four thousand ghosts." He went in and sank onto the cot. Wilma jumped up, purring, and rubbing against him.

"Did something happen?" Juliet sat on the cot next to them. She crossed her legs and tucked her hands into her sweater sleeves, a habit Kyle found endearing. But then, what didn't he find endearing about Juliet? She was smart, feisty, generous, and full of goodwill. And beautiful with those gray eyes, that black hair, those full lips.

"Kyle?"

"Yeah?"

"What's wrong?"

"Bernice came to the café with a big old bruise on her cheek. She said LeCrosse hit her, said he'd withhold food from the baby if she didn't do what he wanted."

"Which was?" Juliet put a pot of water on the flat rocks in the frying pan to heat and pulled a washcloth and towel from a plastic bin under the bed.

"Thank you," Kyle said, nodding toward the lit stove.

Juliet smiled at him, a smile that reached his core, and his fatigue vanished.

"What does LeCrosse want her to do?"

"To get pregnant again."

"So soon?" Juliet's voice rose and she narrowed her eyes.

"That's what I said. When I asked why he'd want her to get pregnant again so soon, she balked. I suggested we get the baby's real grandmother to come and get them."

"And?"

"She said LeCrosse got rid of Twyla because she wouldn't follow the plan. He didn't kill her, just got rid of her."

Juliet shook her head. Kyle could see the worry in her face. They'd had no luck in finding Twyla since she'd last disappeared.

Wilma stretched and jumped from Kyle's lap into Juliet's lap, happy to be right where she belonged. Kyle thought he and the kitten were much alike, happy just to be near Juliet. "Bernice left before I could find out exactly what LeCrosse wanted of Twyla, but I'd bet he wanted her pregnant, too."

Juliet dipped the washcloth in the warm water and rung it out. She sat on the bed next to him and washed his face. The clean heat felt good. Her hands on his face felt good. When was the last time someone had touched him so tenderly while help-ing him tend to a daily task?

His mother's memory crashed in so hard he nearly fell off the bed. Her sweetness, her kindness, her pure, sweet love. Kyle felt love now, right at the center of his being.

"Is the water too hot?" Juliet asked.

"It's perfect." And it was.

"Do you think they're selling babies? And where is Twyla?"

"If we only had answers." Kyle pointed to the pocket-sized tape recorder sitting near the door. "Anything on it yet?"

"I haven't checked it." Juliet handed him the towel and picked the recorder up. "Something's here. The tape has moved." She rewound it and hit play.

He heard shuffling noises and then a voice. "Wilma, kitty, kitty. Come here Wilma. Kitty, kitty." More shuffling. "There you are. Come here." Wilma meowed. And then, nothing.

"Roy?" Kyle asked.

Juliet lifted her eyebrows and nodded.

CHAPTER TWENTY-THREE

The wind whistled through the cracks in the shed walls and played into Juliet's dream. An older boy, dressed in black, sat sullenly in the corner. She walked over to him, a curious cat, and bent down to meet him eye to eye. Red eyes looked up at her. She wondered if his eyes were really that color, or if he wore contacts to hide his true self. As though an expert at examining eyes, she reached out and pulled a thin red piece of plastic off his eye. The boy shut both eyes and wouldn't let her touch the other one. She cajoled him, softening her voice. She'd give him time, encourage him to open up by being open. It worked. He opened his eyes and looked at the floor. She reached out and lifted his chin. He stared at her, one eye red and the other radiant green.

Juliet woke to a damp cold in the shed. She looked over at Kyle on his cot. His brown hair stood up on one side and little puffs of air moved through his soft lips. The blue sleeping bag covered his shoulders. He'd thrown one leg out from under it. Let the prince sleep, she thought. Pulling on a coat and a pair of sweats over the leggings she'd slept in, she grabbed a plastic jug and opened the door.

In the morning sun, the air outside felt warmer than the air in the shed. Something about the dream gnawed at her. What had Gabriella said about an older boy fighting with LeCrosse? Something about his eyes. That green eye. That boy in black.

She'd seen them both before. She walked to the park to fill her water jug. Out of the clear blue sky, the thought hit her. Juliet knew the dream boy and the sullen boy in black at LeCrosse's party-they were both Stephan. Stephan had radiant green eyes like that. Radiant green eyes like Tony and Alice LeCrosse.

Back at the shed, she woke Kyle. "Come on," she said. "We have work to do."

• • •

"You're not afraid of the police," Juliet said. Kyle stood next to her, a protective bear. A fire roared in the wind like the angry sea, flames crashing against the morning skyline.

Stephan stood on the other side of the fire, warming his hands as he looked at her.

"But you are afraid of your father," she added.

Stephan's face turned angry and then soft. He didn't deny it.

"You ran away to protect yourself," Juliet guessed.

"He's not my father," Stephan said.

"Married to your mother?" She asked.

He nodded. "You can see why I wish it wasn't true."

"Was he mean to you?"

"You don't want to know."

"You started the tent camp to protect others from Tony. He used the kids to make toys." Tony and Alice both, Juliet thought, but she had to tread carefully. She knew better than to mess with the love between a person and their mother.

"And more, I couldn't keep the young ones safe at Tony's place and I couldn't convince them to leave. They were too scared to defy him. Half the time they didn't even know what he was doing was wrong. He was a refuge in the terrible storms of their lives. The older kids, eyes wide open and ready to leave, needed a place to go. We provided it." He looked over at Kyle, motioning with his chin, including Kyle in his "we."

"The police?"

"Tony threatened to kill my mother if I spoke to them. I tried to get her to leave him, but she'd gotten too far into the meth and the 'business,' as she called it. He had a strangle hold on her. I watched her die right before my eyes. She became something not quite human."

"One of the rescued teens said an older boy fought with Tony," Juliet said. "You're that boy, right?"

Stephan nodded. "I couldn't stand what he was doing to all of them, and I couldn't stand being so helpless. I hated it when one of the young ones disappeared. I never knew where they went. I fought with Tony. But I could only push it so far. I believed him when he said he would hurt my mother." He kneeled, picked up a stick, and pushed ashes around the edge of the fire pit, getting dangerously close to the flame.

"Two more kids are missing," Kyle said softly. "Twyla and Roy. Do you know where they are?"

Stephan shook his head. He seemed sad, hopeless, Juliet thought. It would have been awful for him to lose his mother to Tony LeCrosse. "Are the twins your sisters?"

"They haven't been around long. Just this year." He looked out toward the waves. "I don't know where they came from. One day they showed up. Mom was thrilled with them. When I asked Tony about them, he kicked me out. Made it clear I was not to come back.

"He didn't like you questioning him," she said. "A boy left Tony and your mom's condo with a couple from Nevada. Any ideas about him?"

"Maybe they were his new parents." Stephan raised an eyebrow.

"New?" Juliet asked.

"I don't know. I've been gone a long time. But Tony is beyond nothing for a buck."

Juliet felt her stomach go sick. The waves rolled in and out, talking, saying catch him. Catch him.

Stephan bit his lip and sucked on it. "As far as Twyla and Roy go, Tony has a cabin. One time they blindfolded me and took me out there and kept me somewhere dark and cold, a shed or a cellar. I lost track of time. When they took me back to the farmhouse, I was good as gold until I had enough food and money to run."

"You didn't go far," Kyle said.

Stephan's face got sad again. "I couldn't. I kept hoping I could stop them."

"Any idea where this cabin might be?" Juliet asked.

"My mom knows. But she'll never tell. She couldn't imagine betraying Tony LeCrosse, not even if the devil himself came up and grabbed hold of her."

Which might be exactly what had happened to Alice LeCrosse, Juliet thought.

• • •

At the Halloween party, LeCrosse displayed his toys. Stuffed bears bore intricate hand-sewn seams, the stitches minute and even. Wind from a tiny fan filled the brightly colored sails of miniature wooden boats. The sails looked like they could have been cut straight from the nylon cloth of the tent town. A copper coiled moon rose above a magical city of clowns, gypsies, and circus animals. Lovely ladies danced with elephants, the big tent open to the stars.

Juliet had dressed in tight leggings, a colorful thrift store skirt and a silk bandana covering her head, posing as a fortune-teller. Not exactly a stretch for her. She set the card table up near the large window overlooking the bay. Ominous clouds added the last touches to her costume. She felt scared after her interactions with LeCrosse at the grocery store, after eavesdropping on him at their lunch, but being there was her best chance to find information about Twyla and Roy, and to help them get somewhere safe.

The condo filled with wild characters: Spiderman climbed the wall next to the window, stepping on the couch and a ladder, hanging dangerously from a wooden beam; Cinderella, Bob Marley, and a certain beautiful cat drank from tall-stemmed glasses in the corner. An entire pack of colorful M&Ms crossed the room to chat with a tomato and a box of cereal.

Batman and the lion walked in together, holding hands, much smaller than the rest of the guests. A whole parade of small people in costumes followed–a princess, an astronaut, a scientist, Big Bird, a cowboy, and a rock star. Alice LeCrosse followed them, looking like the jewel of the sea. A soft green gown flowed to the floor, shimmering in the light like ocean waves in the early morning. A sequined crown covered her auburn hair.

Outside, dark blue-gray clouds promised a storm, mimicking the turmoil Juliet felt inside.

"Only one piece of candy tonight," Alice admonished the children.

One piece would be difficult for the children, since candy dishes on every tabletop overflowed with Butterfingers, Milky Ways, Hershey chocolate bars, and chewy tart candies. Juliet passed on all of it. She knew better than to trust anything to eat or drink at this party. She'd brought her own water and water would have to be enough for now.

Candy wasn't the only temptation. LeCrosse had dressed as a bondsman, in a beautiful leather vest, a pressed white shirt with a red tie, and brown trousers. He looked distinguished and handsome, wise even. Every woman in the room, and some men too, jumped to get him a drink or help carry coats to one of the extra bedrooms.

"Have a card for me tonight?" he asked. "Social Services came asking questions. I assume you sent them." He sat across the table from her, crossed his legs, leaned forward, and smiled.

"You sure you want to know?" she asked, ignoring his accusation, resisting the swell of power he cast over her and failing, the rest of the room falling away. "Tonight's the night the earth opens and souls fly. Anything can happen. All secrets may be revealed."

"What the hell. Try me." His brilliant green eyes glistened. He touched her hand, sending a shiver through her.

She drew in a breath, and let it go, shaking loose of the touch. She shuffled the deck and pulled a card from the center. The reversed Page of Swords. An upside-down young man, dressed in a short tunic, held a sword over his shoulder, ready to swing. Clouds dotted the air behind him, as if he were falling into the sky. Thunder cracked outside. The room went dark and then lit up again. Run, it seemed to say. Run faraway and never come back.

Juliet ignored the storm's warning. "The Page of Swords shows a risk, usually mental or spiritual in nature," she said. "This card is about someone charming and attractive, but immature and dishonest. It could be someone using others for selfish reasons or running a scheme at the expense of others. This person's endeavor will most likely cause great harm to all."

"Could it be you, Juliet?" Tony asked in a fatherly way. "Perhaps your readings alter people's lives in unfavorable ways, doing damage to their souls and yours."

Lightning flashed, lighting up the room again. Juliet felt it pierce her heart, his words striking hard at her own doubt. What if she was doing evil rather than good?

When the lightning flickered again, two older kids dressed as orphans appeared and disappeared around a corner. Twyla and Roy? Pulling away from LeCrosse, Juliet gathered her card deck, put it in her pocket, and followed the orphans.

Alice had a group of children in the hallway. "Would you like to come with us?" She reached out her gloved hand to Juliet.

Like a fool, she took it. The hand didn't feel quite right, as if the woman had a plastic limb underneath her elegant white glove. Alice led Juliet and the children to a large room with yoga mats arranged in rows. Each mat had a yellow pillow and a fleece blanket on it. When Alice let go of her hand, Juliet noticed some gel on her palm and wiped her hand on her colorful skirt.

Alice touched her crown, turning on a revolving light that cast a recurring green glow into the room. "They'll stay the night here," she said. "You're welcome to stay over if you'd like."

Suddenly Juliet felt woozy and tired. Sleep sounded glorious. The room spun around her, the woman's crown revealing and hiding the youngsters. She thought she saw Twyla, her mouth pleading as she tried to reach Juliet.

"We've been looking for her," Juliet said, starting toward the orphan.

"For whom?" Alice stepped in front of Juliet, tilting her crown, turning the pulsating room sideways.

"Twyla," she replied.

"We've lost her," Alice said. "I hope she's somewhere safe."

Juliet looked again at the orphan. Now she wasn't so sure it was Twyla. The moving light of Alice's crown brightened and faded. The orphans came and went, waving frantically at something.

The jewel of the sea again reached out her hand to Juliet.

She felt that plastic again, as if something metallic and not human had replaced Alice's hand. She had to ask now before she faded away. "Stephan is your son. Why did you leave him?"

The hand tightened around Juliet's hand in a stiff but comforting way. "He left me," she said. "He's happier away from this. You can see it gets chaotic."

But it wasn't chaotic. The children had gone to the mats like tiny robots and cuddled into the blankets. She couldn't see the orphans now. "You have a cabin somewhere near the sea," she said, her voice sounding strange in her own ears. Her mouth felt swollen. A giant jellyfish controlled her lips, making the words slur.

Alice smiled. "Sweetheart, your mind works too hard. Relax here with the children. Let yourself dream."

When Alice let go of her hand the room invited Juliet to sleep, a magical wonderland of good fairies. Again, Juliet wiped her hand on her skirt to get rid of the gel. Before she could lie down on a mat, LeCrosse appeared and whisked Alice off, the orphans now in tow.

In their place stood Kyle, dressed as Paul Revere.

"Get your horse and take me out of here," she said, falling into his arms, nearly asleep on her feet.

• • •

The next day, All Souls Day, Kyle turned eighteen. Juliet hadn't prepared a celebration for him, but she'd invited him to join her at the Farmer's Market. The clouds hung heavily over the last market of the season, the fog covering Annie's Court like a thick blanket–the same thick blanket that occupied her head. Two cups of coffee hadn't helped her shake off the party.

Across the aisle from the spot where she and Kyle sat, Alice LeCrosse sat behind a u-shaped counter lined with magnificent wooden toys. A tiny horse reared, lifting his rider into the air. Cows nosed up to a water trough; water spilling into a small bucket and recycling. A little soldier pointed his toy rifle across the market, right at Juliet, filling her with anxiety.

She looked away.

Focus on Kyle, she told herself. That should be easy. He looked handsome today in his blue jeans and gray fleece. She took his hand. Wrapping her fingers around his worked a balm into her, replacing the anxiety with desire. The thought of kissing him sent a warm flush through her. Her body swelled and filled with a mix of peace and anxiety, something that changed with each breath. She knew what she'd like to give him for his birthday.

But that sort of birthday present would have to wait.

At least she had a treat for him. She had bought them each a cinnamon roll and a chocolate cookie, not mandatory they eat them both at the same time. A little mustache of icing lined Kyle's lip. Juliet wanted to kiss it away but restrained herself. Instead, she brushed at her own lip in the universal sign of "you have something on your lip". Kyle wiped at it but didn't get it.

"The other side," Juliet said.

"Is it gone now?" Kyle asked after a second swipe at it.

"Much better."

"But is it gone?"

"Mostly." She rubbed the corner of her mouth.

Kyle wiped his face clean with his napkin. "How are you feeling?"

"Like someone hit me over the head with a sledgehammer. Somehow, I was drugged again. I'm not sure how. I brought my water, and I ate nothing. Maybe they poured gas into that room."

"I would have smelled it, and it would have affected me, too," Kyle said. "You said Alice's hand felt strange, like plastic?"

"Yeah. She had a glove on, and it didn't feel like it was her actual hand underneath. After she held my hand, a gooey substance covered my fingers and palm. I wiped it on my skirt. Maybe something in it went through my skin and made me sleepy."

Kyle nodded. "Why would she give you drugs?"

"To make me question my sense of reality? To control me? Drugs are probably how they control the children in their care. They all went to bed too easily last night. No whimpers, no objections, no questions asked–even with a Halloween party going on in the other room. It's not normal."

"No. Not at all."

"And then, at one point, like little robots, they all got up and followed her."

She felt Kyle's eyes on her.

"It doesn't make sense," Kyle said.

"I thought I saw Twyla and Roy, but then they disappeared. Poof. Just like that." Juliet kept trying to shake the night off. "It's horrible. I can't get this fog out of my head."

"Try some water," Kyle said, pulling two bottles of water out of his bag and handing one to her. "It might help. Why don't you throw the cards for me? It'll pass the time and drum up business." He had a mischievous grin on his face, like by asking something of her, he was giving her a gift. She'd take it. Reading the tarot cards would distract her and ease her discomfort, but she had one stipulation.

"Only if you really want to know the answer." Even in her mental fog, she remembered his reaction the last time she did a reading for him.

"You really believe the cards can know something?"

"We've already had this conversation." Juliet sighed. It had taken many attempts on her grandmother's and mother's parts for her to understand how the cards worked. Finally, she'd understood: The images on the cards brought forth a person's unconscious thoughts. They were a tool for people to find their way, not the way. They helped her and others gain access to what they already knew, what intuition had to tell them.

If she couldn't get it in one try, why would Kyle? He wasn't even truly interested, except through his interest in her. The thought made her smile, and her head began to clear. "The card images don't know things, but you do. When the pictures work with your mind, your imagination, and your experiences, the message becomes clear."

"But you tell people things."

"I watch their body language. They tell me yes or no." Again, Juliet thought of her mother and her explanation of dreams. The dream images work with what the mind already knows. An example of such a dream popped into Juliet's mind and she shared it with Kyle. "One night, I dreamed our house exploded. The next day, the furnace repairman worked on our heating system. Guess what? The valve was stuck open, releasing a small amount of gas. 'You're lucky this place didn't blow sky high,' he said."

"Like your dream."

"Yeah. Part of me likely recognized the smell of gas, minute as it was, and saw the danger. My conscious mind didn't pick it up, but my dream mind did."

"So, your dream warned you?"

"I'm saying there is more to life than what we see. It's mysterious. Shuffle the cards. You're right, it'll pass the time." Juliet scooted her chair forward and leaned her knee against Kyle's. His leg felt warm, and the warmth felt good. She hoped her foggy energy mixing with his didn't mess with the cards.

Kyle shuffled and reshuffled the cards half a dozen times. "Am I supposed to ask a question?"

"If you want." Juliet smiled at him.

Kyle smiled back.

A sweet thrill rushed through her, and she took a deep breath, clearing the fog in her brain. Clouds threatened rain and she wished the sun would come out. He set down the cards and pushed them toward her.

She pulled the first card off the top of the deck. The Page of Cups, upside down. Of course. She'd never had a season with so many inverted cards. What did it say about her? "This first card describes the situation. The upside-down position depicts deception. Things are not what they seem. There are secrets in the heart and it's a situation you should look at carefully."

Kyle had a distant look in his eye. "The fire," he murmured, almost to himself.

She waited.

"What's the next card?" He motioned to the deck.

She flipped it. The King of Pentacles, a kindly, mature man sitting on his throne, holding a single coin. "This card represents the obstacles inherent in the situation. The King of Pentacles is a courageous, generous, and fair person. He's understanding and forgiving. Right side up is a good sign. He's dependable, and likely represents a person who loves you. The obstacle in this case may be your own fears about whatever you believe the king will think of you."

"My father," Kyle said, tears swelling in his eyes.

He motioned for the third card, and she flipped it. The Four of Wands, reversed. Four wands topped with a decorative garland, or in this case, the garland was at the bottom of the card. It didn't matter. The Four of Wands was an especially positive card in either position. "This card represents the action you might take to resolve the situation. The Four of Wands is a good card. It means if you step forward with a sincere heart, the outcome will be good. Because it's upside down, there may be things to settle as you step forward. Clearing up misunderstandings is just part of the process. Any sincere action to resolve the situation is a good action."

He looked at Juliet. "What is the last card?"

She flipped it. Strength. The courageous lion with a loving handler. Right side up. Juliet smiled. Her card. "This card shows what you already know. You have great courage and strength. You've come through many difficulties and come out the other side. Your instinctive, animal nature will help you."

Kyle sat quietly and stared at the market as a light rain fell. Juliet gathered the cards and waited. She knew the power of silence. Finally, he spoke. "My father told me to go to bed. I didn't want him to know I was still awake, so I lit a candle to read by. I fell asleep. I'd left the window open, and wind blew the curtain into the candle. It caught fire. The fire jumped across the ceiling. My sister was sick in bed. I opened the door to run out of my room and the fire shot across the ceiling to Katy's bedroom. I thought my parents had gotten her out already. But I didn't even look."

"Kyle," Juliet said, "it wasn't your fault."

"I didn't even check to see if she was still in her room. If I'd gone back for her, I might have gotten us both out, but I didn't go back. I just ran."

"You were a kid, doing the best you could. It was no one's fault."

He shook his head. "I don't know how my parents will ever forgive me."

She thought about the King of Pentacles. "If your parents ever blamed you, they have already forgiven you. The cards show that."

"I wish I could believe it."

Juliet hated the idea of him leaving. "You'll believe it when you go home."

"Thank you," Kyle said. "You're a good friend."

Juliet smiled, wishing she could help him. She pulled the next card for herself: the Ten of cups, a happy card emphasizing family. How odd to pull a happy card when Kyle looked so sad. Across the market she noticed the woman from Montana watching them, wearing the same broomstick skirt she'd worn a couple of weeks ago. Jealousy hit Juliet hard, and she just wanted to get Kyle away from there.

"Time to pack up," she said, pulling a Tony LeCrosse, feeling half the manipulator.

"Looks like we're not alone," Kyle said. "Alice LeCrosse has already packed up and is leaving. I'm going to follow her. Maybe she'll go to the cabin." He'd borrowed a motorcycle from a co-worker. He put on the helmet and started the engine.

"For others, you don't give up hope," Juliet said.

"No."

"I like that about you." Despite the woman from Montana, and her own devious self, Juliet felt good. She'd pulled the family card. With Kyle, she almost felt like she belonged again. She didn't want anything to threaten that.

CHAPTER TWENTY-FOUR

Kyle's instincts were right. He followed Alice LeCrosse south out of town on a dirt road that went deep into the woods and turned into a driveway. Wet and cold, he stashed the Honda 50 in the brush. Seagulls flew in circles, diving into the water and soaring back into the clouds. He could hear the lapping of the waves, moving in their consistent rhythm. A weathered log cabin sat in a clearing lined by large leaf maple trees, atop ocean cliffs, not too far from the caves. Its foundation tilted, as if it might slide into a hole at any moment. A thick blanket of vines grew up the porch railings, bringing it back a century or two.

Alice went in, leaving the front door ajar. Kitchen noises–pots clanging together, silverware being pulled from a drawer–filtered out to where Kyle sat crouched in the bushes. Watching. Listening. Long tendrils of grass snuck up his pants legs and scratched his ankles. A late season fly buzzed around his head. The soft wind made Kyle's eyes water as he listened to crows cawing in the tall trees. No voices came from the building.

What if Alice saw him? What if she was meeting someone at the cabin? As he watched, Kyle relaxed, convinced she was alone in there, tending to who-knew-what. She wasn't interested in anything outside the cabin, including him. He stretched his legs as he waited for her to leave. But she didn't leave. Time passed. The sun moved across the sky. Sounds inside of the cabin quieted down. His legs ached. He knew he couldn't stay much longer. It was almost time for him to go to work.

Kyle didn't dare miss work. His parents had taught him a strong work ethic. In Montana, he'd helped them with house and yard work. His father had sent him over to the neighbors to help them with weeding and raking. He'd worked for two summers, haying on a family friend's ranch. That job had meant he was up at dawn and working till dusk, the Flathead River rolling by. Kyle had loved summers in Montana. He'd loved the work, and the warm air full of sunrises.

No. He had to make his shift at the Hungry Bear Cafe. He'd come back another time. At least now he knew where the cabin was. Just follow the crows, he laughed to himself, wondering what the image of the crow meant.

• • •

After work, Kyle listened as Juliet played the tape for him. Someone had been at the shed again, and this time, the tape recorder caught more than one voice.

"Leave me alone," a boy yelled.

"Got him? Hold him tight. He's slippery." A man's voice.

"Let me go, you idiot." The boy's voice again.

"No, no, I don't think so," the man said.

Something crashed. A voice was muffled under something– maybe a hand or a piece of cloth.

"Got him?"

"Yeah. He's going nowhere this time."

Juliet stopped the recorder. Kyle looked at her, wishing he could remove the sad look in her eyes. "Roy," she said.

"We have to find him."

"Something we're not particularly good at."

. . .

Kyle told Juliet about finding the cabin. It was south of town, out near the caves, in a clearing lined by large leaf maples, with nothing but the cold weather flies, seagulls, and the crows.

"How can they have so many buildings?" he asked, wondering if the LeCrosses had a real estate business going too.

"Let's go to the cabin when no one's there, break in, and see what we can find," Juliet said. She looked so innocent as she sat cross-legged on her bed. She'd already dressed for sleep in an oversized t-shirt and black leggings. He wondered if she ever wore real pajamas. He hoped to be around long enough to find out.

"Breaking and entering is illegal," he reminded her, shaking himself back to the present.

"We'll just look in the windows then. Maybe we'll get lucky."

"It could just be their summer cabin. Nothing bad there. Look, we could be making stuff up, pretending to be detectives."

She shook her head and blinked her eyes. "Pretend crime. No. We're going to figure out what they are doing, even if we must go inside of the cabin. Pretend or no pretend, we're going to figure out what they have to do with the runaways."

"If anyone goes in, I'll go in without you." Kyle felt that protective urge come over him again, felt his muscles tense. He rubbed his knuckles, ready to fend off any enemy, real or imagined, of Juliet's.

Juliet shook her head and took Kyle's hand. "No. We're both eighteen now, and we're in this together." She looked up at him with those soft gray eyes and the tension left him. His heart felt big as the world.

. . .

"Think anyone's in there?" Kyle whispered. They were shivering in the woods at the edge of the clearing. He and Juliet had ridden the borrowed Honda 50 out to the cabin in the maple grove. They'd stashed it in the forest at a safe distance from the cabin, and walked the rest of the way in. The small log structure looked empty, desolate, and timeworn. It had to be at least eighty years old.

"I don't know. Maybe Roy? Twyla?" she said. "They have to be somewhere."

"Unless they aren't." Kyle said the thing he'd been avoiding. They could be dead.

Juliet narrowed her eyes. "Is it possible they went home?"

Kyle shook his head. "Anything's possible. Warmth and food are pretty attractive. But you heard Roy on the tape. That's not a kid going home. Someone had ahold of him."

"No one seems to be around," Juliet said. "Let's look in the windows."

Kyle nodded, and they walked forward together, holding hands. For a second, he let himself dream: the two of them, married, on a honeymoon where they'd rented a rustic cabin with printed curtains, ready to begin a life together. The surf rolling in and out, the seagulls crying overhead, the wind kicking leaves off trees, and the crows cawing.

"Lift me up," Juliet said. "I'll look in the window."

Kyle cupped his hands. Of course, he would do what she asked. What else would he do? Her good heart and those wide gray eyes got to him. He couldn't imagine leaving her. But he had to go back to Montana. He was old enough to go home and face his parents, something he'd planned from the beginning. If things went bad at home, he could always leave again.

She stepped onto his hands, her weight barely pressing into his palms.

"Sheez," he said. "What do you eat? Air? You can't weigh more than Wilma's cat dander."

"Damn. They've pulled the curtains tight. Not even a glimmer of light shining through." She hopped down.

"We should go. They could show up while we're here." Kyle's brain was working fast. Certain they'd get caught and be in real trouble, he took her hand and pulled her away from the house, moving toward the Honda 50. The dried leaves pressed into the mud under his work boots. Juliet pulled her hand, and he tightened his grip.

He didn't want to love the smile that started in her eyes, those delighted, daring eyes, but he did. She'd somehow entered the closed circle of his heart and he never wanted to let her go.

"I thought we agreed to break in," she said, pulling him back toward the cabin.

"I changed my mind," he said, tugging her close. Once he felt that inkling of love, he feared for her safety. She was too nonchalant about danger, too quick to put herself in peril. Maybe, he thought, she didn't always know what was best.

"Something could be in there that leads us to Twyla and Roy."

"They, Tony and Alice, could show up at any minute or they could have security wired into the building."

"Look at the building. It's old as the hills," Juliet said, mimicking Kyle's unspoken sentiment. "There's no security in there. Even if they have an alarm and it goes off, and they find the Honda, we could just be down on the rocks enjoying the sun, knowing nothing about this place." Her gray eyes twinkled. Mischief looked too good on her.

Kyle shook his head, admiring her ability to think so fast. What if she twisted facts with him, making up quick stories instead of telling him the truth? How could he trust her if she lied? But then, he lied. They all lied. It was Runaway Survival 101.

Juliet let go of his hand and moved to the door. She tried the doorknob. The wooden door opened easily, and she stepped quietly over the threshold. Against his better judgment, he followed her. He'd regret it if she ended up in trouble inside while he sat helplessly outside.

A red-checkered cloth covered a kitchen table, a vase of fake lilies sitting neatly in the middle. The dishes had been washed and put into a white drainer. A white plastic tub sat upside down in the sink, still wet. A brown couch angled toward the kitchen from the tiny living room, where an overly large wood stove and the protective brick behind it took up an entire wall. The simple bedroom housed a bed with a blue and white 1970s bedspread. The whole place smelled clean. Nothing shifty or devious was there.

Juliet shook her head.

"Let's go," Kyle said, pulling the door shut behind them. The creaking door hinges nearly covered the sound of a car coming down the rutted road.

Tony and Alice pulled up to the cabin in a white van. Alice hit the brakes just before bashing through the cabin wall. She jumped out and slammed the door shut. Not a woman Kyle would want mad at him. He and Juliet hid behind a stand of sharp rocks near the cliff edge, barely breathing. The rocks were slippery and cold from the water splashing up. One wrong move, and he and Juliet would tumble into the water.

It was still safer than facing the LeCrosses.

Tony followed Alice into the cabin, looking steamed. They were there after him and Juliet. Kyle felt certain of it. The thought constricted his chest, catching in his throat. Calm down, he told himself. Breathe.

Kyle remembered the time his sister, Katy, was making pictures in the driveway outside their trailer. She'd used a ball of red yarn to make a dog and an elephant, then a house, a little girl, and a mother. She was eight years old and as calm and peaceful as he'd ever seen her. Then Kyle heard a loud rumbling. Someone had opened a gate on the horse property nearby, and the horses were galloping full speed toward their driveway and Katy. "Come here Katy!" Kyle had yelled. She'd looked at him, curious and stubborn. "Now!" he'd yelled. Still, she'd stayed put.

Clear-headed and full of adrenaline, Kyle had run to his sister, picked her up, and carried her back toward the house. The horse stampede barely missed them. The red yarn scattered across a hundred yards; the pictures ruined. Looking at the galloping horses, now at a distance, and then at Kyle, Katy had buried her head into his shoulder and cried.

Once he had saved Katy's life. At that moment, he'd been uncharacteristically sharp and focused, as if something or someone good and clear-headed had guided his mind and body.

He needed that clear-headed guide now. Maybe Katy had come through the memory, like a dream, to help him now. Maybe she forgave him. The thought made Kyle strong. He slowed his breath and calmed himself.

LeCrosse came out, dressed in a black suit like a phantom from another time. Looking both ways, he stepped off the porch and went to the back of the cabin. Something creaked. It sounded like rusty hinges. Another door maybe. After a while, he came back to the front, stood in the doorway, and waited for Alice. Together, they got into the white van. The tires spun gravel as they took off.

After the LeCrosses left, Juliet's ears perked up.

"Hear that?" She asked. "A wild animal trapped."

"Let's go around back," Kyle said. "I think that's a human animal."

They went behind the cabin and found a green tin cellar door. Grass had snuck in between the cement foundation and the tin door. The tin door was hooked to the cabin by two rusty hinges. A silver padlock secured the door. From the way it shone in the western sun, the padlock hadn't been there long. Kyle found an old metal fence post, picked it up, and slammed it against the lock. The lock didn't budge. He tried again, but the result was the same. He picked up a large rock and crashed it down. The padlock held tight.

Under the tin, he could hear a low whining punctuated by blurts and muffled words. At first, Kyle thought whoever was down there might be mute.

"She's gagged," Juliet said, as if reading his mind. "Look." She pointed to the hinges. "We just need to take the hinges off."

"The wood has rotted there. We can pull them out."

"LeCrosse locked the latch, making sure no one could get out," Juliet said. "He didn't think about someone trying to get in and opening it from its connection to the wall."

Kyle pulled the hinges loose with his fingers and flipped the green tin cellar door onto the pine needles and leaves spread across the overgrown lawn. The trap door made a loud screeching sound, like a wild hawk. At the bottom of the dusty wooden steps, he saw a pair of legs. He stepped into the hole and motioned for Juliet to wait.

She didn't. She followed him into the dark hole.

The musty smell nearly gagged him as he waited for his eyes to adjust. What he finally saw told him they'd been on the right track. LeCrosse had brought Twyla to this damp, musty cellar to rot. She sat in a white wooden kitchen chair, her feet taped to the legs and her hands lashed behind. Piles of cardboard boxes littered the dirt floor at the edges. The stark image of Twyla taped to the chair among the empty boxes hit him in the chest. She looked like she'd been sleeping upright for a month. Terrified. And alone.

He untied the blue handkerchief gagging her mouth.

"What happened?" he asked.

"She didn't know how to behave," a man said from above, "just like you."

Kyle snapped his head toward the sound, just in time to see the tin door crash into place.

The cellar went dark. The slamming of the tin door blew dust, and Kyle coughed, unable to breathe.

A scratching sound came from where the door met the wall.

"LeCrosse came back," Juliet whispered.

"He's reattaching the door," Kyle said, working quickly to take the tape off Twyla's legs and wrists, the sticky silver tape holding strong.

"Let us out," Twyla whimpered in a voice that was barely audible.

"Let us out," Kyle yelled. "You won't get away with this." He clutched his fists and tried to push down the fear choking him. He knew his demands were useless. He felt himself go ragdoll limp.

In a small bit of stubborn light from a crack in the door, Kyle could see the dirt smudges under Twyla's eyes. She'd been crying, and her ratty red hair hugged her ears. In the ray of light, she looked small and soft, like a dusty Christmas angel.

Twyla had rubbed her hands raw, trying to wiggle free.

"It's ok," Juliet said. "We'll get you out of here."

"Thirsty," Twyla said.

"How long have you been down here?" Kyle asked, trying to sound casual. They needed a plan to get out of this hellhole.

Before Twyla could answer, a sickly sweet smell inundated the root cellar. As the gas poured in, it didn't take Kyle long to realize that hell was exactly where they were.

CHAPTER TWENTY-FIVE

Sharp threads of rope cut into Juliet's wrists as her eyes adjusted to the dark. She looked around. Kyle and Twyla were also tied at their wrists. Kyle's legs were bound with rope, but Twyla's were taped to the chair again with wide, silver duct tape. The piles of empty boxes against the walls looked like shadowy hills. With shadowy creatures living in them, she thought.

She shook her throbbing head and struggled to sit up, trying to clear the fog from her brain. The air smelled sickly sweet, and she thought LeCrosse must have gassed them. If they didn't get out of there, he'd do it again–or worse.

"Kyle, wake up." She tried to nudge him with her foot, nearly falling back onto the cellar's dirt floor, tightening her stomach muscles to stay upright. "Come on, Kyle. Wake up. We've got to get out of here."

Twyla moved slightly in her chair, but then went still. Her red hair matted to her cheeks. Her head hung down toward her chest. She'd have a serious neckache when she woke up.

Juliet's pocketknife sat snuggly in the front pocket of her jeans, but she couldn't get to it with her hands tied behind her back. When Kyle didn't answer, she turned over on her belly and tried to wiggle the knife free, rubbing her pocket against the floor.

"You look like a dry land whale," Kyle said in a sleepy, sluggish voice. "Without the weight, of course."

"Finally," she said. "Scoot close and reach into my front pocket. Get my knife out. I'll cut these ropes off us."

"You have a knife?" An almost smile in his voice. He bottom-wiggled close to her.

"My right pocket." She pulled her knees up to her chest so he could get past her. "You'll have to feel for it."

Kyle sat close as she leaned back on her elbows. Any other time, this touching might have been a prelude to something more, something sensual and romantic. But today it was purely functional. Survival. His fingers traced her hip down to her pocket and warmth rushed through her body, her heart beating fast. Juliet wanted to be home safe with Kyle while he ran his hand down her hip. He slipped two fingers inside the pocket. She lost her breath for a minute, her fear and her desire mixed together. He latched onto the knife and pulled it out. Leaning forward, he held it in his tied hands behind him, in front of her.

Twyla slept through it all. Maybe she'd been gassed so many times that now the gas permeated her system, making it more difficult to wake up. That idea made it even more urgent that they get her out of there soon.

Juliet turned so she and Kyle were back-to-back. "Cut the ropes off my hands. Then I'll cut you free."

"I don't want to cut you."

"Me either. Just feel for the ropes." She heard him open the knife. Seagulls squawked outside; the wind sounded strong against the sea. "I don't hear any voices. Maybe LeCrosse went to his condo, or back to his farmhouse."

"Or he might be upstairs taking a nap."

"Keeping guard."

"Tell me if it hurts," Kyle said. As he cut, Juliet felt the rope begin to fray. Along with the rope, her hold on reality was fraying as the sickly sweet smell again permeated the air. Before the rope pulled loose, she blacked out again.

In the dream she wore an emerald-green, sequined leotard and stood bare-footed on a bared-back lion. Her mother swung from the trapeze close enough to whisper in her ear. "The lion, strength and kindness, freedom, and courage. You are being helped from above. But you must make the move. It's up to you. Your courage. Your strength." Her mother swung back to the platform and stood there, her wings spread out above the horses, elephants, and tigers. The soft feathers of her mother's wings were now on the roof of the circus tent. Red gates opened, and the crowd drove in.

The lion lifted his head and roared. Juliet's bare feet felt the thick hair on his spine, as if she and the lion were one. Juliet twirled on his back like a ballerina, lifting a leg behind her like a figure skater. She planted both feet on the creature's massive back and did a backbend, like an acrobat. With the lion, she was a ballerina, a figure skater, an acrobat. She finished to loud applause, standing on her hands, head close to the lion's neck, and balancing on his back while he pranced around the ring. Strength and courage, kindness, freedom, love–all of that and more extended from the lion into her. The lion reached his legs out in front of him, bowing his head to the ground, as Juliet lowered her feet to his back and climbed off. Touching his cheek lightly, she thanked him.

Her mother spread her wings and flew off to the white clouds of the sky, pulling the lion, circus, and tent out from under Juliet and dropping her into a pile of fallen tree branches. She stared out onto a barren ground.

No one was around for miles.

• • •

A knee pressed against Juliet's leg. Not pain, but tenderness. She woke up, startled, and sat up too quickly, nearly tumbling back to the dirt floor, disoriented, searching for some clue of recognition.

"LeCrosse was here," Kyle said. "Did he take the knife?"

The cellar. With Kyle and Twyla. She shook her head.

"No," she said. "I must have fallen on it. Just before I passed out. He must not have seen it. We were lucky."

"If you can call being tied up and gassed twice lucky," Kyle said.

Juliet smiled. She could almost see the sparkle in Kyle's eyes. Such good humor at a desperate time. "Let's get the ropes off and get Twyla out of here. I don't know how much more gassing she can take. She must be weak. She hasn't awakened since the first time he gassed us."

"I hope he's gone. I thought I heard a car drive away." Kyle cut at Juliet's rope, scraping the knife against her wrists.

"Ow," she said.

"Sorry."

"It's okay." Minor compared to everything else, Juliet thought. When he tugged the rope loose, she pulled her hands free and rubbed her wrists. She took the knife from Kyle and cut her feet free. Next, she cut Kyle's hands and feet free. He held onto Twyla while Juliet cut her hands and feet free. Together, they gently laid Twyla down on the floor so she wouldn't fall. They'd have to carry her once they figured out how to get the root cellar door open again.

Kyle tried the door to find what Juliet already knew. It was locked. She looked for something to bash the lock with but realized the lock would be too strong. They'd have to try the hinges, which were probably still weak. LeCrosse had most likely repaired them, but he wouldn't have had time to change the rotted wood.

Plus, he was depending on the gas to keep them subdued.

"The chair," she said.

Kyle already had it in his hands. "Stand back." He swung the chair at the cellar door, to no avail. He took a couple breaths and swung again.

The gas has weakened us both, she thought. If LeCrosse is here still, or if he comes back, he'll kill us. Fear welled up in her and suddenly she felt she could move a mountain.

"Let's do it together," she said. "Let's both hold the chair and push it straight up into the door. Maybe we can loosen the hinge screws again."

Kyle nodded. "If LeCrosse is home, he'll be here any minute."

"Yeah. On three?"

"One, two, three," Kyle counted.

They pushed hard, and a smidgeon of light came through. Together, they swung the chair up again and pushed. Working with Kyle, like a real partner, made Juliet smile despite the frightening situation. That LeCrosse possibly loomed somewhere near the dark dungeon was terrifying, but Kyle's brown eyes shining in the dim light and the way his hair fell in his face still made Juliet's heart soar.

"Again?" he asked.

"Yes." It was a word she hoped she'd say often to him.

They shoved the chair up and this time, a blast of light burst through. With the next shove, Juliet could see the cellar's dirt walls and cardboard boxes strewn across the floor. They swung the chair one last time. The wood cracked, and the door swung open, revealing a setting sun turning the clouds pink. Juliet had no idea how much time had passed. Had they slept for a day or for several days? She was weak from the gas and lack of food and water. In fact, she was terribly thirsty.

"Hurry," she said. "Let's get Twyla and get out of here."

Kyle went backwards up the steps, holding the girl by her armpits while Juliet carried her legs. When they walked over to the tin door on the ground they made a loud banging noise, a horrible noise that was sure to draw LeCrosse if he was any-where nearby. Juliet's legs wobbled as she carried Twyla into the woods and out of sight of the cabin. Once they were far enough into the trees to be hidden, they set her down. She jolted awake, sitting up and releasing a muffled scream.

Juliet jumped toward her, a finger to her lips, wanting to si-lence her, fearful of Tony LeCrosse's wrath. If he got to them before they got somewhere safe, they'd be done. Literally done.

She pushed Twyla's hair out of her face. Her mouth looked loose and wrong. Her eyes were frozen in fright.

"Itoy," Twyla said, sounding as if she had cotton balls in her mouth.

"What?" Juliet asked.

"Oyoyoy."

"You're safe now," Kyle said. He looked over at Juliet as if she had the answers and he expected her to interpret.

She shrugged. She knew no more than he did at that moment.

"No. O-oy." Twyla struggled to stand.

Juliet helped her. "She wants something important."

"Roy." This time, Twyla said it clearly.

"Roy?" Kyle flashed his eyes at Juliet.

"The cellar," Twyla said, pulling free and stumbling back to-ward the house.

"No one else is there," Kyle told her.

"The cellar," the girl repeated, staggered forward, and fell.

Kyle caught her before she hit the ground. "Wait here with her," he said to Juliet.

She put her arms around Twyla to restrain her, which was easy. The girl pushed and wiggled but was too robbed of strength to get away. The multiple gassings—and whatever else LeCrosse had subjected her to—had rendered her powerless. Within a minute, Twyla slumped, becoming dead weight. Juliet was all too happy to hold her, closing her eyes and taking deliberate deep breaths as she waited. By inhaling fresh air, she'd recover more quickly.

Kyle ran toward the house, darting through the bushes and quickly disappearing into the cellar. Soon Kyle came bursting through the bushes and trees carrying Roy, cradling him in his arms. The boy looked as light as the heavens, his shredded pants revealing pale, thin legs. Roy's dirty t-shirt, ripped at the neck and waist, showed his shrunken belly. His ribs stuck out, with sunken ravines between each one.

Twyla sat down quietly, leaning against a tree, following Kyle with her eyes as he placed Roy on the ground next to her. He was breathing, but unconscious. "He was alongside the wall, under the boxes," Kyle said. "I have to fix the cellar door, so LeCrosse won't notice anything." He took off again, before Juliet could say anything.

"Let's take deep breaths," Juliet whispered to Twyla. "It will help us feel good again."

The girl nodded, her sad eyes on Roy as she breathed.

It felt like forever to Juliet as she waited for Kyle. When he finally came back, he brought two bottles of water, two browned bananas, and most of a loaf of bread.

"Tonight, we dine," he said.

Juliet grinned at him, feeling silly with admiration. He was her knight in shining armor, her sailor washed up from the sea, her Kyle, her friend, her sweet, sweetheart.

CHAPTER TWENTY-SIX

Since Juliet had foolishly left Detective Benson Picard's cell phone at the shed, Kyle walked to the nearest neighbor's house to call 911 and alert Picard. She stayed with Twyla and Roy. They both needed an ambulance, especially Roy. He hadn't awakened. Juliet was afraid he wouldn't make it.

LeCrosse had not returned to the cabin. Juliet fervently hoped their luck in that department would hold.

The ambulance arrived at the same time as Detective Picard. Tears sprang into her eyes. She was so relieved to see them both. Kyle held her hand, and she was grateful for his warmth. She felt her body shake as she released the fear she felt. She was safe with Kyle. They were both safe with Picard on their side.

They hadn't found LeCrosse yet, Picard said, but officers were searching for him. Juliet listened to his police radio as the EMTs carefully loaded Roy and Twyla into the ambulance. Then, the word came. The cops had found Tony and Alice LeCrosse sharing a bottle of single malt scotch in their condo, as if in celebration. They'd arrested both.

She looked at Kyle as he squeezed her hand and pulled it to his chest. His smile looked tired and ragged. Tired and ragged was okay if they were both safe. And they were both safe. Relief once more filled Juliet's heart. They'd found Twyla and Roy and gotten them help. Hopefully, they would both make full recoveries.

A curly-haired, burly man stepped out from the back of the ambulance and walked over to them. It was Arnold, the lumberjack from LeCrosse's party.

"They'll be okay, thanks to you," he said. "They have low oxygen levels and probably would have died soon if you hadn't gotten them out of there. We've got O2 masks on them now. That'll start clearing the poison out of their systems. You did good. You two are a good team."

"Thank you," Juliet said, beaming at Kyle. He hugged her close and gently pushed the hair out of her eyes, kissing her forehead. She settled into the nook in his arm, protected, warm, completely at home.

"How are you involved here?" she asked Arnold. "You were at one of his parties."

"And gave me a ride to Seattle and back," Kyle said.

"Yeah, I had to make LeCrosse believe I was one of his people. But I never went beyond simple intimidation."

"You're undercover?" She heard the pitch of her voice rise.

"I can't really say."

"You pushed Roy out of the van that day," Juliet said. "You're the reason he escaped."

"I can't really say," Arnold repeated, smiling as he stepped into the back of the ambulance and closed the door.

Juliet could still see his face in the rear window as the siren blared, and the ambulance raced off.

. . .

The LeCrosses quickly ratted out Georgy My Boy, blaming him for everything and offering to make a deal for information regarding his whereabouts. The police picked George up. He easily turned back on the LeCrosses. They found George guilty of child endangerment and severely addicted to drugs and alcohol. They took him straight to the state mental hospital's secure unit where he could get sober and clean while awaiting trial.

George also told the police about the farmhouse where they kept the children waiting to be farmed out to childless couples. For a price, the price sometimes going as high as $50,000. The number Juliet had heard was for a child, not a building. While the children waited for their new parents, they sanded and painted toys, nothing too intricate for most of them. The more elaborate work was done by either those children with talent or by LeCrosse himself. The toys provided a front to introduce the children to possible new parents.

George didn't understand the problem, Picard explained to Juliet and Kyle. Most of the kids had run away from abusive homes. At least this way, they'd be safe and have someone to watch over them. Social Services went to the farmhouse and retrieved them. They took them to safe, temporary shelters, until they could locate their parents, or good homes for them. They also started a search for the children who had been already sold to childless couples.

When Detective Picard searched the cabin grounds, he found six cans of veterinary gas–enough to knock out three rabid bulls for a week. He located the equipment LeCrosse used to forge birth certificates once a new set of parents were located. Sitting neatly on the kitchen table, Picard found fake birth certificates for Roy and Twyla, along with picture IDs. Ally LeCrosse and Randy LeCrosse. Alice and Tony were listed as the children's parents.

Clever twists on their names, Juliet thought as she relaxed in the shed that evening. As if falsely claiming teens as their own would be so simple. As if these youngsters didn't have strong spirits and wouldn't fight back. Tony had disregarded all they'd survived already. What was the saying? What doesn't kill you makes you stronger? Well, those kids were strong–much stronger than either Tony or Alice.

See if your black magic can bend prison bars, Mr. LeCrosse, Juliet thought.

She smiled and looked over at Kyle. He slept soundly on the bed next to where she sat. He didn't budge even when she got up and made tea. The whole ordeal had frightened and exhausted them both. She couldn't imagine how terrified the children in LeCrosse's home had been. She hoped they'd find strength as they healed and grew. She hoped what hadn't killed them made them stronger.

• • •

Picard contacted Roy's mother and grandmother in Eugene, Oregon, and they came to get him from the hospital. He went to live with them again, under the close watch of social services. It wasn't perfect, but maybe–with some support–they could be good parents. His mother, scared by losing Roy, had gone to drug treatment for opioid addiction. She was on a long, fragile road to recovery, which gave her family new hope. When she came to get her son, her eyes were clear, her cheeks were pink, and she had a little meat on her bones. Mother and son ran to each other and held on all the way through signing the release papers.

Juliet, Kyle, and Twyla walked them to the car.

"He's a master toy maker," Twyla told Roy's mother. "He has a real gift there, and you'll want to help him pursue it. Give him a piece of wood and some material, and his dolls will talk. His creations will dance magically through time. They are little extensions of himself, laughing and running, all heart and soul."

Roy's mother nodded. "I'll get him a good mentor."

Juliet was sure she meant it, for now anyway.

Tony and Alice LeCrosse hadn't yet gone full bore into trafficking infants. They had simply seen an opportunity with Bernice and took it. Picard helped Bernice find the people who had illegally adopted her daughter. With legal help, she got her child back. Her mother, the baby's true grandmother, had agreed with Bernice that she and Bernice would raise the child together. Bernice would need the help, and it was a beginning.

Twyla went to a group home in Seattle. Her mother was in rehab. Once her mother finished treatment, they would start the process of rebuilding their relationship. Hopefully, Twyla would one day live with her mother again. For now, she'd return to school and build a future, something that might be secure with or without her mother's sobriety.

Kyle woke up and rubbed his eyes.

"Tea?" Juliet asked.

He nodded. She poured his tea and put it on the crate they used as a table. She sat by him and rubbed his hair, messing it even further. "We didn't mention Stephan to Detective Picard," she said.

Kyle shook his head. "Stephan?"

Juliet laughed. "Yes, I suppose he'll find his own way."

"His mom will go to prison. They've been ensnaring children and young teens for a while, according to Picard." Kyle sipped his tea. A worried look crossed his face.

"What is it?" Juliet asked.

"The tent town. What will happen to it? Stephan had said the police ordered them to pack up and leave."

Juliet shrugged. "So far, the police have left it alone."

•   •   •

Before Juliet and Kyle went with Picard to gather a box of toys and other evidence from the farmhouse, Detective Benson Picard handed the teens both a set of rubber gloves and invited

them to sign a paper saying they'd come along as student officers. She gave him a funny, blank look that probably baffled him
as much as his calm expression baffled her.

"It's common practice to have students ride with officers," he
said.

"What does it mean if we sign?" She looked at Kyle, who had
already signed the paper.

"It means you're interested," Picard said. "That's all. But you
should think about it. You should think about going to the academy."

"You should," Kyle said.

"Okay," Juliet agreed, but she wasn't so sure.

They found boxes of stuffed bears dressed in hard plaids,
hunter orange and the rubber boots of fishermen. A family of
half-finished cats lounged on a small, pillowed bed. An entire
town made from copper coils lit up with the touch of a soft
breath. Acrobats flew on trapeze handles and walked tightropes.
A full tent camp, near a tiny wooden shed, sprawled across one
workstation. Juliet shuddered to see it. A magician, a miniature
LeCrosse in perfect form, pulled a rabbit out of the hat.

A tiny Alice tamed a lion. The image of strength and courage,
Juliet's card. They were more alike than she had known, she
thought, opposite sides of the same card. Both had been mesmerized by LeCrosse's attention. Juliet felt that horrible shudder
again. She understood Alice too well, having fallen under
LeCrosse's spell. Juliet hadn't quite broken the spell. But she had
sensed his dark cruelty. That knowing had partially saved her.
LeCrosse going to jail saved her the rest of the way. She hoped
she'd never cross paths with him again.

"He's a real artist," she said.

"He is," Kyle said. "He could have had it all."

"We think he cooked meth for the kids," Picard said, "to keep
them working long hours. Then, sedated them when they

became unruly. After they rested, he'd give them meth again. They did trivial work while waiting to go with new parents."

"Were the twin girls at the farmhouse?" Juliet asked. She didn't understand it, but she thought they had been on LeCrosse's good side and part of the operation. The few times she saw them, they seemed calm and happy enough.

"They were," Picard said. "According to Twyla, they were the pet children of the couple. They supposedly got whatever they asked for. They've gone with Social Services."

"It's a sick operation to be a pet in," Kyle said, rubbing his hand through his hair. "To be described as a pet at all gives me the creeps."

"What about the boy who went with the couple from Nevada?"

"The car was caught on video," Picard said. "An APB has been put out for the license plate. He'll be found and when he is, he'll go into foster care until his parents can be located. We have a lot to sort out here. But we will sort it."

"Will the kids get help to recover?" Juliet asked.

"Yes, hospitals and outpatient programs. Besides the twins, three more children, ages 9-13 were at the Farmhouse barn. We hope we've got them all."

"Picard," she said, almost in a whisper. "Look."

"A bookcase." The detective raised his eyebrows at her. "It's a shop, not the type of space with a bookcase."

"Maybe LeCrosse read to them as they worked," Kyle said.

Juliet ran her hand across the books. Titles like *Murder and the Thief*, *The Trials of Ancient Egypt* and *A Short History of World War II* filled the shelves. Not exactly story time books. She pulled on the edge of the bookcase, and it moved easily away from the wall. The lower front of the bookcase hid the wheels. Juliet pushed the bookcase aside and revealed a door behind it. She knocked and tried the door. It was locked. No sound came from the inside.

"Is there a key?" Kyle asked, looking, but not finding one.

"Let me at it," Detective Picard said. He hauled back and slammed his body against the door, creating a jagged split in the doorframe. He stepped back again, gently, like a tender bear. After a moment of slow, deliberate breathing, he charged forward, ramming the door, shoulder first and following with the bulk of his torso. A loud, splintering crack echoed throughout the workshop as the hinges broke free and open space appeared on the other side. Once more, Picard loaded up his body like a great cannon and slammed into the door, this time shooting straight through it to the other side.

Sunlight from high windows lit up a cloud of dust particles. For a minute Juliet felt like one of them, light and airy. Insignificant. She walked slowly into the hidden room. Despite the high, sunny windows, the room felt dark and stagnant, like the death card, the sad knight on his white horse. Even though she knew he carried a mystical white rose, a symbol of true love, she felt no love here. She felt the opposite: cruelty, power, control. She ran her fingers down the wall and turned on the light. A single uncovered bulb hung from the ceiling.

Brightly colored yoga mats lined the floor, like they had at the Halloween party. A blanket, a pillow, and a stuffed animal sat on each one. The room was stuffy, almost suffocating in its airlessness. Dust lined the baseboards. The walls were dotted with dark images, like Rorschach inkblot tests. Juliet's heart broke when she realized blood had splattered against the wall and dried.

She tried to stop the flood of images rushing into her mind. A head slammed against the wall, a cheek broken open from a fist, teeth knocked out. The children had not been treated kindly. If only they could have gotten to them sooner.

In one corner, several rubber masks lay crumpled on the floor. Juliet remembered the man from the white van with the cleaning symbol on the side. What seemed like a lifetime ago, the man had kidnapped Roy from the street. When she went after him, she'd tried to scratch his face, but her fingernails had bounced off a rubber mask. She'd never forget the chill that went through her then. She understood the terrible danger that Roy had faced, knowing it must have been LeCrosse who grabbed him that day on the street.

Now, in this room, she felt that awful brutality again. This closed-in, closeted chamber seemed to suck the life, the love, out of her, leaving only black emptiness. Something close to evil lurked in the corner with those dark masks. It took her breath away. She shivered, a light breeze from nowhere crawling over her.

Yes, it was like the death card. But that card represented change, one time ending and another time beginning. That ending was the bright spot in all of this. "Your time is over, LeCrosse," Juliet said. "You are finished."

· · ·

With the money she'd earned from Picard, Juliet rented a cheap apartment from Antonia, one of the real rentals Antonia had bought through the years. Her landlady was thrilled to have Juliet in a real home with running water and a reliable heating system, especially with winter coming. She'd brought a big pot of soup over and left both the soup and the pot as a house-warming present. Wilma had greeted her by purring and rubbing against her legs.

Juliet also enrolled in the cadets' program. She'd start the program next year. In the meantime, she'd stay put. With the market closed, Juliet figured she'd wait tables at the Hungry Bear Café or work at a retail store for the holidays.

She looked around at the apartment's white walls, thought about what color to paint them, and shuffled the tarot cards. Feeling silly about asking the cards such a trivial question as what color to paint the walls, she decided against it. Use your brain, she told herself.

Still, shuffling the cards calmed her. The sound and rhythm of it helped her think. Juliet knew their images so well; she imagined them talking to her. Reading tarot cards is my way of using my brain, she said back to herself.

The phone rang. She still had the cell phone Picard had given her.

She walked over to the counter and picked it up. "Hello." She answered it, even though she didn't recognize the number.

"Juliet?" A hauntingly familiar voice came through the receiver.

"Aunt Gloria?" Juliet couldn't believe it was her.

"Yes. How are you?"

"Fine. I'm fine. How are you?"

"Doing better these days. It's good to hear your voice, honey."

"Good to hear yours, too. How did you get this number?"

"It's kind of a long story. A girl named Gabriella said a Detective Picard and a girl named Juliet were helping runaways on the west coast."

"You're friends with Gabriella?" Was the world really that small?

"No. I saw her Facebook post about Annie's Court and the people there who helped her. People had shared it and it landed on my page. I tracked down the detective and he gave me your number. I have news about your father and Harrison."

Juliet's stomach dropped. She stared at the white walls, wishing she'd already painted them blue or lavender, anything soothing. "I never knew my father. He left when I was a baby, remember?" She didn't mean to sound bitter. She wasn't bitter toward Aunt Gloria. Any bitterness she harbored was toward her father for leaving her and her mother on their own. And, well, maybe she was a wee bit bitter with Aunt Gloria for choosing Layne over her.

"He was killed," her aunt was saying. "They found his body in a shallow grave on the other side of the border. Next to Harrison's."

"What?" Juliet thought her heart was going to explode.

"That's why he disappeared."

"How?"

She heard Aunt Gloria take in a breath. "They were both shot, years apart, but with the same gun."

"But why?" Juliet had to force the words out. She sat down hard on the kitchen chair.

"According to the detective, they'd both done undercover work, trying to stop the flow of drugs from Mexico into the U.S. Someone didn't like it, and stopped them."

Juliet could barely breathe. All these years she'd blamed her father. He'd been trying to do something good. And he'd been shot for it. He hadn't left them, she realized. He'd been killed. She'd hated Harrison too, her mother's cowboy, the only father she'd ever known, for leaving them. She did not know what they'd been through, or what they'd faced. Her chest swelled with regret. It was too late to apologize to them. "Aunt Gloria?"

"Yes?"

"I'm sorry I didn't let you know I was safe."

"I wish you had. I was so worried. I searched hospitals and called police departments all over the West. I called..." She heard her aunt's voice catch in her throat. "I called morgues. I'm sorry I didn't believe you about Layne. I'm sorry I blamed you."

"Are you still with him?"

"He's gone. That's a good thing. But the bad thing is that I lost you. I'm thankful you're okay. From what Detective Picard said, you're quite the amateur sleuth."

"I guess I helped."

"Baby?"

Juliet's eyes welled up. No one had called her baby since her mother had died. "Yes?"

"Will you come home for the funerals?"

"I will," Juliet said. "Aunt Gloria?"

"Yes?"

"Thank you for finding me."

"I love you, sweetheart. I always have."

As Juliet hung up, someone knocked on the door. She opened it to Kyle's smiling face. He held a bouquet of sunflowers.

"Congratulations on your place, and on getting into the police academy," he said.

"Thank you. Come on in. I'll make us some tea."

"On a real stove? You sure you know how to use one?"

"Smarty pants. I also have some good chicken stew Antonia dropped off earlier. If you're nice, I'll heat it up too." She filled the teakettle and put it on the stove, proud of her new home.

Kyle sat at the table. "I'm going to Montana," he said, his voice so low she barely heard it.

She thought she hadn't heard it right. "What?" Juliet tried to hold back the sharp stab of fear. He was going back to be with the woman from Missoula. She should have known that what they had was too good to be true.

"When we were in that cellar," Kyle continued, "I realized your tarot cards were right. I love my mom and dad. In the cellar, I was terrified I'd never see them again. I should have gotten my sister out of that fire. But I didn't. I was afraid I'd die in there."

"You probably would have."

"I didn't even try," he said. "I ran away because I couldn't face how cowardly I'd been, and I couldn't face my parents' shattered lives. They were out of their minds with grief."

"So, your parents lost two children instead of one."

"It wasn't fair to them. A private investigator from Missoula came to The Hungry Bear and gave me this." He put an envelope on the table. "A plane ticket home. My parents sent it. I leave tonight."

"The woman with the bushy hair and long skirt?" Juliet was determined to keep her cool, even though her heart had fallen into her lap. She followed it with her eyes. It was raw and throbbing, way too open. "She's not your girlfriend?" She raised her eyes under lowered lids.

"What?" Kyle looked perplexed.

"The woman from Missoula? She's not a past girlfriend?"

Kyle laughed and shook his head. He tilted it toward the ticket. "I just met her. She said it took a while to find me. Everyone was so hush, hush about me."

Juliet let go a breath of relief, but the relief didn't last. She hadn't expected to love Kyle, but she did. Once he went to Montana, girlfriend, or no girlfriend, he'd never come back. She'd been to Montana and seen it in all its glory. She struggled to find the words, to tell him how she felt. If she didn't tell him, he'd be gone forever. Her raw, open, fallen heart ached at the thought of losing him.

"It's a round trip ticket." He flashed a mischievous grin. Wilma jumped up on the chair near him. "I rented an apartment here with the money Picard gave me. My boss at The Hungry Bear promoted me to assistant cook. That job comes with more money, so I'll be able to keep the apartment."

Juliet looked up as the late fall sun beamed through her window. Even the sun approved. "Where is it?"

"Next door," he said. And like an old pro, he reached over and pulled "The Lovers" card from the tarot deck.

Juliet shook her head in disbelief, walked around the table, and kissed him. He pulled her close. His lips felt tender and strong. Fresh ocean air blew in through an open window. And Juliet knew exactly who Kyle loved.

Kyle loved her.

They held hands and waited for the tea water to boil.

THE END

ABOUT THE AUTHOR

Photo by Judith Bromley

Milana Marsenich lives in Northwest Montana near Flathead Lake at the base of the beautiful Mission Mountains. She enjoys quick access to the mountains and has spent many hours hiking the wilderness trails with friends and dogs. She has an M.Ed. in Mental Health Counseling from Montana State University and an MFA in Creative Writing from the University of Montana. She has previously published in *Montana Quarterly*, *Big Sky Journal*, *The Moronic Ox*, and *Feminist Studies*. She has three novels out. *Copper Sky* was a Spur Award finalist. *The Swan Keeper* was a Willa Award finalist. *Beautiful Ghost* is the sequel to *Copper Sky*. Her book, *Idaho Madams*, is popular history. Her short story *Wild Dogs* won the Laura Award for short fiction.

NOTE FROM MILANA MARSENICH

Word-of-mouth is crucial for any author to succeed. If you en-joyed *Shed Girl,* please leave a review online—anywhere you are able. Even if it's just a sentence or two. It would make all the difference and would be very much appreciated.

Thanks!
Milana Marsenich

We hope you enjoyed reading this title from:

www.blackrosewriting.com

Subscribe to our mailing list – *The Rosevine* – and receive **FREE** books, daily deals, and stay current with news about upcoming releases and our hottest authors.
Scan the QR code below to sign up.

Already a subscriber? Please accept a sincere thank you for being a fan of Black Rose Writing authors.

View other Black Rose Writing titles at www.blackrosewriting.com/books and use promo code **PRINT** to receive a **20% discount** when purchasing.